A Lucy Novel

Lucy Out of Bounds

Other books in the growing Faithgirlz!™ Library

The Faithgirlz! Bible
Nonfiction

Dear Nancy, The Skin You're In, Body Talk, Girl Politics, and
Everybody Tells Me to Be Myself but I Don't Know Who I Am

The Sophie Series

Sophie's World (Book One)
Sophie's Secret (Book Two)
Sophie Under Pressure (Book Three)
Sophie Steps Up (Book Four)
Sophie's First Dance (Book Five)
Sophie's Stormy Summer (Book Six)
Sophie's Friendship Fiasco (Book Seven)
Sophie and the New Girl (Book Eight)
Sophie Flakes Out (Book Nine)
Sophie Loves Jimmy (Book Ten)
Sophie's Drama (Book Eleven)
Sophie Gets Real (Book Twelve)

A Lucy Novel Series

Lucy Doesn't Wear Pink (Book One)
Lucy Out of Bounds (Book Two)
Lucy's Perfect Summer (Book Three)
Lucy Finds Her Way (Book Four)

Check out www.faithgirlz.com

A Lucy Novel

Lucy Out of Bounds

Nancy Rue

ZONDERVAN.com/
AUTHORTRACKER
follow your favorite authors

In memory
of Rocky Carter-Rue, our curmudgeon kitty

We want to hear from you. Please send your comments about this
book to us in care of zreview@zondervan.com. Thank you.

ZONDERKIDZ

Lucy Out of Bounds
Copyright © 2008 by Nancy Rue

Requests for information should be addressed to:
Zonderkidz, *Grand Rapids, Michigan* 49530

Library of Congress Cataloging-in-Publication Data
Rue, Nancy N.
      Lucy out of bounds / by Nancy Rue..
         p. cm. – (A Lucy novel ; bk. 2) "Faithgirlz."
      Summary: Eleven-year-old tomboy Lucy feels betrayed by everyone when a bobcat stalks the
neighborhod, her best friend Mora suddenly becomes boy-crazy about Lucy's best friend, and the
town considers selling the soccer field where she plays.
      ISBN 978-0-310-71451-4 (softcover)
      [1. Soccer–Fiction. 2. Schools–Fiction. 3. Single-parent families–Fiction. 4. Blind–Fiction.
5. People with disabilities–Fiction. 6. Household employees–Fiction. 7. Christian life–Fiction. 8.
New Mexico–Fiction.] I. Title.
      PZ7.R88515Luh 2008
      [Fic]–dc22
                                      2008028030

Published in association with the literary agency of Alive Communications, Inc., 7680 Goddard Street, Suite
200, Colorado Springs, CO 80920. www.alivecommunications.com

Zonderkidz is a trademark of Zondervan.

Art direction and cover design: Sarah Molegraaf
Interior design: Carlos Eluterio Estrada

Printed in the United States of America

11 12 13 14 15 16 17 18 /DCI/ 24 23 22 21 20 19 18 17 16 15 14 13 12 11 10 9 8 7 6 5 4

So we fix our eyes not on what is seen, but on what is unseen.
For what is seen is temporary, but what is unseen is eternal.

— 2 Corinthians 4:18

Why J.J. Is My Best Friend Even Though He's a Boy and Boys Are Mostly Absurd Little Creeps

Lucy stuck her pen through the rubber band in her ponytail and looked at her cat Marmalade, curled up in the rocking chair. He blinked back out of his orange face as if he'd heard what she wrote and was very much offended.

"I'm not talking about you, silly," she said to him. "You're a Cat-Boy. That's different from a Human-Boy." She grunted. "If you can call most boys human."

Untangling her pen from its blonde perching place—and wondering how it got into a snarl just sitting there for seven seconds—she went back to the J.J. list.

- ∾ He lives across the street so we can send signals to each other if one of us is grounded. Usually it's him. Only, today it's me.
- ∾ He doesn't think it's lame to ride bikes.
- ∾ He loves soccer as much as I do, and he doesn't care that I'm better than him. We both want to be professionals someday.

Marmalade yawned—loud—and licked his cat-lips.

"Okay, okay," Lucy said. "I'm getting to the important stuff."

- ∾ He doesn't feel my back to see if I'm wearing a bra and think it's funny—like SOME boys do. Ickety-ick.

She scowled. The last time Aunt Karen visited from El Paso, she kept talking about how it was time for Lucy to get a bra. Had Mom worn one when *she* was only eleven years old? That probably wasn't something Lucy could ask Dad without dying of embarrassment. She squeezed her pen and went back to the page.

- If I'm kicking stones and J.J. asks me what's wrong and I say I don't want to talk about it, he says okay and we go kick a soccer ball instead.
- He never looks at me like I'm from Planet Weird. Which some people do. Like Mora when I say I'm never wearing a bra. Ever.
- When J.J. gets me in trouble, he always tells my dad it was his fault. Except for this last time. Because I wouldn't let him, because J.J. would have gotten in way more trouble than me, so I took the blame, which is why I'm grounded for a whole day.

Lucy dropped the pen and shook her hand, letting her fingers flap against each other. That was a lot of writing. Inez, her weekday nanny, always said Lucy's lists were her way of praying, so even though she might be hand-crippled for life, she did feel better.

Marmalade obviously did too, because he was now curled in a ball like a tangerine, breathing his very plump self up and down in the middle. Sleep-wheezing sounds were also coming from the half-open toy chest, where Lollipop, Lucy's round, black kitty was snoozing.

It must be incredibly boring being cats. Feeling better seemed to make them want to lick their hairy paws and go to sleep. It made Lucy want to bounce out the door and get a soccer game going, or ride her bike in the desert with J.J., or at the very least go check out whatever her dad was clanging around in the kitchen.

But you couldn't do any of those things when you were grounded. At least the March wind had stopped beating against the house and the long shadows were making stripes on her blue walls. That meant the day of groundation was almost over, and tomorrow she could start fresh.

Lucy carefully nestled the Book of Lists on her pillow and got to her knees on the bed, propping her chin against the tile windowsill to gaze out at Granada Street. It was a sleepy Saturday, except for the sound of the hammers a block over on Tularosa Street where workers were turning the old, falling-apart hotel into a restaurant.

The cottonwood trees that lined her street were letting loose a swirl of white fibers, and between those and the new spring leaves, she couldn't see J.J.'s house as well as she could in winter. It was impossible to tell if he was sending her any shadow signals with a flashlight from behind the sheet covering his upstairs window. J.J. making a bunny with his fingers meant, "I'm hopping on over." Devil's horns meant, "Januarie"—that was his sister—"is driving me nuts."

Dad's clanging in the kitchen stopped in a too-fast way. Marmalade uncurled like a popping spring and stood on the seat of the rocker with every orange hair standing up on end. Marmalade never moved that quickly unless there was food involved.

Lucy scrambled across the bed and got to her door, yelling, "Dad?"—at the very same moment her father said, "Luce?"

She sailed across the wide hallway—not bothering to ride the yellow Navajo rug on the tile the way she usually did—and almost collided with Dad in the kitchen doorway. His hands were spread out to either side in their "Now, Lucy, calm down" sign. But his face looked about as calm as a cat in a kitty-carrier. His triangle nose and squared-off chin formed white, frightened angles that made Lucy's mouth go dry.

"What's going on, Dad?"

"I'm not sure. I need your eyes."

He tilted his salt-and-pepper-crew-cut head toward the back door. "I heard something I didn't like in the yard. I don't want you to go out there."

"Why?"

"Because I think it's some kind of wild cat."

"In our *yard?*"

Dad rubbed his palm up and down her arm. "I'm probably over-reacting, but let's check it out."

Lucy lunged for the door.

"Window, Luce," Dad said.

She dragged a chair to the sink and climbed up on it. Her father had been blind for four years, and she still couldn't figure out how he knew absolutely everything she was doing—or was going to do—before she even did it. J.J. couldn't either. He thought she could get away with a whole lot more than she ever did.

Leaning across the sink, Lucy slid the Christmas cactus aside on the windowsill so she could support herself with her hands. The backyard was already a puzzle of shadows, and at first, she didn't see anything unusual except—

"Uh-oh," she said.

"What?"

"Looks like Artemis got into the garbage again. That bag that had that disgusting Thai food Aunt Karen brought is all over the place." She started to pull away from the window. "I'll go out and pick it up."

"Keep looking," Dad said. "I closed the cans with those big bungee cords. Artemis couldn't have gotten them undone."

Lucy didn't remind Dad that Artemis, their hunter cat, was practically Terminator Kitty when really nasty trash was involved. She got one knee up on the sink and peered past the red-checked curtains again.

"The bungee is still on the lid," she reported. "She ripped into the side of the trash can."

"She didn't."

"Well, there's a big ol' hole there."

"Do you see claw marks?"

Lucy pressed her forehead on the glass, and a chill wormed its way up her back. Right where the gray plastic had been ripped away, thick gashes scrawled down the can as if someone had made them with a big nail.

"Yeah," she said. "And they aren't Artemis's. Or Marmalade's—or Lolli's—or Mudge's—"

"It's a good thing we only have four cats," Dad said, "or we could be here for days." The dry, Dad-calm was back in his voice. "You keep watching. I'm calling Sheriff Navarra."

Lucy pulled her other knee up and settled into the sink. It was a good thing she'd done all the dishes and wiped everything dry in an attempt to get out of groundation, although that never worked on Dad.

From this position, Lucy could survey the whole yard, which fanned out from the big Mexican elder tree in the middle to the fence surrounding the house like a row of straight gray teeth. The umbrella was still down on the table on the patio, and the chairs leaned with their faces against the house, waiting for enough spring in the air so she and Dad could come out and sit in them. The gate on the side sagged as always beneath its fringe of cautious wisteria vine just coming into bloom—the same kind of plant that covered the toolshed and had started to creep up the dead tree by the back fence.

"Whatever it was, it's gone now," Lucy said.

Dad closed his cell phone against his chest and dropped it into his pocket. Two fierce lines formed between his eyebrows. "That's a definite bummer."

"How come?"

"The sheriff's on his way. He's going to think we're imagining things. Okay—be like the kitties. Look for movement. Up high—not on the ground."

Lucy pulled her eyes to the top of the fence, the roof of the toolshed, the rickety arch over the gate. Nothing moved. Not until she went back to the dead tree, where a shadow was passing over it.

"What?" Dad said.

"I think I saw something—"

"Shhh!"

Lucy froze and let Dad tilt his head and listen. People said a blind man didn't really have a better sense of hearing than anyone else, but Dad could practically hear a cobweb fluttering in a corner.

"Do you see Artemis?" he said.

Lucy searched the top of the fence again, where Artemis Hamm normally inched, tightrope-walker style, when she was stalking a mouse or a quail who was just trying to keep her kids in tow. No sign of Artemis.

And then Lucy heard what Dad must have heard: the low growl of their huntress feline, the kind she made when some other cat was trying to horn in on the prey she'd done all the work to catch.

"Under the dead tree." Dad put both hands on her shoulders. "Is Artemis down there?"

Lucy saw her cat's mottled coat, the one that looked like God couldn't make up his mind on what kind of cat he wanted Artemis Hamm to be. She crouched at the bottom of the dead tree, staring up as if it had come to life.

Because it had. Lucy gasped as she watched one paw and then another, each the size of Artemis's head, creep its way down the spongy bark, smothering its woodpecker holes, until pointed, tufted, devilish ears came into view.

"It's a bobcat!" Lucy said. "Dad—he's going after Artemis!"

Dad let go of Lucy's shoulders, and she scrambled down from the sink—but not before he got his hand up.

"You stay in this house, and I mean it," he said.

"He'll get Artemis!"

"He'll get you too. I'm calling Sheriff Navarra again—"

The rest of whatever he was going to say was lost in a screech so horrible even Dad looked bolted to the floor. Lucy hoisted herself back up onto the sink and flattened her face against the window. The big cat was almost to the ground, but there was no helpless Artemis flailing in his mouth.

There was only J.J., facing the animal with a shovel in his hand and a smear of sheer horror across his face.

2

Even in the dusk, Lucy could see J.J.'s almost-too-blue eyes, sharp as hatchets on his narrow face. Shags of dark hair fell over his brows, but J.J. didn't shake them off like he usually did. He didn't move a lanky muscle. He just stood frozen with the shovel.

The bobcat seemed to be in the same state, as if it were carved into the bark of the dead tree. Lucy couldn't see Artemis anywhere, but the big cat apparently didn't care. Its eyes were fixed on J.J., unscared and hungry.

"Da-ad?" Lucy said in a voice she could hardly hear herself.

But Dad was already on his cell phone again.

"J.J.'s out there," she whispered.

"Sheriff—Ted Rooney again—listen, we're seeing this thing now—"

Lucy didn't want to call to him any louder. What if the bobcat got freaked out and jumped J.J. and—But the cat didn't look at all put off by the human who faced him. Even as Lucy watched, frozen herself, it took one soft step, and then another, right at him.

"Lucy, what do you see now? I need to tell the sheriff—"

"It's going for J.J.!" Lucy hissed.

The bobcat moved closer, as if he were enjoying scaring the spit out of the boy. Although the shovel jittered in J.J.'s hands, he didn't back up. There was no place to go except against the toolshed, where he would be cornered.

"It's doing *what?*" Dad said. "J.J.'s out there?"

The cat lowered itself until its belly dragged the ground, and it set another paw in front of it. Lucy looked wildly around the kitchen for something—anything—and her eyes lit on the one item that was always there.

"Lucy—what's going on?"

Lucy scrambled from the sink and snatched her soccer ball from its net bag on the hook by the back entrance. With her father still firing frantic questions, Lucy flung open the door and set the ball on the back porch. With all her soccer might, she smacked it with a perfect push pass. The ball drove across the yard and landed squarely in front of the bobcat.

The long tufts of hair startled in the big cat's ears, and for an instant, its spotted lips lifted and revealed four long, pointed teeth. In the same instant, J.J. came to life and waved the shovel. The bobcat backed down onto its haunches and sprang up the dead tree. As Lucy watched, heart hammering in her ears, the cat made a silken climb and disappeared over the back fence.

The shovel thudded to the ground, and J.J. tossed his hair back to peer across the yard at Lucy.

"Score," he said.

And then he ran for the back porch, probably faster than Lucy had ever seen him move before—and she'd seen him do some pretty impressive sprints down the soccer field.

"Lucy." Dad's voice shook. "What is going on?"

"Got him, Dad. He's outta here."

"Where's J.J.?"

"I'm good." J.J. turned sideways in that skinny way that made him hard to see and slipped past Lucy and her father. As he looked over their heads out into the dark, his ice-blue eyes weren't as cool as Lucy knew he was trying to act. His Adam's apple was going up and down.

Dad, on the other hand, wasn't even trying to be calm. "What in the world just happened?"

"The cat was gonna get J.J., so I—"

"She just about nailed it right in the head with the soccer ball—"

"One at a time."

J.J. shrugged and, as always, let Lucy tell the story. When she was done, Dad's lips pressed together in a tight white line. This was a definite oops situation.

"I tried to tell you, Dad, but you were on the phone," she said.

"Didn't I say not to go outside?"

"Yeah, but J.J. was cornered."

"And you could have been too. This is not okay, Lucy, and——"

The sound of a car skidding onto the gravel at the side of the house whipped all three of their heads toward the window. J.J. leaped to it like he was escaping from a firing squad. The way Dad's eyebrows shot up made Lucy decide to stay where she was.

"It's the sheriff." J.J.'s eyes went wild again. "I think I gotta go home."

"I think you gotta stay here," Dad said. "You're not in trouble, J.J."

Lucy was pretty sure *she* was—again—so she was grateful when Sheriff Navarra tapped on the glass on the back door.

"I will get it," Dad said. "You two wait right here. And I do mean here."

"The sheriff came through the yard?" J.J. muttered as Dad stepped out onto the back porch. "There's a wild cat on the loose, and he walks right in?"

"I bet he doesn't believe it was really out there," Lucy muttered back. "You know, 'cause my dad can't see."

J.J. grunted. "Your dad sees everything."

Lucy peeked out the window in the door and wondered if Dad now "saw" Sheriff Navarra parking his beefy hands on his hips and cocking one bushy eyebrow like he was about to hear a whopper. The hair on the back of Lucy's neck bristled under her ponytail.

The two men talked outside while Lucy and J.J. pressed their ears against the door's window. When the sheriff started down the steps, Dad inched the door open and practically knocked them both down.

"Come on," Dad said, "but stay behind me."

They stepped out into what was now a starless, black night. The sheriff was striding across the yard, leaving Dad to make his own way. Lucy held out her arm to him, and he curled his fingers around it. She could feel how sweaty they were, even through her sleeve.

By the time they got to the dead tree, the sheriff was already shining his flashlight on long gouges that striped its side.

"Those weren't there before," Lucy informed him.

"You have, what, nine or ten cats?" Sheriff Navarra's dark eyes glittered, the way his son Gabe's did when he was about to put Lucy in her girl-place.

"We have four," Lucy said. "And none of them have claws big enough to do that."

She didn't do what she would have done to Gabe: smack him with a soccer ball first chance she got. She did scoop up her ball, which was lying near her feet, and prop it against her hip.

"Let's have a look," Dad said, and ran his hand up and down the old tree, letting his fingers sink into the gouge marks. He whistled under his breath.

"Hey."

Lucy joined J.J., who was pointing at a patch of bare ground. A foot with four toes and a pad the size of Lucy's fist had left its perfect stamp.

"I know none of our cats did that," she said. "It's a giant footprint, Dad."

Sheriff Navarra skimmed his light over it. "I think 'giant' is exaggerating a little. The wind could have distorted one of your—"

"I saw the bobcat!" Lucy said. "And so did J.J. And Dad heard it. I'm sorry we didn't have time to take a video. I was kind of busy saving J.J.'s life—"

"Luce." She could hear an almost-chuckle in the back of Dad's voice. "Why don't you and J.J. go back to the house, and we'll finish up here."

"Finish up" meant the sheriff would pat Dad on the head and then go tell everybody the Rooneys were looney tunes or something. At least that's what Lucy thought as she stomped toward the house, picking up pieces of garbage as she went and stuffing them into the trash can. Sometimes the sheriff could be cool, like when he did stuff for their soccer team and helped J.J. when his dad was mean to him. But sometimes Sheriff Navarra could be just like his kid: all puffed up and acting like he was the only one who knew anything.

She turned to say that to J.J., but he wasn't there. Lucy stood on the bottom of the back steps and squinted. He was just coming out from behind the toolshed, head down like he wanted to be invisible. The sheriff was too busy yakking at Dad to notice him.

"What were you doing?" Lucy whispered when J.J. reached her.

"Finding this. On the back fence." He pulled his hand out of the pocket of his jeans and produced a handful of hair. "This Mudge's?"

"Too dark."

"Artemis?"

"Too long."

"Sucker?"

"You mean Lollipop? Are you kidding? She lives in my room." Lucy stroked the hair lying over J.J.'s palm. "It's sure not Marmalade's."

"I'm keeping it."

"No. It's evidence." Lucy pulled it through his fingers and marched to the sheriff, who was putting his flashlight in its holder as importantly as if it were his gun.

"This was on the back fence," she said, holding it out to him. "And it didn't come from any of our cats." She glanced quickly at Dad. "Sir."

The sheriff grunted, but he took the hair. "Too fine to be a dog's."

"I don't know any dogs who can jump that fence." Lucy tried to avoid the "tone" Dad was always warning her about.

"I'll check it against a bobcat pelt I've got at home," the sheriff said finally. "Meanwhile, it can't hurt to publish a warning, tell people there's a *possible* wild cat diggin' through garbage cans. I'll notify Wildlife Management." He wrinkled his face. "What died in your trash, anyway?"

Lucy left that for Dad to explain. "Let's go sit on the porch," she said to J.J.

"Front porch," he mumbled.

She wasn't sure whether that was to get away from the sheriff or from the scene of a very scary thing that had almost happened to him. She didn't ask. She never did. She just led the way through the house to the front porch, stopping only long enough to grab a Ziploc bag full of Inez's homemade tortilla chips from the kitchen and her favorite battered jean jacket from the coatrack.

They sat side by side on the shallow brick steps, which were painted the color of cream to match the Rooney's adobe house. The temperature was in the forties now that the sun had set, and the few lights on in J.J.'s house made it look like a cold, lonely kid with no friends. Lucy didn't like to go in there. It always smelled like wet dog, even though Mr. Cluck had never let Januarie and J.J. have pets. Inez, Lucy's nanny, always said a house had to be tendered or it became sad and angry. Lucy was pretty sure Mrs. Cluck had never been able to be tender to her house. She was too busy protecting her kids.

Lucy and J.J. didn't talk at first but just chewed until J.J. said, "I got you in trouble again."

"It's okay. Groundation's not that bad. Besides, tomorrow's Sunday. I still get to go out for church, and we don't have soccer practice anyway." She passed him the bag. "You didn't get grounded or anything yesterday, huh?"

"My mom never punishes us, only my dad."

He sighed. Lucy was hearing a lot of relief coming out of him lately.

"Do you *have* to do those visit things with him?" Lucy said.

"Weasel Lady says I do. I'm not gonna."

"Who's Weasel Lady?"

"That person from the court. She looks like a weasel." J.J. pulled at his nose to make it long and pointy.

She gave him a poke with her elbow. "Y'know, you could have told me that's what you were hiding from when you dragged me into the museum yesterday. I shoulda known you didn't really care about a bunch of junky pottery. Nobody does."

"Sorry."

"I don't get it." Lucy took the bag back from him and pawed through for a chip that didn't have any broken-off corners. "You don't have to be alone with your dad. That lady from the court's always there, right?"

"Doesn't matter. I don't want to see him."

Then he clamped his teeth together, and Lucy gave up. When J.J.

was done talking about something, he was done. It was time to change the subject.

"So why'd you come over here?" she said. "Did you hear that cat and hunt him down in the backyard so you could be a hero and save Artemis's life?"

J.J. looked at her from under his shag of hair.

"Okay, so, no," Lucy said.

"I was bored."

"You coulda signaled."

He put his fingers above his head like evil horns. Lucy nodded.

"Januarie wouldn't leave you alone."

"Worse."

Lucy stopped with a chip halfway to her mouth. "Is she in trouble?"

"No, she's just a moron."

J.J. always thought his little sister was a moron. At least since their dad had been taken out of their house, J.J. had stopped wanting to lock her in the garage or duct tape her mouth shut.

"Why is she a moron today?" Lucy said.

"She wants to wear makeup like your aunt."

"I know," Lucy said, groaning.

"She found a Sharpie and drew on eyebrows with it. Down to here." He put his fingers to his temples.

"Oh, nuh-uh! You're making that up."

J.J. shook his head.

"That stuff doesn't come off."

"She looks like a freak. Any soccer on tonight?"

J.J. didn't have a TV at his house, although there were probably enough parts of old televisions in his junky yard to make several. The Clucks didn't have a phone either, which was another reason J.J. and Lucy always sent signals. Besides, it was more fun.

"I don't know if there's a game on or not," Lucy said. "We could go find out."

But before she could get up, the sheriff's car pulled away from the side of the house, spewing gravel, and Dad opened the front door.

"Time to come in, Luce."

"Can J.J.? We wanna watch—"

"I think it's time for you to head on over to your place, J.J."

That was Dad-speak for, "You and I are going to have a serious talk, Lucy." Otherwise, he would have let J.J. stay as long as he wanted. Everybody was taking care of J.J. and Januarie these days.

"See ya," J.J. said.

Lucy made a phone with her fingers, the sign for "Signal me."

But J.J. had already slipped into the dark like he was stepping soundlessly into an envelope. Dad always said that was the half of him that came from his Apache mom. Right now, Lucy didn't want to hear what *else* Dad might say. She dragged the tops of her feet, one by one, across the tile in the front hall as she followed him into the living room. He sank into what they called the Sitting Couch, and Lucy knew there was no point trying to escape to the Napping Couch over in the corner, where Marmalade was taking his Saturday night bath. When he didn't join them on Dad's lap, his favorite spot in the world, Lucy figured even the cats knew this was not going to be a fun conversation.

She perched at the other end of the Sitting Couch. "I bet I know what you're going to say."

"I don't think you do, because if you did, you wouldn't have done any of the things you've done in the past couple of days."

There was no chuckle in Dad's voice, no sunlight smile on his face. Lucy pulled her knees up to her chin.

"The sheriff says I need to get better control of my daughter."

Lucy opened her mouth, but Dad put a hand up. His sightless eyes were aimed at her feet, but she knew he was seeing the protest on her face.

"I'm not one to be taking parenting tips from him," Dad said. "His own kid isn't perfect."

"Gabe? Ya think?"

"But I'm telling you this because I'm not the only one who sees that you—" Dad stopped and closed his eyes, as if he were sorting out something that had gotten confused. She often wondered if he could see things inside his head the way he remembered them from back when he could see.

"Look, champ, Sheriff Navarra pointed out to me that you are very mature in some ways. You're soccer captain. You helped pull the whole town together to get behind the team. But he said that also makes you—what was the word he used?"

It probably wasn't a very long word. Lucy chewed at the inside of her mouth so she wouldn't say it out loud. She was obviously in enough trouble already.

"It was something in Spanish, actually," Dad said, "but it means strong willed. Sometimes that serves you well, and sometimes it doesn't."

"The sheriff said all that?"

"No, I did." Dad rubbed his hand over his mouth. "You make up your mind about something, and that's it. You go after it. Your mom was like that."

Lucy let go of her knees. "Then that's a good thing."

"It can be. But not when what you make up your mind to do isn't the right thing."

"I don't get it."

"I know, which is why you need to listen to your dad here." He tried the smile on her, but Lucy was past that now. She folded her arms.

"I'm listening," she said.

"Even though you could have been hurt, you did a good thing saving J.J. tonight. I know you would do anything for him. But unlike tonight, 'anything' isn't always the best thing."

Lucy pulled her ponytail to the top of her head and let it go. "I don't even know what you're talking about, Dad."

"It hasn't escaped me that you only get in trouble when it's about J.J. That whole thing with you going with him to the museum when he was supposed to be at a supervised visitation with his father, and then you covering for him, saying it was your idea—"

"It—"

"Wasn't—and I know it. You wouldn't go into Old Man Esparza's museum if Mia Hamm were in there."

Lucy snatched up an orange-striped pillow and hugged it fiercely. "J.J. doesn't want to see his dad—and I don't blame him. He was awful to him."

"Which is why his dad can't live with his family right now, and why the court is trying to get the man some help for his anger issues." Dad reached across the couch and found her hands. He pried one of them loose from the pillow and held it between his. "Nobody is going to let J.J.'s dad hurt him again. You don't have to protect him."

Lucy didn't answer. It wasn't really a question anyway.

"So here's the deal," Dad said. "If you get into trouble with me because of J.J. again, I'm going to have to forbid you to see him."

Lucy pulled her hand away, and her arms and legs flew out as if they'd come off her body. "Dad—*what?*"

"It's the only way I can think of to keep you from getting in the way of what's right for J.J. and his family."

"Okay." Lucy collected her limbs and stood up. "I get it. Is it all right if I go to my room?"

Dad left a you-might-change-your-mind pause. When she didn't, he nodded.

"You hungry?" he said.

"No." She edged toward the hall.

"Champ?"

"Yeah?"

"I'm just trying to take care of what I love."

Usually she liked it when he said that. Right now it rubbed at her like Inez's cheese grater. With an "uh-huh," she fled to her room.

The Book of Lists was right on the pillow where she'd left it. Lolli had her black head resting on it, but when Lucy stormed in, she escaped into the toy chest Lucy kept propped open for her. Usually it was Januarie or Aunt Karen or one of the other cats she was hiding from—not Lucy herself, who never got as prickly and hot in the neck as she was right now.

She flipped open the book and pulled the cap off the pen with her teeth.

Things I Just Don't Get, God

she wrote.

~ Why Dad doesn't understand that him thinking I can't

do stuff just because I'm only 11 bugs me as much as it bugs him when people think he can't do stuff just because he's blind.

~ Why the court thinks J.J.'s father is ever going to be a good dad. I personally think he's evil in his soul.

~ Why the court gets to be the boss of J.J. anyway.

~ What I would do if I couldn't hang out with J.J. My girlfriends are fine, but nobody gets me like J.J. And nobody gets him like me.

Lucy folded her arms around the Book of Lists. Dad said her mom was going to write in it, when she got back from Iraq, all the things she wanted Lucy to know about being a girl. But the explosion in the hotel in Baghdad made sure she didn't come back, and now it was up to Lucy to fill up the book with whatever she could discover. She closed her eyes and prayed like Inez had taught her that whatever Mom would have said would find its way to her.

One thing she was sure of as she slid the green book under her pillow. Her mom wouldn't want her to stop hanging out with J.J.

She was even more sure when she looked over at J.J.'s window and saw the shadow of his arm, bent at the elbow and swinging back and forth. That was the signal for "Hang in there."

Lucy would have stayed in her room for the rest of the evening, but the phone rang and Dad yelled for her to see who it was.

She was in the living room on the second ring, but she waited until the third one to pick it up. When Aunt Karen's name came up on caller ID, Lucy was always tempted to tell Dad it was a telemarketer and they shouldn't answer it. But Aunt Karen always left a message that was longer than you could listen to, and besides, Lucy just didn't lie to Dad. She handed him the phone.

"She wants to talk to you, champ," he said after a few minutes of "Uh-huh" and "Oh, is that right?" Lucy was pretty convinced he was only nice to her because she was Mom's sister. Lucy couldn't think of any other reason.

Especially not when Aunt Karen followed "Hi" with "I've been meaning to ask you—are you still wearing that beat-up old jeans jacket?"

Lucy hesitated. Now, Aunt Karen she might consider lying to.

"I don't know why I'm even asking," Aunt Karen said. "We're so going shopping next time I come up, and then we are going to burn that hideous thing. But that isn't why I called." Lucy could imagine her licking her lips the way she did every other minute. Lucy curled up in a corner of the Napping Couch and scooped Marmalade onto her lap. She might as well get comfortable, because this was sure to be a long, one-sided conversation. She sometimes wondered if she put the phone down and went and made popcorn and came back whether Aunt Karen would even realize she'd been gone.

"You remember the coach from the El Paso team," she was saying now, "the one who said you were talented, blah, blah, blah."

Lucy would never forget it. She'd loved hearing it, but it also meant Aunt Karen used it like a weapon to try to force Lucy to come and live with her every chance she got. Lucy would rather live in J.J.'s junkyard.

"I had lunch with him today, and he says you should know about this program—"

"I know about the El Paso League," Lucy said, between teeth gritted like J.J.'s.

"No, this is a different thing: the Olympic Development Program." She sounded like she was reading from something. "'The US Youth Soccer Olympic Development Program, or ODP, is a national identification and development program for high-level players. The program identifies and develops youth players throughout the country to represent their state association, region, and the United States in soccer competition.'"

Aunt Karen paused.

"I wish it was in English," Lucy said.

"Okay—they pick the best players in the different age groups and make up these, like, pre-Olympic teams and, let's see—" Lucy could tell she was reading again, "'develop their skill through training and competition. From the state pools and subsequent teams, players are identified for regional and *national* pools and teams.' Do you get it?"

Lucy sat up straight. "They train kids for the Olympic soccer team? For real?"

"Yes, and Coach Baldwin says we should definitely look into it. It says here you can try out in a state association where you're eligible, but you can't try out in more than one state."

"I only live in one state." She couldn't help feeling a zing up her spine. The Olympic soccer team? "What would I have to do to get in that?" she said.

"They have open tryouts. Let's see … oh, and some state associations combine scouting techniques and invitations to certain players with the open tryouts. I'm going to see—"

Aunt Karen sounded more like she was talking to herself than to Lucy.

"How good do you have to be?" Lucy said.

"*Superior,* is the word they use—in technique, tactics, athletic ability and fitness, and attitude."

"Oh," Lucy said. She wasn't sure what all that meant, or even if she could remember it. But she did understand "superior." That meant better than just about everybody else.

"There are camps you go to—all kinds of different things. I'm totally looking into this, Lucy."

"Okay," Lucy said.

"Fabulous," Aunt Karen said. That was a word she seldom used to describe anything connected to Lucy.

The Olympics. Superior soccer. High-level players.

Lucy wrote it all down in the Book of Lists and held it close to her when she crawled into bed. Slowly, sleepily, worries about bobcats and J.J. and Dad faded into nothingness, replaced by the vision of herself scoring that final winning goal to the wild cheers of the whole world and ducking her head to receive her gold medal.

She had to start tomorrow. At recess. She had to work on her techniques and tactics and whatever else it was Aunt Karen had said she needed to do. It was time to start being superior.

Oh yeah: *please, God, will you help?*

3

By the end of Monday morning, Lucy was sure that "Please, God" was already working a little bit. If she'd had time to write in her Book of Lists even before recess, she would have put down this list:

1. J.J. is going to be so jazzed when I tell him about ODP. Maybe he'll even forget about the Weasel Lady and his dad.

2. All four cats showed up for breakfast, which means nobody was the bobcat's kitty-and-eggs.

3. Janvarie really does look like a freak with her eyebrows colored in with Sharpie. I cracked up when she showed up to walk to school this morning — only I tried to hide it because she has enough problems at her house.

4. When I told Mr. Auggy about the wild cat, he said tomorrow we could look up bobcats instead of having a vocabulary test.

5. Dad packed me a peanut butter and pickle sandwich, my favorite, which means he isn't mad at me. Even though I'm still pretty mad at him for even threatening to make me not hang out with J.J.

That last one was probably why she couldn't completely stay in a good mood. If she didn't keep thinking about the ODP, she had a vague feeling of wanting to rip somebody's nose hairs out. She kept it from erupting into full tweezers mode in class all morning, even when Oscar asked the same question fifteen times at least and Carla Rosa pointed out, loudly, that Lucy had a booger coming out of her nose. Lucy just told herself Oscar couldn't help it because he was a boy, and Carla Rosa couldn't help it because she had some—what did Mr. Auggy call them?—learning disabilities.

Finally—*finally*—it was lunchtime, and then there would be soccer with Coach Auggy and her team, the Los Suenos Dreams, and she could start seriously working on being a superior player. She hung back so she could tell J.J. about it without anybody else hearing yet. But before she could even get her mouth open, he said:

"Did you get in trouble?"

"I didn't get grounded," she said. She felt like she was measuring her words out in teaspoons.

"Then what?"

"Just a warning."

"About what?"

Lucy pushed through the door into the cafeteria and pretended she *really* needed to get to that peanut butter and pickle sandwich, but her mouth was suddenly too dry to chew it. How could she tell J.J. they couldn't hang out together if she tried to help him again? Why did all this other stuff have to keep interrupting the good parts?

She had never been so glad to have Januarie join them, devouring Lucy's lunch bag with hungry eyes. But J.J. grunted and glared, and by the time they got to the playground to meet Mr. Auggy and the team, Lucy felt like she needed a zipper she could undo to let all the ickety-icks out. Telling J.J. was going to have to wait.

"Red Light, Green Light!" Mr. Auggy called out. He opened a big net bag and tossed a ball to each of them.

"Hey, where'd we get all them?" Oscar said.

"Compliments of Pasco's Café." Mr. Auggy tossed one to Carla Rosa, who took it in the chest because she was staring at pretty much nothing. She did that in games sometimes too.

"Pasco's jealous because Benitez bought our uniforms and everybody thinks he's all that." Gabe Navarra parked his meaty hands on his hips—and reminded Lucy of the sheriff.

"Everybody have a ball?" Mr. Auggy said.

Lucy, J.J., Carla Rosa, and Emanuel all nodded. Gabe juggled three over his head while Veronica and Dusty squealed to grab at the balls and Oscar tried to grab at *them*. Mr. Auggy tooted cheerfully on his whistle, and Dusty hurried to join Lucy.

"Boys." She rolled golden-brown eyes in her creamy, heart-shaped face. But Lucy knew she kind of liked Gabe teasing her. Dusty was Lucy's best girlfriend, but—ickety-ick.

"Gabe—yo," Mr. Auggy said.

Gabe bounced a ball lightly on Veronica's fudge-brown head of thick hair—and she giggled—and it took another thirty seconds for Mr. Auggy to get everybody in a line across the practice field with their balls. Lucy was really ready for that zipper by then. How was she supposed to get ready for Olympic tryouts with all this going on?

"I'll be the traffic light down here," Mr. Auggy called from the other end of the field. "You're all the cars."

"I'm a Ferrari," Gabe said.

Veronica giggled. "I'm a Mustang."

"How 'bout you're a Volkswagen bug—"

"How about you shut up," Lucy muttered.

"Guess what? If Mr. Auggy heard you say that, you'd get a—" Carla Rosa let out a loud buzzing sound.

"I'm going to yell 'Green light!'," Mr. Auggy was saying, "and I'll turn my back to you. You all dribble like mad dogs until I yell 'Red light!' Before I turn around, you have to put a foot on your ball."

"It's gonna get away from some people." Gabe gave Veronica a wicked grin, which made her squeal, "Stop it!"

"If it does, that person has to go back to the beginning," Mr. Auggy said. "The winner is the person who crosses the line first. Anybody want to tell me why we're doing this drill?"

"Because it's cool!" Oscar said.

"That too. And?"

Lucy shot up her hand. "Because it teaches you to keep the ball close but still dribble fast—which we have to do—" She gave her team a hard look. "—if we're ever gonna win a game."

"You heard the captain." Mr. Auggy made a big deal out of turning his back to them. "Ready? Green light!"

Lucy gave her ball a small, sharp tap with the inside of her left foot and then with her right, keeping them close together like she always did so nobody could take the ball from her, even though they weren't practicing guarding right now. She liked to work on as many of her skills as she could at the same time. That's what you had to do if you were going to be a superior soccer player. She was already several steps ahead of Gabe, who was the fastest besides her, so she switched to using the outside of her feet so she could cut and change directions.

"Red light!" Mr. Auggy shouted.

Lucy brought her ball back and under her foot and looked at the rest of her team. Carla Rosa swatted at hers like she was trying to kick a fly and fell face first on the dirt.

"Oops—Miss Carla's down," Mr. Auggy said. "A little help please."

Lucy went over and stuck her hand out to Carla Rosa, who smiled up at her, red curls peeking out from under the white cap with the big sequins that she always wore.

"You have to keep the ball close to you," Lucy said.

"Guess what? You told me that a hundred times." Carla Rosa's smile faded, and Lucy felt a pang. Carla always did better if Lucy told her what she did right instead of what she did wrong. But at the moment, that was a little hard to do.

"It's okay." Dusty hooked her arm through Carla's. "I have to go back too."

"No, you don't," Lucy said. "You caught your ball."

Dusty bugged her eyes at Lucy and kept moving with Carla to the starting line. Veronica was still only a few feet from it, one foot on her ball, lower lip hanging open as she rebraided her ponytail.

"That's as far as you got the whole time?" Lucy said.

"My hair came undone."

"How are you going to get faster that way?"

Veronica wrinkled the caramel-colored skin on her nose. "I don't want to be fast. I want to be cute."

"Green light!" Mr. Auggy called out and turned around.

Lucy took off like a shot, dribbling around the plodding Oscar and between J.J. and Emanuel in their own personal race and past Gabe who was juggling his ball with his feet, his knees, his head and making no progress toward the line at all. Lucy crossed it before Mr. Auggy could yell "Red light!" again.

"We have a winner! All right, Miss Lucy!" Mr. Auggy put his hand up to high-five her.

"Man, nobody does that anymore," Gabe said.

Mr. Auggy didn't seem to hear him, or there would have been a buzz.

"Miss Januarie," Mr. Auggy said, "could you come over here?"

Across the touchline, J.J.'s eight-year-old sister lifted her pudgy face as if she'd been waiting all her life to be called on. Double ponytails wagged in the wind.

"You be the traffic light for a while," he said to her. And then he gave her a second closer look. Veronica and Dusty giggled into their sleeves.

Oscar squinted. "Januarie, Dude, you look like Mr. Potato Head with those eyebrows."

Januarie turned to them, lip already sticking out like a sofa, and whined, "Shut UP!"

Everybody yelled "Buzz!" which was what Mr. Auggy always did when one of them said anything ugly to somebody else. If they said something good, they got a "Ding!" He really was the best soccer coach on the planet as far as Lucy was concerned, even if he was the only one she'd ever had.

Mr. Auggy nodded toward the rock Januarie had just vacated. "Join me, Miss Lucy."

"Busted," Gabe said.

Mr. Auggy buzzed him and Oscar went "Ha-ha!" and Lucy gritted her teeth. How come she was the only one who was taking this seriously, but she was getting the talking-to?

She sat, stiff as the rock itself, next to Mr. Auggy.

"What's up, Captain?" he said in his low, kid-teacher conference voice. He wasn't a very big man — he was smaller than Dad — and he had young hair, shiny and light brown and falling over his forehead. He was like another kid, only way smarter, which was why Lucy always felt like she could tell him what she really thought instead of just what a grown-up might want her to say.

"First of all," she said, "we're trying to get good so we can actually *win* a game, and everybody's messing around."

"I think everybody's just having a good time. We can have fun while we're doing a drill." He gave her his small smile. "You're usually the first one to praise your players."

"Not to sound snotty, but I don't see what I can praise right now."

"You might want to look a little harder next time." He nodded toward the field, where Oscar was facedown on the ground and Gabe and J.J. were dribbling around him while Veronica squealed and Dusty crossed the line and Januarie wailed that she had forgotten to yell "Red light." "Look at that. They fall apart without you, Captain."

He blew his whistle and jogged back to the team. She hadn't even had a chance to tell him what was second of all. He would totally see her point if he knew about the Olympic Development Program.

But right now, he was buzzing Oscar for tripping Gabe and dinging Carla Rosa because she was the only one not screaming something. Lucy tightened up her inner zipper. This wasn't going to be so easy.

"So, like, what is up with you?" Dusty said to her after school when she and Veronica and Januarie were walking to Lucy's house. It was just across Second Street from Los Suenos Elementary, and they went there almost every day before their practice at the real soccer field across the highway.

"You're all crabby," Veronica said.

"Yeah," Januarie chimed in. Lucy knew she hadn't even noticed her being crabby because she was way over in the third-grade wing all day, probably being teased about her makeup job. It was hard for Januarie to be eight when all she wanted in the world was to be eleven like Lucy.

"I don't know what's wrong," Lucy said. That made her feel crabbier than ever since, of course, she did know.

"Yes, you do, *Bolillo*," Dusty said.

Lucy liked it when Dusty called her that. I meant she wasn't Hispanic, like Dusty and Veronica and Gabe and, partly, Mr. Auggy, and she wasn't Indo (Native American), like Oscar and Emanuel and the half of J.J. and Januarie that was Apache. Lucy and Carla Rosa were two of the few bolillos in their school, or even the whole town. Dusty always told Lucy in private that she was her favorite bolillo.

Veronica fell into step beside Lucy, who was walking her bike. "You know, but you don't want to talk about it."

"It's better if you get it out," Dusty said, joining them on the other side. "That's what my mom always says."

"Lucy doesn't have a mom," Januarie said.

"Duh-uh." Veronica slung her arm around Lucy's shoulder. "But she has us. Come on—dish."

"Huh?" Lucy said.

"Spill it. Tell us why you were being all bossy on the soccer field."

Lucy felt like the inside of a sandwich—and it really wasn't all that bad a feeling. Still, she didn't want to "spill it" in front of Januarie. And since she had to watch out for her like she was a little sister, she couldn't just run her off. Lucy stopped, leaned the bike against her leg, and dug into the pocket of her jeans.

"Here, Januarie." She pulled out two folded-up dollar bills. "Go down to Claudia's and get us some candy for after practice. Pick whatever you want."

Januarie put her chubby hands on what were becoming some pretty round hips. "Claudia sells flowers, silly. She doesn't have candy."

"She does now," Veronica said. "She started Friday. Suckers in bouquets and stuff like that."

"For reals?" Januarie licked her lips, and Lucy was sure she was going to start drooling any minute.

Veronica said, "I got a chocolate rose—"

Januarie was gone. Veronica and Dusty moved against Lucy like pieces of Velcro.

"Give it," Dusty said.

Lucy chewed at the inside of her lip. She really wanted to tell Mr. Auggy about the ODP first, because he'd make sure everybody knew how important it was to her and she wouldn't have to be the one to make them stop messing around. Still, they were both looking at her like they couldn't wait for her to share her whole entire life with them. There *was* that other problem —

So she told them the J.J. story. She finished with, "If I get in, like, this much trouble with J.J. — " she held her thumb and index finger close together — "my dad's not gonna let me hang out with him anymore. Like, ever."

Veronica looked like someone had died as she hung her lower lip even farther down than usual. "That's so unfair."

They stopped outside the side gate to Lucy's yard. From behind the pointy century plant, Mudge, the big brown tabby, gave a low warning growl.

"That's how you feel about your dad right now, huh?" Dusty said, nodding at him.

"Yeah," Lucy said. "And it's all funky because I usually really like my dad."

"I know. When I'm mad at my dad, I like my mom better, and when I'm mad at my mom, then I'm daddy's girl."

Lucy didn't point out that she didn't have that choice. She couldn't ever remember being mad at her mom before she got killed, and she couldn't imagine that she ever would have.

"Well, there's only one thing to do." Veronica folded her arms, which lately seemed too long for her body.

"What?" Lucy said.

"You just have to hang around with J.J. as much as you can now, in case your dad gets mad at you and — " She snapped her fingers — "J.J.'s outta here."

"Wow," Dusty said. "Good idea."

Before Lucy could even give her opinion, Veronica's face glowed like she'd just stepped into a spotlight. "There he is right now!"

Lucy followed her gaze across the street to where J.J. was standing in his yard bouncing his soccer ball off of his head. If he dropped it, he'd never find it again in that mess.

"Hey, J.J.!" Veronica called out. "Why don't you come over!"

"What are you doing?" Lucy said between her teeth. "It's all girls over here. He's not gonna come!"

"Wanna bet?" Dusty said.

J.J. had already vaulted his fence and was loping toward them with his head tilted and his arms dangling. Lucy knew if he opened his mouth to say something right now, his voice would go all high-pitched the way it did when he was feeling weird. She suddenly felt pretty weird herself.

"I bet Inez has sopapillas ready," Veronica said when he got to them. "Come eat with us."

"Okay," J.J. said.

Sure enough, the "kay" part went up into that range where only dogs can hear. For no reason she could figure out, Lucy's face began to burn.

They filed into the Rooney's kitchen, Veronica chattering away and J.J. giving Lucy question-mark looks from under his shag of hair and Dusty rubbing Lucy's back like she was preparing her for a boxing ring or something. It didn't surprise Lucy that Inez gave them a very long look.

Inez Herrera was the Spanish nanny Dad had hired a few months ago to be with Lucy after school. At first, Lucy didn't see why she needed a "babysitter" when she and Dad had gotten everything done by themselves before and she hadn't gotten into *that* much trouble being on her own every day until Dad got home from work. It was especially annoying because Aunt Karen was the one who sort of made Dad do it.

But now Inez cooked their suppers five days a week and did the shopping and the laundry and the cleaning and sometimes brushed the kitties—except Mudge who didn't let anybody but Lucy touch him—and told Lucy things even Dad didn't know about growing up. She was kind of like a member of the family who arrived at 8:00 a.m. and left at 6:00 p.m., and it was sometimes lonely when she wasn't there making tea and folding socks and talking about people in the Bible like they lived next door.

Right now, Inez eyed all of them with her very black eyes beneath straight-across bangs and silently put a plate of sopapillas on the table, next to a gravy boat brimming with honey.

"We brought J.J.," Lucy said. Like that wasn't obvious.

"Always there is plenty." Inez's words sounded sliced-off because English wasn't the language she learned as a little kid. Her granddaughter, Mora, on the other hand, did know English and spoke it longer and faster even than those guys on TV who tried to sell you stuff.

Mora was doing homework at the table, which Inez always made her do after she picked her up from her sixth grade down in Alamogordo. She slapped her notebook closed and surveyed them all in that way she had, like she was deciding if everybody in the room was cool enough to be in her presence. They must have all passed, because she shrugged and moved her backpack from the chair next to her.

Nobody could say Mora wasn't pretty, at least when she wasn't in a bad mood. She had the same hair-like-black-silk that Lucy's Hispanic girlfriends had, only she seemed to have more than both of them put together, and it perfectly matched the enormous eyes that took over the top half of her face. Aunt Karen said Mora should be a model. She never said that about Lucy, who didn't want to be a model—but Aunt Karen wanted her to *want* to do stuff like cover up her exactly sixteen nose-freckles with makeup. Which she was never going to do because Mom had had exactly sixteen freckles too.

Lucy refocused on J.J., who was looking at the arrangement of chairs like he hadn't sat in all of them practically his whole childhood. Finally, he started to fold into one of them. He seemed really tall all of a sudden.

"Not that one!" Mora cried. "That orange cat's in it. He'll scratch your eyes out."

J.J. blinked at her and picked up Marmalade and dumped him onto the floor. Mora looked very impressed.

"Sit," Inez said.

They all dropped into chairs. Lucy selected one of the pillows of dough from the plate and bit off an end so she could pour honey into it. When she reached for the gravy boat, she realized everyone was looking at her, and then at J.J. And nobody was saying anything.

Except of course Mora. "These are so fattening," she said to J.J. "I just want half."

"Who will have the tea?" Inez said.

Lucy pushed her mug forward. Ever since she found out her mom had liked hot tea, she had a cup with lots of milk and sugar every day. Mora leaned toward J.J.

"I would so rather have a Starbucks, wouldn't you?"

"I don't know," J.J. said. The "know" went up into the stratosphere. "I never had it."

"That's where my mom and I always go when she's in town. She's in California right now, but when she comes back, my life is going to get a *lot* better."

"How come you don't go to California with your mom?" Veronica said, as if she wished Mora would go right now.

Mora tore off a microscopic piece of sopapilla and rolled it between her fingers. "I'm going to, next time she comes. She has a huge job there. It's way important, and she had to get settled in first—Oh!"

Everyone jumped as Mora flew out of her chair, eyes bulging.

"What?" Lucy said.

"He's stalking me!"

Mora pointed to the top of the cabinets where Artemis Hamm was creeping slowly along, head down, eyes in slits.

"First of all, he's a she," Lucy said. "Second of all, she isn't stalking you. She just wants to go out and hunt, and she can't, so she's practicing in here."

"So put her outside," Mora said. "She's creeping me out."

"We don't want the bobcat to get her," Lucy said.

She thought Mora's eyes were going to pop out of her head. "Bobcat? You have a bobcat now?"

All three girls dissolved into giggles. Mora turned to J.J. "What are they talking about—*you* tell me."

J.J. mumbled about half the story, but it was apparently enough to get Mora to the edge of her seat. By the time he fumbled to the end, she was almost in his lap, in Lucy's opinion.

"You are so totally brave," Mora said.

"You know what?" J.J. said. "I gotta go." Lucy couldn't even hear the "go." He scraped back his chair on the tile and looked at Lucy like he had another bobcat coming at him.

"See you at practice," Lucy said.

He escaped through the back door. It had barely closed behind him before Mora sighed dramatically. "He is so hot."

"What is 'hot'?" Inez said, arms folded.

"You know, Abuela. Cute."

"Yeah, well, forget about it, Mora." Veronica slung her arm around Lucy's shoulder again. "He's Lucy's."

Mora gazed at Lucy as if she'd just shown up. "You guys are going out?"

"No!" Lucy said.

"Yes!" Veronica said. Dusty echoed her faintly.

"Okay, I don't think you know what 'going out' means." Mora perched at the edge of her chair and fanned out her fingers, pulling them back one by one as she went on.

"One, you talk on the phone." She cocked an eyebrow at Lucy, who shook her head. J.J. didn't even have a phone.

"Two, you meet at the movies and sit by each other. I know you don't do that."

"Hello!" Lucy said. "How would I get there?"

"Exactly. Three, you hug."

"Ickety-ick!"

"There is no hug the boys, Mora," Inez said.

"Do you even write notes to each other?" Mora said to Lucy.

"No."

"Then you're totally not going out."

She smiled as if she'd just won a prize and tore off a big hunk of sopapilla, which she shoved into her mouth. Something in the look she gave Lucy as she chewed made Lucy feel like she needed a sweater. When Januarie burst through the door, cheeks bulging as much as the paper sack in her hand, Lucy could have hugged her for the second time that day.

"No more J.J. talk," Veronica said to Mora out of a hole she formed out of the side of her mouth.

"Muchachos," Inez said. "They are trouble."

No kidding.

4

One thing did make Lucy feel less like going after somebody's nose hairs with the tweezers. While she and Dad were waiting for the cheese to stop bubbling on the blue corn enchiladas Inez left for them for supper that night, gravel spit outside on the driveway and Lucy looked out the window to see Sheriff Navarra climbing out of the cruiser.

"Are the police after us again?" Dad said.

Lucy didn't grin along with him as she let the sheriff in the back door. She secretly hoped Artemis would attack him from behind the broom where she was hiding. But Sheriff Navarra wasn't looking quite as puffed-up that evening. When Dad offered him some of their enchiladas, he shook his head and folded his arms.

"He says no," Lucy said to Dad.

"I just came by to let you know I compared that hair to a bobcat pelt I had."

"We appreciate you doing that," Dad said.

The sheriff cleared his throat. "It matched. I thought it probably would."

You *so* did not, Lucy wanted to say. But she fought to hold herself back.

"Bobcats are usually pretty shy," the sheriff went on. "This one appears to be aggressive."

Lucy lost the battle. "Ya think? He tried to take out our cat!"

Sheriff Navarra narrowed his black eyes down into dashes. "Which is why if you see the animal again, you won't go tearing out there trying to be a hero. You call me. You hear?"

You are so not the boss of me, Lucy wanted to say. But the way Dad was shooting his eyebrows into his hairline made her bite it back and nod at the sheriff.

"Was that a yes, Lucy?" Dad said.

"She hears me." The sheriff had his thumbs in his belt now, and was poking out his chest. "I've got Wildlife Management on alert. The cat'll have to be destroyed."

Artemis stuck her head out around the broom and slit her own eyes down, as if to say, "Uh, which cat did you say you were destroying?" She did, in fact, let out a long, low growl.

"Get Artemis, Luce," Dad said.

Lucy scooped her up, but she let her continue to snarl at the sheriff. Just so he knew.

When he was gone, Lucy gave Artemis a final squeeze and let her go. Artemis parked herself next to Lucy's leg and rubbed it with her head. Then she trotted off, job done.

"Luce," Dad said.

"I know. I was a smart-mouth. I'm sorry."

"It's hard not to be, but—"

"I won't do it again, I promise."

"I feel your pain. I had a tough time not saying 'I told you so' myself."

He smiled his sunlight smile and raised his palm. Lucy high-fived him and didn't inform him that, according to Gabe, hardly anybody did that anymore. It felt good to be her and Dad again for a minute. It was like having the zipper open.

The enchiladas were still warm when Lucy cut into them and arranged one and some lime Jello on Dad's plate. She was about to take her first bite when Dad said, "So, did you and Aunt Karen talk girl stuff again last night?"

Lucy looked at him, her mouth half open in front of the fork. He was poking at his enchilada as if he suddenly didn't know how to eat it.

"I know she's always trying to get you to do the girly thing," he said. "You hold your own on that pretty well. But I was just wondering—"

"Wondering what?" Lucy said.

Dad poked at his plate some more.

"You have enchiladas at six o'clock," Lucy said. "Lime Jello at twelve —"

"I know where everything is." Dad shook his head, and Lucy saw a red spot form at the top of each cheek. "I just think I need to come out with it. Your Aunt Karen says you need a bra. What do you think?"

Lucy stuffed her mouth so she wouldn't have to answer. Dad, of course, waited. She prayed for the phone to ring. For the bobcat to return. For the roof to cave in.

When none of that happened and her mouth was empty and she hadn't died of embarrassment, she said, "I don't want one, Dad."

"I didn't ask you that. I asked if you thought you needed one."

"No! Dad, please don't make me go shopping with her for a bra. I'll do anything. I'll be so polite to Sheriff Navarra —"

"Luce, it's okay." Dad looked like he was trying not to laugh. Or cry. "When you're ready, you let me know and we'll make other arrangements. Okay?"

Lucy didn't even ask what those might be. This was definitely time for a change of subject. She got up on one knee in the chair.

"Did Aunt Karen tell you what we did talk about? About the Olympic Development Program?"

The rise of his eyebrows told her no.

"Yeah, it's this program where there's camps and everything. If I get in, I could be on the Olympic soccer team."

"Your Aunt Karen told you all this?" Dad said.

"Weird, huh?" Lucy pushed her plate aside so she could lean farther across the table. "Maybe she's starting to get me, Dad — you know, not trying to convince me to move to El Paso and be all girly with her."

Dad nodded, but he didn't look like he really agreed. "She didn't say anything to me. I'll have to ask her about it."

"But doesn't it sound cool?" Lucy said. "Mom would really like it, wouldn't she?"

She found herself nodding her head so hard her eyes blurred. But it didn't get Dad nodding his.

"Mom would be proud of you no matter what, champ," he said.

"Yeah, but she wanted me to be a soccer star. You told me that."

"She wanted you to be happy." Dad put up his hand as if he could see Lucy opening her mouth to protest. "This does sound exciting, Luce, and I'll get more information from Aunt Karen."

You'll let me try out, won't you? Lucy wanted to say. But she didn't. This wasn't the reaction she expected from Dad, and suddenly she didn't want to talk about it anymore.

The list-prayer that night was short:

Things I Wish You'd Tell People for Me, God

- Soccer is WAY serious for me, and I need to totally focus on it.
- I am not "going out" with J.J.
- I don't need a bra.

Before she snapped the light off, she took a peek under her favorite soccer T-shirt, just to be sure she was right. She was.

She was about to snuggle down when a flash of light caught her eye. She scrambled up to the windowsill.

Across the street, J.J. was opening and closing his hand and turning the flashlight on and off. Code for "MAJOR Problem." At least he wasn't making his fingers run, which meant his dad was coming and he was out of there. Still, the "MAJOR Problem" signal was a call for an immediate meeting, preferably in Lucy's toolshed. She started for the door, and then she remembered: *If you get into trouble with me because of J.J. again, I'm going to have to forbid you to see him.*

Lucy found her own flashlight under her bed and flashed it twice — for no — at the window. J.J. flashed his again, fingers working, but again Lucy flashed twice and then threw herself under her covers and pulled them over her head. When did everything get so complicated?

The next morning, J.J. showed up on his bike outside Lucy's gate without Januarie. His shoulders were tightened almost up to his ears.

"Where's—" Lucy started to say.

"With the Weasel Lady."

"Why?"

"Don't know. They say I *have to* have meetings with her."

"Because of your dad?"

J.J. grunted.

Lucy got on her bike and wheeled it slowly across the street. J.J. rode a circle around her. His shoulders were starting to come unhunched.

"Isn't it better than meeting with just him?" she said.

"She's supposed to teach me."

"Teach you what?"

"How to talk to him or something."

"Oh."

"I hate him."

"I know."

"I wish Mr. Auggy was my dad."

"He sort of is right now."

J.J. made one more circle and then said over his shoulder, "Race ya."

As Lucy took off after him and sprayed him with dirt at the bike rack, she decided maybe Dusty was right. Maybe it did help to just get it out.

Until J.J. got off his bike and gave her a sideways look and said, "How come you didn't meet me last night?"

Lucy took her time slinging on her backpack. "I couldn't."

"Your dad?"

"Yeah."

It was the truth, but on her tongue, it tasted like a lie.

"I gotta go talk to Mr. Auggy," he said. And then he walked off with his lanky arms swinging, and Lucy thought things would be so much easier if it was all about soccer.

In class, just as he'd promised, Mr. Auggy passed out books about bobcats and told everybody to find five interesting facts.

Lucy didn't mind that. She had a lot of practice making lists. What she didn't like was reading out loud in front of people. To her, it was like dribbling an invisible ball. Maybe Mr. Auggy would just let them turn in their papers, and he would read them. He was nice that way.

She curled up on the floor in the corner, next to J.J., and read silently about how bobcats had powerful jaws and long, pointed canine teeth, but she didn't write that down. She'd already seen that for herself—up close. The same went for the big ears and the spotted coat and the tufts of hair at the tips of their ears. She was skimming over all of that when she came across something that slowed her way down.

"In one small mountain town," the book said, "a bobcat entered a store, walked around, curled up behind the counter, and purred happily like a house cat."

That sounded like something Marmalade would do.

Lucy read on. "They stalk their prey and then pounce on it."

If that wasn't like Artemis Hamm, she didn't know what was.

"They are carnivores (meat-eaters) and prefer rabbits and rodents."

Lucy found herself grinning. That was Mudge all over.

"Bobcats are loners who seldom wander into each other's ranges, especially the females."

And that was totally Lollipop.

Lucy gnawed at the end of her pen. So that bobcat that was after Artemis wasn't really so different from her own kitties, except that it had bigger teeth and, according to the book, could kill its prey in one powerful bite.

She poked her hand into the air.

"Question, Miss Lucy?" Mr. Auggy said. He was smiling the small smile he always used when somebody in the group did something that proved they really weren't the dumb class.

"How come those Wildlife people have to kill bobcats when they come down here? They're just hungry."

"Why don't you find out?" he said, over the ringing of the lunch bell. "I want all of you to take what you've learned about bob-cats—maybe learn some more—and a week from today, be prepared to present it to the class. We'll all be experts."

Lucy tried not to groan out loud, but she was absolutely roaring on the inside. Why did they have to get up in front of the whole class?

"You like this idea?" Mr. Auggy said.

"Dude, yeah," Oscar said. "It's better than a stupid vocabulary test."

Mr. Auggy buzzed him, but he was still smiling his small smile.

Ugh. One more thing to distract her from soccer.

But as soon as they went out for recess, everything else went out of her mind.

Mr. Auggy had them work on shielding, so he divided them into their two smaller teams. Lucy, Oscar, Veronica, and Gabe each had a soccer ball. J.J., Dusty, Emanuel, and Carla Rosa were the defenders trying to get the balls from them. J.J. and Lucy paired up like always, and Lucy had her body between him and the ball, keeping it close to her feet and away from J.J.

J.J., however, was the best defender on their whole team. Lucy sometimes wondered how he could be gangly as a puppet on strings when he was just walking around falling over stuff, but on the soccer field, he was totally balanced and hardly ever missed one of her fakes. The second she let the ball get a little too far away, he'd pounce on it. Kind of like Artemis. Kind of like that bobcat.

Right now, he was at her back, almost swimming around her with his arms. She swung her hip out, and he grabbed her shirt, his eyes still drilled into the ball. Lucy pretended to start taking off to the right and then darted to the left, dribbling like a mad dog, as Mr. Auggy always said. But J.J. was right there — everywhere at once, in fact. Their feet were suddenly tangled, and they fell like one person with their ankles still wrapped up. Lucy could feel J.J.'s wiry arm across her back.

"Get off me!" she said, laughing from the pit of her stomach.

J.J. rolled to his back, mouth open in a silent guffaw, which was the way J.J. always laughed. You never actually heard him make any noise — you just saw his chest going up and down. That was the Apache half of him too, Dad always said.

"Oo-ooh, Lucy Goosey. Huggin' in the dirt with your boyfriend."

Lucy got up on her elbows and gave Gabe an eye-roll.

"A little help for Miss Lucy," Mr. Auggy said.

Gabe stuck his hand down, but Lucy smacked it playfully and

scrambled to her feet by herself. J.J. glared at Oscar, who was trying to pick him up by the armpits.

"So what did we learn from that?" Mr. Auggy said, smiling his small smile.

"That Lucy Goosey and the J-man are goin' out," Gabe said.

"We are not," Lucy said.

"That's not what I heard."

"This is soccer practice, not Match dot com." Mr. Auggy nodded at J.J. "You don't want to make your move until you're sure you can get the ball. Defense is all about patience and what we call 'containment.'"

J.J. nodded as if he actually understood that. Lucy made a note to herself, because that must be one of those tactic things she'd have to know about for the tryouts. When she told Mr. Auggy about the ODP, he'd probably teach her more important stuff. That had to happen soon—maybe right after recess.

Mr. Auggy blew his whistle, and everybody paired up again. Gabe dribbled right up beside Lucy and made a kissing noise.

"You are such a little creep," Lucy said.

He wiggled his eyebrows. "But you don't think J.J.'s a creep."

Lucy wrinkled her face in disgust. Where was this coming from all of a sudden? And then she heard Veronica giggle, and she knew.

J.J. tapped the ball deftly away from her and took off down the field. Okay, she had to concentrate, or else the soccer ball was going right up Gabe's nose. And maybe Veronica's too. She had to get this straightened out so she could focus. Instead of waiting to talk to Mr. Auggy after recess, she stomped directly to the sixth-grade hall.

The elementary school didn't have lockers, only cubbies for storing their stuff. Veronica's was next to Dusty's, but at the moment, Veronica was down the hall chasing Gabe, who had snatched off her striped headband and taken off with it.

"Did you guys tell Gabe me and J.J. were going out or something?" Lucy said to Dusty.

Dusty pulled her arms out of her hoodie with the sparkle-stars on it and folded it neatly. "Veronica did."

"But it's not true!"

"I know, but Veronica doesn't get you being friends with a boy. She thinks it has to be like a date."

"We're eleven!"

Dusty tucked her folded hoodie precisely into her cubby, on top of a stack of color-coded binders. "She didn't tell the part about your dad, though. That's a secret just between us three, right?"

That felt like a hug to Lucy, and she let her arms come unfolded from across her chest.

"Don't worry," Dusty said. "Me and Veronica have been friends since like kindergarten. I know her. She'll get tired of talking about you and J.J. and start on something else."

The warning bell rang, and Lucy peeled off her sweatshirt and wadded it up. "I wish she'd think about soccer."

"Good luck with that. Veronica only plays soccer because we do."

"And because Gabe does." Lucy shook her head as she crammed her ball of a jacket into her cubby, squishing a nest of papers into the back. "She could be really good if she'd just take it serious."

"Not gonna happen. She's totally not into it like us, Bolillo."

Another word-hug. It was one of those moments when Lucy wanted to be with Dusty forever—or at least not have to split up to go to their separate classes. She wanted to tell her all about the Olympic program—maybe she'd want to try out for it too—

But there was no time right then. Dusty and Veronica were in regular sixth grade down the hall from the cubbies. Lucy was in the support class out in the portable building with Oscar and Emanuel and Carla Rosa and J.J.—and Mr. Auggy. At least there was that. And at least Gabe wasn't in there. Okay—the list of things to be happy about was getting longer.

There was no time after school either. It was Tuesday, and that was the day Inez did Bible study with her and Mora. That was another reason Dad had hired her, and at first, Lucy had thought it was a waste of the time she could have been spending practicing her step-overs—or flossing Lollipop's teeth—or anything that had something to do with her actual life.

And then she'd learned that the Bible did. So even though Veronica and Dusty didn't get to come over on Tuesdays and she had to get to practice late, she was okay with it. And today they were starting a new story, which meant Inez would tell stuff instead of making them read out loud.

When Lucy had the milk and sugar all regulated just right in her tea in the butterfly mug that was her mom's, and Mora had stopped whining, like always, that she would rather be watching *Oprah*, and Inez had taken her cell phone, her iPod, and her electronic diary away, Inez folded her cinnamon-colored hands on the tabletop and closed her eyes and began.

"Senor Laban, he has two *hijas*—"

"Daughters," Mora said to Lucy.

"Yeah, I got that."

"The older one, she is called Senorita Leah, and the younger one, she is Senorita Rachel."

Mora didn't point out, the way she usually did, that the Bible didn't really use Senor and Senorita. Inez would just have told her she saw her own world in the characters' when she read the Bible.

"Now, Senorita Leah, she has the weak eyes."

"What does that mean?" Mora said.

"She was blind like my dad?" Lucy said.

"She does not see so well." Inez squinted. "Like this."

"Attractive," Mora said.

"But Senorita Rachel is very beautiful, and she has the nice figure. Can you think what that was like?"

"Hello, yes!" Mora tossed her hair back. "People were probably all, 'Too bad Leah's a dog and Rachel's drop-dead gorgeous.' It had to really be awful to be Leah."

Lucy's neck bristled. "Why do you think she was ugly just because she was blind?"

"Oh, no offense to your dad or anything, but I bet Rachel had way more friends. Guys were probably asking Leah if she could hook them up with Rachel all the time."

"And I bet Rachel was a snot too."

"Why? Just because she was cute?"

"No, because people were telling her she was, twenty-four hours a day."

"You see this. Good." Inez opened the leather cover to her Bible, all creased and worn like the skin around her eyes. "We begin."

Mora gave her hair another toss. She was probably thinking she was like Rachel and Lucy was Leah. She obviously hadn't figured in the superior soccer part.

Inez swept her eyes across a page of the book of Genesis and then looked up. "One day, here comes Senor Jacob, a young *guapo*—"

"Was he hot?" Mora said.

"*Si*. Yes. *Muy* hot. He is the nephew to Senor Laban, and he goes to work for him on his farm. Senor Laban raises the sheeps."

Mora put up one of the hands she was always using to place periods at the ends of sentences and put quotation marks around things. "Let me guess. Jacob saw Rachel and he thought *she* was hot—"

"The minute he sees her, it is love."

"Nuh-uh," Lucy said.

"Oh, yes. He goes to her and he kisses her—and he begins to cry." Ickety-ick.

"He cried?" Mora sank her chin onto her hands. "That is so sweet. Where are the guys like that?"

Far away, Lucy hoped.

"So did they get married?" Mora said.

"No, no, no. Senorita Rachel, she is only twelve years old."

"No way!" Lucy said.

"*Si*. But Senor Jacob, he will wait. He makes the promise to work for Senor Laban seven years, and then he can marry Senorita Rachel."

Mora's fingers sprang out like fans. "Seven years? Are you serious?"

"Think of you when seven years have gone by."

Lucy did a quick calculation. "I'll be eighteen."

"I'll have my driver's license," Mora said. "And my own car—probably even my own apartment."

Lucy didn't mention that probably *she'd* be playing soccer in the Olympics. She didn't think that was the point of this story.

"You will be very different than today," Inez said, "because that is a very long time." She nodded soberly. "This is a big sacrifice for Senor Jacob."

Mora nodded. "He could have been dating a lot of other girls all that time."

"But he waits for Senorita Rachel, because he has deep love for her. And when seven years pass—and not one minute longer—Jacob tells Senor Laban he is ready for his bride."

Mora's eyes sparkled. "Did they have, like, this huge gorgeous wedding?"

Lucy squirmed. Could they not talk about anything else? Maybe the *whole* Bible wasn't about her life.

"Yes," Inez said. "Everyone is there, and the bride is in a beautiful gown and veil—"

"I knew it," Mora said.

"And the marriage ceremony, it is perform. But—there is a surprise." Her black eyes darted mysteriously from Lucy to Mora.

"What surprise?" Lucy said.

"Behind the veil is not Senorita Rachel, but Senorita Leah."

"What?" Mora nearly came out of her chair. "What happened?"

"Senor Laban, he is ashame for his older daughter that she does not yet have a husband."

"Well, hello! Who was going to marry a blind chick?"

"So he switched them and didn't tell Jacob?" Lucy got up on one knee. "That's just—wrong."

"*Si.* Senorita Rachel does not get her Jacob. Senor Jacob is tricked. He does not know until the next morning."

"Okay, now I just don't get how that could have happened," Mora said.

"And Leah's married to some guy that doesn't even love her." Lucy sank onto her foot. "That's like the worst part of all."

"No, it's totally worse for Rachel," Mora said. "Her dad just took her boyfriend away from her. I would have pitched a royal fit."

Lucy was sure she would have, and for once, she might not have blamed her. What kind of Bible story was this anyway?

Mora now had her hands on her hips, like she was ready to demand justice. "So what did Jacob do?"

"Senor Jacob is angry. He demand Senor Laban give him Rachel."

"Yes!"

"So he divorced Leah?" Lucy said. That seemed kind of mean, since it wasn't even her fault.

"No." Inez appeared to be choosing her words carefully, the way she picked just the right chiles to put in the sauce. "Senor Jacob, he marries Rachel too."

"He had two wives?" Lucy and Mora said together.

"*Si.* It is done in Bible times."

Lucy and Mora blinked at each other.

"And to have Senorita Rachel too, Senor Jacob promise to work seven more years for Senor Laban."

"Okay, that Laban guy was just evil." Mora ripped a corner off of a sopapilla as if it were Laban's head.

Inez softly closed the Bible cover. "I want you think now. Before next time. Think of things that are no fair for you. Things that make you want to stomp the feet and scream."

That had to be the easiest assignment Lucy had ever had. But she couldn't go there at the moment. She could hear Mudge yowling at J.J. and Januarie at the back gate, where they were waiting for her to go to practice at the "real" field they'd discovered back in January, and which the whole town had helped them fix up so they could play teams from other towns. So far, they'd only had one official game, but just practicing at the big field with its actual goal areas and bleach-ers—where she imagined her mom cheering her on—that made the soccer dream come closer. Especially now, with the ODP to work for. Already shaking off the business with Mora, Lucy grabbed her sweat-shirt and her soccer ball and went for the door.

"I'll walk you out," Mora said, instead of making her usual beeline for the TV. "I have something for Januarie." And then she dug in her pocket as if she were trying to figure out just what it might be.

Before Lucy could maneuver her bike through the gate, Mora was on the other side, whispering in Januarie's ear. The little round face glowed, as if Mora were a rock star offering Januarie her big break. It just didn't take much to impress Januarie.

"Least she's not whisperin' in *my* ear," J.J. muttered as Lucy hiked up onto her bike. "She's scary."

"Come on, Jan," Lucy said over her shoulder. "We're already late."

"Go ahead," Mora said. "She'll catch up."

"No, she won't," J.J. said, still mumbling to Lucy.

Januarie could barely *keep* up on the little pink bike Mr. Auggy had gotten for her at a yard sale and fixed up with pieces he'd found in their yard. Lucy and J.J. set off at a crawl, practically pedaling backward.

It was hard to stay prickly though. It was spring-windy, and the tendrils on the yucca cactus were bent over like canes. The yuccas were the ones that couldn't make up their minds whether to be cacti or palm trees, and they were one of Lucy's favorite New Mexico things to see. A mama quail led her four babies across the street in a line, leaning forward with the little curl sticking up from the top of her head. Lucy loved that too. It was finally spring—her and J.J.'s best time of year.

"This weekend," J.J. said. He must be thinking it too. "Bikes on the desert."

Lucy wiggled her front wheel back and forth. "Or—I have a surprise."

J.J. didn't squeal or beg to know what. He just pretended to ride into her and then jerked his wheel away. "Yeah?" he said. He was so ungirl-like.

"Yeah," Lucy said. "I could be in the Olympics."

"Nuh-uh."

"Yuh-huh. There's this program I could get into where I could train. There's camps and stuff—"

"Where?"

"I don't know. I have to try out first. And before that, I have to practice way more than we do already. But I figured you could help me."

J.J. didn't say anything.

"It'll be fun. Maybe you could even try out too. Hello! Why didn't I think of that before? You could totally make it."

Still J.J. said nothing. He just shook his shag of hair over his eyes and rode a little faster.

Behind them, Januarie called, "I'm coming!"

Lucy looked back to see her chubby legs pumping furiously. The pink and white fringe sailed out from the handgrips, and bedraggled pink feathers fluttered from one ponytail. That must have been what Mora dug out of the bottom of her pocket.

"She looks like a psycho chicken," J.J. said.

Lucy felt a flood of relief. Okay, J.J. wasn't mad at her. He was just thinking. He did that more, now that Mr. Auggy was working with him.

So Lucy laughed. "Don't tell her that. Look at her, she thinks she's all stylin'."

"Whatever," J.J. said.

A tumbleweed flew across Highway 54 as they crossed, and Lucy watched for cars like she always promised Dad she would do. She'd talk to J.J. about ODP later, after he'd turned it around in his mind. Besides, right now she had to make sure Januarie went ahead of her, since she was paying way more attention to her feathers than to the traffic. It was a good thing she was just the water girl and errand-runner, because there was no way she could have concentrated on soccer today.

And neither could anybody else, as far as Lucy could tell. At least not Oscar, Gabe, or Emanuel, who had apparently taken up teasing Lucy and J.J. as their new sport.

"Here comes Mr. and Mrs. Cluck!" Oscar said, punching Emanuel, who punched him back. "Oooh!"

"Were you guys holding hands?" Gabe said. "You were holding hands—I saw you."

"Guess what?" Carla Rosa said. "You could get in trouble for that."

"We weren't holding hands!" Lucy said.

But J.J. didn't say anything. In fact, he just juggled a soccer ball with his foot and acted like he didn't hear them.

Huh. Maybe she should try that too. Pretend they didn't exist. Wouldn't that be nice at the moment?

"Miss Lucy," Mr. Auggy said, "I want to try something with you today."

Yes! She hadn't even told him about ODP yet, and he was already going to show her how to score more goals.

He blew his whistle for everybody to take their places, and Lucy headed for hers as forward. But he pointed to the middle of the field.

"I'm going to let you play midfield," he said.

"Go, Lucy!" Veronica did a little dance, as if she actually knew what Mr. Auggy was talking about.

"Midfield?" Lucy looked back at the goal line and lowered her voice. "But I'm your best shooter."

"You're good at everything, but this is a special position." Mr. Auggy turned to the team. "Lucy's going to be center midfielder. That means she's like a link between the defenders—J.J. and Dusty and Emanuel—"

"Go J.J. and Dusty and Emanuel!" Veronica said.

"And the forwards—Gabe and Veronica and Carla Rosa."

"Go Gabe and—"

"We get it," Gabe said.

Mr. Auggy's small mouth twitched. "Lucy will get the ball where it needs to go."

"So she's like the boss of us," Carla Rosa said.

"No way!" Oscar looked like somebody had just woken him up from his sleepy position as goalie.

"She just has a way of seeing the field that makes her perfect for the job," Mr. Auggy said.

"So that means she gets the ball to me, and I score." Gabe's dark eyes were sparkling.

"That's not what it means!" Lucy looked at Mr. Auggy. "Does it?"

"You can run up and make an attack if you see an opportunity," Mr. Auggy said, "and you can go all the way back to protect your goal too, but it's usually a good idea to hold your position."

"That's what I'm talkin' about!" Gabe backed toward his forward place. "Bring it on, baby."

"Now remember," Mr. Auggy said as he tossed the ball to Dusty to throw it in, "no matter where you play, all of you are responsible for shooting, passing, and defending. When your team has the ball, everyone is on the attack. When the other team has the ball, everyone is on defense. Got that?"

Everybody nodded. Gabe was expanding by the second and looking like he'd already scored three goals in the last ten minutes.

"Mr. Auggy," Lucy said, "I really need to talk to you."

But Mr. Auggy was already running off the field, and the ball was coming in.

Lucy felt herself zipping up again.

5

Things That Aren't Fair, God
Or How Everything Totally Changed in Three Days

- Januarie has started making commas and stuff with her hands and talking about Starbucks and Oprah and acting like her and Mora are identical twins.

- Mora is rolling her eyes at me all the time and making fun of us not having cable and all the other stuff she used to do when she first started coming here, before we kind of got to be friends. Now it's like we're not. At all.

- Gabe says something about me and J.J. every seven seconds, even though there is no me-and-J.J. the way he thinks there is. Oscar does it too, because he thinks it's cool. Carla Rosa doesn't get it, so she just keeps saying, "Guess what? They're making fun of you." Ya think?

- I have to play center midfielder now, so Gabe's always in front of me and I have to get the ball to him so he can score and I have to keep track of Carla Rosa behind me and make sure everybody else is where they're supposed to be and I don't know how to do all that yet. How is that going to get me picked for the Olympic program?

～ Every time I tell Mr. Auggy I want to talk to him, something happens. Like Januarie has a crisis. Or Oscar gets buzzed. Or he's counseling J.J. When is it going to be MY turn?

Lucy stuck her pen under her nose and curled her upper lip to hold it in place like a moustache. She showed that to Artemis, who didn't seem to think it was funny. The cat just continued to pace back and forth on her windowsill.

"I guess your whole world has changed too," she said to her. "It's the pits, isn't it?"

Lucy closed both the Book of Lists and her eyes and flopped against her giant stuffed soccer ball. She usually liked going to school on Fridays. That was the day Mr. Auggy actually let them play a game against each other at recess instead of just doing drills. But there was going to be teasing, and it was getting harder to ignore it, the way J.J. did.

She stroked the front of the green book, tracing the raised leaves with her fingers. Then she rolled over and flipped it open and chewed the end of her pen. She was never sure she was doing it right, and she wished for about the millionth time that her mom had left her an example.

One thing was for sure: if her mom were here she would already have Lucy signed up for the ODP. She wouldn't let talk about bras and boys get in the way. She would definitely tell Mr. Auggy Lucy shouldn't be playing midfield.

Lucy sighed. Mom wasn't there. Only Dad, and he just kept saying he needed more information, and Aunt Karen had picked now to suddenly not be in their face all the time. Lucy was about to add all that to the list when she heard Dad outside her door.

"Luce, your fan club's at the gate."

"My what?" She slipped the book under her pillow.

Dad poked his salt and pepper head in. "Sounds like more than just J.J. and Januarie out there waiting for you." He slid his fingers across his braille watch. "Time to get a move on."

He was right. Veronica and Dusty were waiting at the gate with J.J. and Januarie. Mudge was growling at all of them from beneath the century plant. He didn't like change either.

"Surprise!" Veronica said, among other chatty things. Her face was morning puffy, but she still talked as much as she did at noon.

"We wanted to walk with you too, Bolillo," Dusty said.

Lucy left her bike parked inside the fence and fell in between the two of them. "Come on, Januarie," she said.

But Januarie sniffed the air like a poodle and walked apart from them as if they smelled bad.

"What's with her?" Dusty whispered.

"What's with J.J.?" Lucy whispered back.

Because J.J. was making circles in the middle of Second Street on his bike and not talking to any of them.

"That's easy," Veronica said out of that hole she could make with the side of her mouth. "He totally likes you, but he doesn't know how to show it."

"Of course he likes me," Lucy muttered. "He's been like my best friend since we were seven years old."

"This is different." Veronica slanted her eyes wisely toward J.J., who was now doing a wheelie by the bike rack. "I know about these things."

And not only did Veronica know about them, she couldn't seem to talk about anything else. She picked up the subject again that afternoon when the girls were all at Lucy's kitchen table eating Inez's nachos.

"Did you see how he was showing off for you when we were playing soccer at recess?"

"Who?" Januarie said, stuffed cheeks puffed out.

Lucy kicked Veronica under the table.

"You're not talking about Mr. Hottie, are you?" Mora curled a long string of cheese around her finger.

"Who's Mr. Hottie?" Januarie said.

"Don't you have something to do?" Mora said to her.

To Lucy's surprise, Januarie didn't collapse her face into a pout. She just said, "Oh, yeah," and disappeared down the hall.

"How did you get her to do that?" Dusty grinned. "Can you show us?"

Mora leaned over the nachos. "Were you talking about J.J. just now?"

"Yes," Veronica said.

Lucy pulled the plate toward herself. "But could we not? I'm sick of it."

"You see?" Mora made several circles in the air with the tip of her finger before she finally pointed it at Lucy. "You're not mature enough for a relationship."

At the sink, Inez grunted. Lucy let her clump of cheese and beans and salsa plop to her plate and wiped her hands on the back of her jeans.

"I'm gonna go get changed for practice."

"Okay, okay," Mora said quickly. "We'll talk about something else. Wanna hear about my dance team? We're learning a new routine—I'll show you. We can totally use it when we cheer for your next game."

She leaped from the chair and planted herself in the middle of the kitchen floor and struck a pose Lucy was sure was going to throw her hip out of joint.

"It's better with music," Mora said, "but I'll just count it out. Five-six-seven-eight—"

Her leg kicked up and her hips swiveled and Dusty and Veronica were totally into it. Even Inez leaned against the kitchen sink and nodded in time. When Lucy was sure Mora was immersed in entertaining everybody, she slipped down the hall to her room. The door was closed.

She stopped, hand on the knob, and pressed her ear to the wood. A drawer scraped, then another one. Lolli gave a frightened mew. Artemis growled.

Lucy flung open the door and nearly knocked Januarie on her startled fanny. She put both hands to her cheeks as they turned the color of Inez's red hot chili peppers.

"What are you doing?" Lucy said. "Are you going through my stuff?"

"I was looking for—" Januarie scrunched her face up as if she was trying to remember something. "The rest of that candy. From that day you sent me to Claudia's."

"Well, for Pete's sake, all you had to do was ask. And besides, it's almost gone. You ate most of it that same day."

"Oh," Januarie said. "Yeah."

"Yeah — so — go ask Mora for candy. She's like your new best friend."

The fleshy face burst into a smile. "She likes me now. She didn't used to, but she says I'm her little buddy."

"Really."

Januarie nodded happily and bounced from the room. Lucy closed her drawers and fished her cleats and shin guards from under the bed and felt strangely lopsided inside.

Things didn't straighten themselves out the next morning either. Lucy smelled food before she even opened her eyes, and she knew it wasn't Dad's cooking that was wafting its delightful way up her nostrils. She sat up and identified scrambled eggs and green chiles, an Inez breakfast.

She was right. Inez was at the stove, and toast and her homemade quince jam were on the table. Mora was in a chair, wrapped in a sleeping bag, glowering like Mudge.

"What's going on?" Lucy said.

"Senor Rooney call me late last night," Inez said. "He have to go to the radio station suddenly early today and be gone all day. He ask me to come."

Lucy shook the bedhead out of her ponytail. "Is everything okay?"

"No," Mora said. "It's eight o'clock on a Saturday morning and I'm up and Abuela wouldn't even stop at Starbucks and get me a latte — so, no, everything isn't okay."

Lucy felt herself grin. Mora could be kind of funny when she was cranky — just as long as Lucy didn't have to deal with her.

"There's only one thing good about it," Mora said, untangling her long arms from inside her cocoon and reaching for a triangle of toast. "I'm going to soccer practice with you, which means I get to see J.J. And I came prepared."

Lucy froze with her knife stuck in the jam jar. "Prepared for what?"

Mora wiggled her eyebrows. "You'll see."

Poor J.J.

Lucy gobbled down her eggs and went to her bedroom window and wished J.J. would show up at his so she could send him a warning to run like a mad dog for the soccer field.

No such luck. He was there at the back gate when Mora burst out ahead of Lucy. She was wearing pink sweats and carrying a bright white backpack with her name painted on it in silver. The thing was bulged with whatever it was she'd come prepared with.

"Hi, J.J." Her giggle-filled voice made Lucy think of fingernails on a chalkboard.

"Hi," J.J. said, and took off on his bike.

Lucy shot after him. She did look back to see if Januarie was keeping up on hers, but she and Mora were following on foot. Januarie made a grab for Mora's backpack, and Mora jerked it away and delivered a look that could have sliced bread.

"I don't think Januarie is Mora's little buddy today," Lucy said to J.J.

J.J. just grunted.

"You want to hear about the Olympic Development Program?"

"You told me."

"We could practice after this practice."

"Maybe," he said, and clamped down his jaw.

That had to be good enough for now.

So Lucy tried to enjoy the sleepy morning as they rode. The air was windless, which just didn't happen in March in Los Suenos, and in between the cars swishing past on the highway, she could hear the birds singing rustily and the new leaves chattering under their breath. It was a perfect day for playing soccer, and she was going to do her best today. No being distracted by Gabe and his teasing. No worrying about whether Mora was hurting Januarie's feelings. No talking about boys with Veronica. She'd make sure she got to talk to Mr. Auggy about the ODP so he'd change his plan for her. Today, it was going to be all about superior soccer.

They were in their two small teams, so Lucy and Emanuel were the midfielders, each for their own team, and the other players had to be both forwards and defenders, depending on who had the ball. Oscar and Carla Rosa were hanging around being goalies. It seemed to Lucy that they never really expected anybody to get close enough to score. Maybe today she could change that.

The ball went back and forth from one team to the other. As usual, it was hard for her team to keep it with J.J. all over the place. Lucy called for Veronica to pass it to her, and she did, although sometimes it went in totally the wrong direction and wound up right at Emanuel's feet.

"Oops! Sorry!" Veronica said. "We'll get it back!"

"We" meant "Lucy." Like always. Lucy got behind Emanuel and waited for the ball to get too far away from him. When he tried to pass it to Dusty, she was on it.

"To me!" Gabe shouted.

Lucy looked his way, but Dusty was already between him and Lucy. Veronica hadn't run up yet. If Lucy could get past J.J., right in front of her, she could make it to the goal, where Oscar was busy chewing on a toothpick.

She dribbled around J.J., faking to the left just as he dodged to her right.

"To me!" Gabe called out again.

He was clear now and much closer to the goal than she was. J.J. had jockeyed around in front of Lucy. If she dribbled through, she might score. If she passed to Gabe, it was a sure thing.

If you have an opportunity to attack, go ahead, Mr. Auggy had said. *But—*

It was the "but" that got her. And she wasn't happy about it. Planting her left foot so it pointed a few feet ahead of Gabe, Lucy swung her right leg with her hip into a hockey stick shape, and pushed the ball squarely in the middle with the inside of her foot. Even as her right leg followed through, she watched Gabe run at the ball and kick it crisply into the net before Oscar could even get the toothpick out of his mouth.

"Perfect!" Mr. Auggy shouted.

"Oscar wasn't perfect," Carla Rosa said. Like she should talk.

Mr. Auggy looked at Lucy.

"Um, no fair blaming the goalkeeper," she said. "It's everybody's job on his team to keep the ball from getting there."

Mr. Auggy's small smile got big. "The captain's right. And did you see the way Miss Lucy passed the ball to Gabe instead of going for the goal herself?"

Gabe raised both arms as if an entire crowd of fans were calling his name.

"Oh, brother," Dusty said, grinning.

"Nice going, both of you," Mr. Auggy said.

Lucy knew she should feel good about her sweet self. But somehow, she didn't. She really needed to talk to him. Maybe over break.

Mr. Auggy called for one, and everybody headed to the big cooler that Januarie was in charge of. She always made a huge deal out of calling out their names one by one and handing them their water bottles when they could each have easily reached in and gotten their own. But Mr. Auggy and Lucy let her be in charge since that kept her from whining about not being allowed to play, because she seriously wasn't any good.

When Januarie called J.J.'s name, though, Mora said, "No—I have his."

Everyone stared as Mora produced a container of Gatorade from her backpack and presented it to J.J. like it was the World Cup.

"Guess what?" Carla said. "That's not fair. We only got water."

"Um, no thanks," J.J. said. His face was as many colors as Artemis's fur. He snatched a water bottle out of Januarie's hand and slunk to the bleachers with it. Mora shrugged and followed, backpack swaying over her shoulder.

"You better go beat her up, Lucy Goosey," Gabe said. "She's after your boyfriend."

"Like Bolillo would punch anybody out." Dusty giggled. "What is this, WWE?"

She laughed even louder, and Veronica snickered into her hand. Lucy felt laughter bubbling up her own throat.

"What's so funny?" Gabe said.

"You," Lucy said. And then she laughed some more, even though she didn't know exactly why. Dusty's husky giggle wound around hers, and Veronica's high-pitched one bounced across the top, and even Carla Rosa let out a shriek, probably just because it felt good.

"I don't get it," Gabe said.

"It's women, Gabe," Mr. Auggy said. "Don't even try. You all ready to get back to work?"

So there was the answer to that problem, at least, Lucy thought as she headed for midfield again. If she just laughed at Gabe, he didn't know what to do. And it was way easier than ignoring and a lot more fun than feeling like she was going to bust through a zipper.

"You have to be kidding me right now," Veronica said.

Lucy looked up from adjusting her shin guard to where Veronica was pointing. J.J. was stalking toward them, head down, face like the inside of a watermelon. It matched the shirt he was now wearing, which had silver printing across the front.

Dusty shielded her eyes with her hand. "What does that say?"

"BECKHAM ASKS ME FOR SOCCER TIPS," Lucy read.

Carla Rosa cocked her sequin-covered cap. "I don't get it."

"David Beckham's only the best soccer player who ever lived." Gabe snorted. "Like he's so gonna ask the J-man for advice. Where did he get that anyway?"

"That chick gave it to him." Oscar sidled up to J.J., who was now bouncing the soccer ball with his knee like he was trying to render it unconscious. "Is *she* your girlfriend now?"

J.J. didn't answer. Gabe joined him on the other side and groped for the ball. J.J. faked, ending up with his back to him.

"Lucy Goosey's gonna get jealous," Gabe said.

Still no answer from J.J. Gabe smacked at the ball with his palm.

"Guess what? You can't use your hands in soccer," Carla Rosa said.

"Is Carla Rosa your girlfriend *too*?" Gabe said. "Dude you got a lot of women—"

"Leave him alone."

Lucy groaned inside as Mora marched up to Gabe, one hand on her hip, the other writing a lecture in the air.

"Huh?" Gabe said.

"Why don't you just leave him alone?"

Lucy was sure J.J. would have flushed himself down a toilet if there had been one close by. She looked at Veronica for help, but her mouth was hanging open, and even Carla Rosa wasn't in there with a "Guess what? J.J. doesn't need you to fight his battles for him."

Dusty tugged at Lucy's sleeve and mouthed, "Do something, Bo-lillo." Which Lucy knew she'd better before somebody else came unzipped.

"Leave him alone, Gabe," Oscar said in a high-pitched voice that actually sounded like Mora's.

Gabe turned on Oscar, but Lucy stepped in between them and peered around Gabe's bulky form at Mora. She was puffed up, fist clenched, teeth bared like the grill on a pickup truck. She looked skinny and hilarious.

"Mora, who are you, She-Hulk? Like Gabe is so gonna take you on!" Lucy waggled her finger at Mora the way Mora herself always did it to her. "For openers, you're in *pink*. You look more like a bottle of Pepto-Bismol."

There was a long silence while everybody seemed to be deciding what they were going to let out of their mouths. They all seemed to come to their decision at once, and a babble of laughter rose from the field. From everyone, that was, except Mora.

Her big brown eyes bulged so far from their sockets that Lucy was sure she would soon be holding them in her hands, and her neck stretched up like a Slinky.

"You are in so much trouble, Lucy Rooney," she said. "You don't even know."

She turned on her snowy white heel and stomped across the soc-cer field, hips wiggling back and forth so hard Lucy was afraid she'd lose control of them. Lucy plastered her hands over her mouth so she wouldn't laugh. Veronica didn't make that effort. She just collapsed against Dusty as if she couldn't breathe.

"All right, the show's over," Mr. Auggy said. Lucy wasn't sure where he'd been through it all, but he obviously hadn't appreciated it from wherever he'd been standing. "Take a lap to warm back up."

The team broke into a group trot, still chortling. Except J.J., who just looked relieved. Lucy started to join them, but Mr. Auggy said, "Miss Lucy."

Out of the corner of her eye, Lucy could see Mora disappearing around the bend in the road that led away from the field, but she didn't dare take her eyes completely off of Mr. Auggy.

"I don't know what's with the girl drama all of a sudden," he said, "but it's interfering with practice. You think as captain you can keep it off the field?"

Lucy stared at him. What had she been trying to do for, like, the whole week?

His smile was so small it was hardly there. "What do you think, Captain?"

"I can do that," Lucy said. "But, see—"

"Good. Let's get your team back into position."

Mr. Auggy blew his whistle, and the team turned happily from laps. As they all reassembled on the field, Mr. Auggy held an arm out to J.J. and walked with him several steps from the others. Lucy was sure she looked just like Veronica, mouth hanging open.

What had just happened?

"That was so funny, Lucy," Dusty said when Lucy dragged herself out to midfield. "You totally got Mora."

"She was like, 'What?'" Veronica did a perfect imitation of Mora's big eyes and waggling fingers.

But Lucy didn't laugh. "That was just stupid girl drama," she said. "We have to get serious about practice now."

Dusty and Veronica's faces went blank. When Mr. Auggy blew his whistle again, they scampered away like squirrels, leaving Lucy at midfield by herself.

They worked on defensive drills so Oscar and Carla Rosa could get some goalkeeping practice. It wasn't as much fun as playing, and after a while, Gabe's eyes kept wandering off the field.

"Hey," he said, pointing toward the driveway. "Nice ride. Who drives a Toyota Celica?"

Lucy almost groaned. It was a silver one, with Texas plates.

"It's your Aunt Karen, Lucy!" Januarie cried. She started for the car, but the driver's door came open like a slap and she stopped. So did Lucy's heart.

Aunt Karen came toward the field, arms pumping. Lucy knew that look. It meant Lucy had done something completely unacceptable and the whole world was going to hear about it. But she hadn't seen Aunt Karen in two weeks. What could she possibly have done?

"What's Mora doing with her?" Dusty said near Lucy's ear.

Lucy looked past her furious aunt and saw Mora's face through the windshield. That answered that question.

"Ms. Crosslin," Mr. Auggy said. Lucy didn't see how he could sound so pleasant.

"I'm taking Lucy home," Aunt Karen said, instead of hello or anything else polite. She leveled her eyes at Lucy. "Where's your stuff? Let's go."

"Busted," Gabe said.

"Gabe, hush up," Mr. Auggy said.

Nobody buzzed him. In fact, nobody said anything as Aunt Karen gave Lucy a push off the field.

6

Lucy took a vow of silence in the backseat—until Aunt Karen turned right on Highway 54, away from Lucy's house.

"Are we taking Mora home?" She tried not to sound hopeful. Mora hadn't even glanced at her since she'd climbed into the backseat, but even the back of her head looked victorious. The sooner Lucy got away from her, the better.

Aunt Karen's eyes met Lucy's in the rearview mirror. "No, I'm taking both of you to Mesilla Valley Mall."

"In Las Cruces? That's, like, an hour away."

"Which will give you plenty of time to get out of jockette mode. Hand her the bag, Mora."

Mora leaned forward and tossed a plastic grocery bag over her head. Lucy ducked so it wouldn't hit her in the face.

"What's this?"

"Try looking inside."

Mora gave a faint "Du-uh," which made Lucy want to bonk her on the head with the bag. She peeked in and pinched back a protest. If she shoved anything else down inside her, she really would burst, but for Pete's sake—a hair scrunchie with silver tinsel? And lip gloss?

"This won't go with my soccer clothes," Lucy said, as if she cared what matched what.

"We'll take care of that when we get there. Why do you think we're going to the mall?"

Aunt Karen looked at Mora, who looked back at her as if they shared some adult secret Lucy couldn't possibly understand. Lucy closed the bag with a knot and stuffed it under the seat. Then she folded her arms and glared out the window.

She hardly ever got out of Los Suenos, and when she did, it was usually an adventure where she stored up things to tell J.J. He had never been away from Tularosa County in his life. White Sands, the wide swath of land whose snowy-white ground looked like a beach without an ocean, normally stirred up thousands of J.J.-and-Lucy fun possibilities in her mind. But today the golden, late-afternoon shimmer of the sun on the sands blurred behind her tangle of questions.

Why did Aunt Karen rip her out of soccer practice to go shopping all of a sudden?

And why was Mora coming with them?

And when was Aunt Karen going to yell at her for whatever it was Mora had told her Lucy did — and get it over with?

But Aunt Karen and Mora just chattered away like two chipmunks in the front seat all the way through White Sands and into the Mesilla Valley. The rocky spires of the Organ Mountains were wasted on Lucy as she gnawed at her fingernails. By the time Aunt Karen pulled into the mall parking lot, Lucy was ready to blurt out, "Okay — whatever it is, I did it. Now can we just go home?"

Aunt Karen twisted to look at her and sighed as only she could — as if Lucy had completely let her down. "You could have at least brushed your hair." She pawed through her bottomless purse for a moment and then shook her head. "Forget it. The stores will be closed before I get all the tangles out of that mess."

Mora giggled. Aunt Karen smiled as if she appreciated it. Lucy wished for a fast train to Acapulco. She'd never been to Mexico, but it had to be better than this.

Aunt Karen's heels clicked on the pavement as she led Mora and Lucy toward the entrance to Dillard's. With her purse slung over her shoulder and her choppy dark hair blowing back in the breeze and her arms swishing leather as they swung, she looked like a woman in a commercial. Lucy couldn't have felt more spastic, following along in her muddy tennis shoes and dirt-caked sweats. Usually she couldn't have cared less, and the fact that she did now bothered her the most.

"Just so you know——" Aunt Karen sailed through the automatic door. "We're here to get you an Easter dress." She dropped a smile on Mora. "I'm treating you to one too."

Mora's eyes bulged until they reminded Lucy of a pug dog. "Are you *serious?*"

"Well, I have to do something to convince you that this entire family isn't terminally rude." Aunt Karen stopped at a display of jeweled belts, and although she fingered them automatically, her eyes were on Lucy. "Before I buy you a thing, Lucy, you're going to have to apologize to Mora."

"For what?" Lucy said.

"Keep your voice down." Aunt Karen looked around. "We don't have to make a spectacle of ourselves."

It was all Lucy could do not to say, "You started it!" Instead, she jammed her hands into the pockets of her sweat jacket and stared at her shoes. One of her laces was undone. She bent down to tie it, but Aunt Karen pulled her up by her hood and put her face close to Lucy's.

"We don't make fun of people in our family," she said. "That is not the attitude they're looking for in the ODP, I can tell you that."

Before Lucy could even open her mouth, Aunt Karen turned her around to face Mora, who at least had the wisdom to look embarrassed. If she had seemed any less humiliated than Lucy felt, Lucy would have bolted right out of Dillard's.

"Apologize," Aunt Karen said. "Now."

Lucy wished she had a crowbar to get her teeth apart enough to speak. As it was, she said between them, "Whatever I did, I guess I'm sorry."

"Is that good enough for you, Mora?" Aunt Karen said.

"Yes," Mora said. She looked ready to bolt right behind Lucy. Two women stopped on the other side of the rack, and Lucy was pretty sure they weren't interested in fancy belts.

"Are you sure? Because if you don't feel like that's sincere——"

"I'm good." Mora nodded until Lucy thought her head might come off. "Seriously, it's fine."

Aunt Karen gave her one more long look before she let go of Lucy's hood. "All right," she said. "Let's go shopping!"

And then Aunt Karen flashed them both a smile, hiked her bag up on her shoulder, and took off for the girls' department. Lucy considered heading off in the other direction, but she followed. Mora practically ran to keep up with Aunt Karen, and it was pretty clear to Lucy as the first six dresses came off the rack and were held up to them that Mora wasn't going to cross Aunt Karen in any way. The more prickly Lucy felt, the more Mora seemed to mold right into whatever Aunt Karen said or did.

When Aunt Karen plastered a sheer flowered thing that looked like a pajama top against Lucy and said, "Now this would be precious on her, don't you think?" Mora ignored the bullets Lucy shot at her with her eyes and assured Aunt Karen that it would be adorable. When Lucy tried it on and felt like she was wearing somebody else's outfit, Mora agreed with Aunt Karen that it was made for her. Lucy endured it, because what other choice did she have?

But when Aunt Karen frowned and said, "I think I know the prob-lem—she needs a bra with that," and Mora said, "I know where the lingerie department is," Lucy backed up against the mirror, shaking her head until her ponytail slapped her in the eye.

"No way," she said. "I don't care what you do to me. I am *not* wearing a bra."

"Oh, for heaven's sake, Lucy, I'm not submitting you to torture. You have to wear one eventually."

"No, I don't."

Aunt Karen looked at Lucy as if she'd just said there was no such thing as gravity. "Of course you do. Every woman does." And then she committed her worst act yet. She said, "You do, don't you, Mora?"

"Oh yeah."

Mora pulled up her T-shirt and displayed a pink thing, decorated with a rose bud and a bow in the center. Lucy felt sick.

"I've had mine for, like, six months," Mora said. "We have to wear them for dance."

"I am not wearing one of those," Lucy said.

"I'm thinking probably a 30-A to start with," Aunt Karen said. "Maybe a 32—she has a broad back. What size do you wear, Mora?"

They were *not* having this conversation, in the dressing room at Dillard's, with other women in the nearby stalls, probably laughing their heads off. Lucy wriggled out of the dress and stuck her arms and legs into her wearing-out sweats and headed for the door. Aunt Karen was right on her heels.

"Where do you think you're going, Lucy Elizabeth?" she said.

"To the car."

"No, you are not."

Aunt Karen tried to grab her arm, but Lucy maneuvered away like she was dodging somebody's bad corner kick and landed against the checkout counter.

"Can I help you ladies?" the woman behind it said.

"We'll take these," Mora said, and tossed the dresses beside the cash register.

Aunt Karen didn't take her blazing eyes off of Lucy. "We're not finished shopping."

"I am," Lucy said.

"You're getting a bra."

"My dad said I didn't have to."

Aunt Karen let out an ugly laugh. "You could run around naked for all he knew. He is not the person to be deciding whether you need a foundation garment."

"He said when I was ready he'd make other arrangements."

"What's he going to do, take you himself?"

"Stop it."

Aunt Karen did, because Lucy was breathing like a horse. She wanted to kick so badly that she had to dig her heels into the Dillard's carpet.

"Stop talking about my dad like he's a moron," Lucy said.

"I didn't say he was a moron—"

"He can do anything for me you can do."

Aunt Karen shoved her purse into her armpit and parked the other hand on her hip. Behind her, Mora was staring at the floor. The cashier had her hand out like she was waiting for the credit card.

"He can't do everything I can do for you, Lucy," Aunt Karen said.

"He can do everything I *want* done for me." Lucy hated the tears she could hear coming. "I'll wear the dress, but I'm not shopping for a bra with you."

"How will you be paying for this today?" said the counter lady.

Lucy didn't wait for the answer. She marched, blurry-eyed, through the store. By the time she got to Aunt Karen's car, the tears were gone and she could breathe again. Now all she was was mad.

When Aunt Karen and Mora got to the car, Mora slipped into it like she wanted to disappear. Aunt Karen put her hand on the back door so Lucy couldn't follow her in.

"This isn't over," she said between her teeth. "But I'm not going to embarrass Mora anymore. Drop the attitude, and be nice for the rest of the evening."

Forget getting into the backseat. Lucy was ready to walk all the way back to Los Suenos.

But she buckled in, and she stared out the window as Aunt Karen started up the Celica and sang out, "We're going to need shoes, but I bet you two are starving. We should have dinner," just as if they hadn't staged a family feud right in the middle of a department store.

Lucy was too furious to be hungry. But at least they left the mall and the dresses and the bras and the humiliation behind. Aunt Karen took them straight to the Old Mesilla Plaza—which was usually a fun place to poke around because it was a village built in the 1800s. But Lucy was beyond fun, even when Aunt Karen led them into the Double Eagle.

"This was a home," she explained to Mora when they were seated at a linen-covered table. "It's a hundred and fifty years old."

"Nuh-uh." Mora gazed up at the chandelier that twinkled above them.

"They say it was haunted. They always say that about old buildings—like that hotel in Los Suenos they're turning into a restaurant. Of course, I don't believe that."

Mora shook her head. "No, this is too beautiful. I never saw anything like it."

If Lucy had thought she'd seen Mora's eyes bulge as far as they would go, she was wrong. When the server brought them each a stemmed glass with shrimp hanging over the rim, the brown eyeballs threatened to drop right into the cocktail sauce. For somebody who claimed to have been everywhere and done everything with her high-class mother, she was sure impressed with the Double Eagle.

Aunt Karen, of course, loved that. She seemed to love everything about Mora—including the fact that she was an informer. After the chilled salad plates had been swept away, Aunt Karen tapped her shiny, squared-off fingernails on her bread plate and leveled her eyes at Lucy and licked her lips.

"So, I understand you have a boyfriend now."

Lucy nearly spewed her ginger ale across the table.

"I'm glad you're showing an interest in boys. In fact, I'm so relieved I can't even tell you."

Lucy pointed *her* eyes at Mora. "Did you tell her I have a boyfriend?"

"It's not like everybody doesn't know." Mora peeled the crust from a piece of bread. Aunt Karen would have smacked Lucy's fingers if she'd done that, but she didn't correct Mora.

"There's nothing to know!" Lucy said.

But Aunt Karen was shaking her head. "Let's not even go there. What I want to talk about is your choice in men." She arched a long comma of an eyebrow. "J.J. is okay as a friend, but, Lucy, you need to set your sights a lot higher for boyfriend material."

"*What?*" Lucy looked again at Mora, who was rolling a hunk of bread into a ball with her fingers. She didn't say a word in J.J.'s defense. Wasn't she the one who'd called him Mr. Hottie?

"It's not like you're going to actually date anytime soon." Aunt Karen laughed as if that were hilarious. "But I just want you to be particular about who you do go out with when the time comes, and it isn't too soon to start getting that mind-set. Think somebody smart, with a good family, somebody who wants to make something of him-self. Like the boys you'll meet at those ODP camps."

"Is that the kind of guy you date?" Mora said to her.

Aunt Karen smiled. "I like athletes, yes, and I'll tell you what else—"

Lucy couldn't listen. The thought of herself dating was enough to wrestle with right now. She was eleven! She didn't even want to wear a bra, much less think about J.J. like — *that*!

While Aunt Karen and Mora reviewed every guy her aunt had ever gone out with, Lucy considered what she'd said earlier, about her not having the attitude she was going to need for the Olympic Development Program. Did that mean she had to let everybody say whatever they wanted to say to her and do whatever they wanted her to do and be what they wanted her to be? She pushed her salad plate away. It was too confusing. And all she wanted was to do superior soccer.

She made up her mind right then, as a steak appeared in front of her and Mora looked as if she were going to faint with the joy of it all, that she was going to do exactly that. And nobody was going to stop her.

Lucy decided to start that night when they finally got home — and Inez had taken Mora off with a chilled look at Aunt Karen and her choice of Easter dresses. While Dad and Aunt Karen were talking in the kitchen, Lucy felt under her pillow for the Book of Lists.

It wasn't there.

It wasn't where she'd left it, where she always put it. Fear licked at the inside of her chest. Where was it? She lifted the pillow all the way up, pulse racing. If somebody took it — if somebody read it —

Only the blue and yellow striped sheet was under the pillow — no book. Lucy tossed the pillow behind her and was about to yank the whole bed away from the wall when she heard a thud. Lolli dove for the toy chest, and Artemis crouched on the windowsill, ears back, staring at the floor.

Lucy snatched up the pillow and felt around. There was something hard inside the pillowcase. She yanked it out and held the Book of Lists against her chest while her breathing slowed down. Losing it would be like losing Mom all over again. And maybe that would be like losing her own self. Because nobody else seemed to know who she was.

Clutching the book so it wouldn't fly out of her hands, Lucy curled up against the big stuffed soccer ball and began with what she did know — and that was who she *wasn't* — a bra-wearing individual.

Dear God, Why Bras Should Be Made Illegal
~ They look like they pinch.

- I bet they make you feel like you can't breathe.
- Boys know you're wearing one and they say stupid stuff and I'll want to smack them, only I can't because Mr. Auggy says as captain I have to set an example and not have drama. I need good Olympic soccer attitude.
- A bra is a sign that you're becoming a woman — and I don't even know how to be a girl yet.

Lucy pulled the book up to her forehead and closed her eyes. She could still kind of smell her mom—Kit Kat bars and lavender soap. She remembered that. And the way Mom had taught her to dribble a soccer ball when she was only four years old. And how she said Lucy was going to be a winner.

Did a winner—a superior soccer player—have to wear a bra and a flimsy pajama-top dress and look for a boy with ambition, when she didn't even like boys?

Or did superior mean scoring goals and leading her soccer team to victory and giving the whole town a reason to be a better community, like Dad said? Being picked for ODP? What was wrong with that? Why couldn't a girl just do that?

Lucy felt something push against the Book of Lists, and she peered over the top to see Artemis Hamm patting it with her paw.

"You know what?" Lucy said to her, "I don't think that bobcat's coming back. I think we should just let you out so you can be happy." Lucy sat up and gathered Artemis into her arms. "Everybody oughta just be allowed to do what they do the best, and you're the best hunter."

She tucked Artemis under her arm and crossed the room and opened the door. Voices in the kitchen stopped her in the hall.

"You're overreacting, Karen," Dad said. "Lucy's loved J.J. like a brother since the first time she saw him."

"You can't see her, Ted. She's not a flat-chested little girl anymore."

Lucy pressed her hand against her chest. Good grief, could Aunt Karen embarrass her just a little bit more? She might never be able to be in the same room with Dad again.

"I know she's growing up," Dad said.

"I tried to buy her a bra tonight, and she pitched a fit—I mean a *fit*."

No, she did not just say that. Lucy headed back toward her room, until Aunt Karen said, "You've done okay with her being a little girl, but now you're facing hormones, boys. I know I said I wouldn't bring this up again, but—"

Lucy squinched her eyes shut. She knew what was coming.

"I just think with her starting to get interested in males—and the wrong kind of guy, I might add—you just really need to consider letting her come live with me."

Lucy heard her father chuckle. "I think boys are one area where I know more than you do, Karen. I was a boy once."

"Did you ever have to figure out how to shave your legs and armpits?"

What?

"And don't tell me you shave your face. It isn't the same—"

Who cares?

"Have you even had the talk with her?"

What talk?

"They did that at school," Dad said.

"You're going to let the school handle the delicate issue of becoming a woman? Mr. Augustalientes is going to guide her through?"

Artemis growled, and Lucy realized she was squeezing her. She let her down and waited for Dad to call for her to leave the cat alone. But evidently they were too involved in the conversation about embarrassing things to even notice.

"We'll be fine," Dad said.

"You're making a mistake. The hormones are starting to kick in, and she's acting out. She has no idea how to be around other girls—"

"Karen—enough."

Lucy didn't like it when Dad used that tone with *her*, but she loved it when he brought it out for Aunt Karen.

"What I want to talk about," Dad said in that same don't-mess-with-me voice, "is this Olympic soccer program you've got her all excited about."

Lucy grew still.

"The Olympic Development Program," Aunt Karen said. "It's an amazing opportunity for her."

"I had my assistant look it up on the Internet. It sounds huge."

"It is."

Lucy realized she was holding her breath. She tried to let it out softly so she could still hear them.

"Then why didn't you discuss it with me first?" Dad said.

"I wanted to see if she would get enthused about it. What would be the point in going over it with you if she wasn't even interested?"

Dad's laugh wasn't the sunshiney one Lucy was used to. "Did you actually think she wouldn't go nuts over anything that had to do with soccer? What are you up to, Karen?"

"Up to?" Aunt Karen took her turn at a hard laugh. "You don't want me to push being feminine on her, but when I try to help her with something athletic, you jump on me for that too."

"I am the one to make these decisions with her, not you. She's still a kid, and this program requires—"

"Which brings me right back to what I was saying: she isn't a little girl anymore, and I'm sorry, but you can't see that."

"What I want to 'see' is her being allowed to have a childhood. Now, not another word to her until I have a chance to think this through. Am I clear?"

Lucy pulled back into her room. Now she didn't like the tone so much. She didn't like it at all.

But as she crawled into bed and pulled the covers over her head, Lucy could still hear him in her head. What if Dad said no? What if she had to give up the whole dream because he thought she was still a kid?

It was hard to settle into sleep, even with Artemis purring beside her. She wasn't used to being on Aunt Karen's side, looking over a big wall at Dad.

7

Lucy stayed in bed the next morning long after she was awake, thinking maybe Dad would sleep in too, and they wouldn't go to church and out to lunch at Pasco's and to the radio station—the stuff they usually did on Sunday. They were all things she loved, but they meant spending the whole day with Dad, knowing that any second he might tell her what he told Aunt Karen, and more. That would make it closer to NO.

But she couldn't get away with pretending to be asleep when Artemis Hamm, Lolli, and Marmalade were all circling her bed and meowing for their breakfasts. She could hear Mudge yowling in the backyard too.

"You feed the four-legged critters, and I'll feed the two-legged ones," Dad called from the kitchen.

Lucy sat straight up. "Aunt Karen didn't spend the night here, did she?"

She heard Dad chuckle. "No, it's safe to come out."

Lucy wasn't so sure about that.

But Dad just asked her questions about soccer practice and dinner at the Double Eagle while they ate their cereal. Lucy gobbled hers down as fast as she could and then took as *long* as she could getting dressed. The new dress went into the bottom of her underwear drawer, next to the Book of Lists. She still wasn't sure she was the one who had stuck it inside the pillowcase, even by accident, and she wasn't taking any chances.

Church took longer than it used to, now that more people were going there and most people had prayer requests during the sharing time. Dad grinned through the whole thing. He'd told Lucy more than once that people coming together was started by Lucy's soccer team and the way people put their squabbles aside to fix up the field and sell concessions and make sure the kids had uniforms and cleats and shin guards. The town council had even refused to sell the soccer field to a big corporation that wanted to put a gas station there. With all of them there on Sundays now, Reverend Servidio seemed to think he could make his sermons longer, as if each person should get five minutes apiece or something. He wasn't as interesting as Inez.

But the service went by way too fast for Lucy that day. All too soon, everybody was filing out, and she and Dad were on their way down the street to Pasco's Café. Maybe if there were a lot of other people there to talk to, they wouldn't be alone, and then maybe she could get out of going to the radio station afterward. She did actually have that bobcat report to do for Mr. Auggy. That might make a good excuse.

Lucy thought she was in luck at first. Almost every chair in the café was filled, and except for the four old ladies playing bridge, everybody was talking to each other between tables. The bridge ladies just drank their Diet Cokes and fanned their cards and didn't say very much. Lucy wondered if they were actually having fun. It just seemed to her that a game should be a little more lively. The women were all square-shaped and wrinkly like old leather, and they all had short hair that stuck out from the wind. It didn't do much to make Lucy want to grow up, if that was where you landed. But if you did grow up, couldn't you make your own decisions about the important stuff?

"When are we going to see another soccer game?"

Lucy looked up at Felix Pasco, who was shaped like a playing card and wore his hair combed straight back and shiny as Aunt Karen's car.

"Did you tell your dad about the changes I've made? My stage—" He pointed to a raised platform that had appeared in the corner since the last time Lucy had been in. "I'm bringing in musicians on Saturday nights—getting people out socializing more." He smiled at the end of the sentence, like he did at the end of every sentence, whether what he'd just said was happy or not. "We can use it for our next victory celebration."

What victory? The Los Suenos Dreams hadn't won a game, which was why she needed to get on with her own career.

"Good for you, Pasco," Dad said. "I like the sound of that."

"Tell him what else." Pasco poked Lucy's shoulder. "It's the least you can do since you abandoned me."

He smiled again. Lucy didn't. As much as she loved going home to Inez after school, she missed coming here like she used to every afternoon, to have a grilled cheese sandwich with two dill pickles and listen to the spin of the lazy ceiling fans and the hum of the ice cream freezer full of Blue Bell ice cream — before she knew what being grown-up was going to involve. Her mouth went dry, and she said quickly, "Pasco has a picture of our team on the wall. And the banner from our game."

"I should get the prize for the most support of our young people," Pasco put in, and then moved off to refill the old ladies' Diet Cokes.

Dad leaned forward and smiled his sunlight smile. "Is it tacky?" he whispered. In spite of herself, Lucy warmed up.

"The frame's gold, like some rich lady's jewelry," she whispered back.

Dad chuckled.

"And he's got the banner hanging over it—"

"Let me guess. He's got something behind it — a Navajo blanket—"

"How did you know?"

"It's Pasco." He tilted his head. "Does it make you proud of your team?"

It was going to take a lot more than that to make her proud of the Los Suenos Dreams right now. But she said, "Sort of," and switched the subject to, "He's also got little twinkly lights around all the posts now."

"Pure class," Dad said.

Lucy felt suddenly sad — that he couldn't see it — that she loved him so much, and yet was afraid he was going to spoil the most important thing in the world to her. She was glad when the breakfast burritos arrived and they could talk about whether they were as good as last week. When Dad had his mouth full, Lucy said, "I don't know if I can go to the station with you today. I have a ton of homework."

Dad chewed, longer than it took to get down a bite of burrito, Lucy was sure, and then set his fork aside.

"You're avoiding me," he said.

There was no point in denying it. But did they have to talk about this stuff *here*? The ladies playing bridge were already peering at her over their cards, and Pasco could pop by the table at any time, ready to spread what he heard all over town.

"Okay," Lucy said.

"It won't take long. I just have to do a PSA."

PSA—that was a Public Service Announcement.

"Okay," Lucy said again. At least if they were talking about his work, they couldn't talk about anything else.

On weekdays, Dad's associate producer, Luke, picked him up at the corner of Granada and Second Streets. On Sundays, Dad and Lucy had to call a taxi, usually driven by some sleepy-looking guy who had a cheek full of chewing tobacco.

Lucy was always glad Dad couldn't see the KIRO radio station, because it was just plain brown on the outside, and the room where he did his broadcasts was lined, even on the walls, with gray carpet—shag wallpaper, Dad called it. She hoped he had a picture behind his eyes of a bright yellow room with red sunbursts painted on the ceiling.

The place was Sunday-quiet; a radio show was coming through by satellite so nobody had to be in the broadcast room. Dad sat in a swivel chair at his U-shaped desk where speakers were suspended by chains above his head and a microphone hung near his mouth and his headphones waited on the counter for him to put them on.

Lucy liked to be there when he was live on the air, although that happened when she was in school, so she didn't get to do it often. It was just that it was easy to think he could see when he was there, talking to people who called in, playing CDs between the pieces about everything from girls in school in Iraq to a harmonica contest in Arkansas. KIRO was public radio, which Dad loved. He had been a talk show host before he became a foreign correspondent for National Public Radio—and then got hurt in an explosion in Iraq and came home blind, without Mom—

He always said he liked live broadcasting from a station much better because he could be involved in the lives of people who called in.

Lucy had heard him say things to folks, like, "Man, get your GED." "You should have some blood tests run, just to be sure." "Apply for that job — you can do it." He would gesture with his hands as if the listeners could see him. Lucy liked it that *other* people were the ones who couldn't see when they were having a conversation with him.

"Okay, Luce," he said. "There should be a blank CD in my in-box. Luke said he'd leave it there."

Luke was his eyes at work, Dad always said, just like Lucy was his eyes at home. He did the things you had to be able to see to do, only he didn't work on Sundays so Lucy was his helper then. Usually, she just handed him the right CDs that he'd recorded so he could make a master one for each piece he'd interviewed and researched for, even though they all had labels in braille. Sometimes she read stuff to him, notes from Luke, things like that.

But today, Dad leaned back in his chair and said, "Mr. Auggy tells me you're learning about bobcats in class."

Lucy squirmed in her own swivel chair. "Yeah. We're supposed to have a project done for tomorrow."

Dad bent his head as if he were looking at the ceiling. " 'Supposed to.' Does that mean you haven't finished yours yet?"

"Uh-huh." More squirming.

"Does it also mean you haven't started it yet?"

"I have all the information."

"Luce, come out with it. You know we can talk about anything."

Lucy felt the sadness again. That used to be true, but now —

"Champ?"

The tears were shining over her eyes again. What was *wrong* with her? Dad was being all nice, not talking about what she'd been afraid he was going to talk about, and all she could do was almost cry.

"You okay?" Dad said.

"We have to do a presentation," she blurted out. "And I can't stand up in front of people and talk."

"Ah," Dad said.

"I guess that's one way I'm not like Mom, huh?" She swallowed hard. Why had she said that? Now she wanted to cry even more.

"Actually, you're wrong about that. Your mother was very shy with an audience in front of her. But she had things to say, and she could say them over the radio where no one was looking at her."

Lucy smacked at the few tears that had managed to escape onto her cheeks. "For real?"

"Have I ever lied to you, Luce?"

No. He hadn't.

"Why don't you let me help you?"

"How?"

"Just talk to me about bobcats." He gave her chair a soft push with his foot so that she twirled away from him. "You don't even have to look at me. Pretend you're talking into that other microphone."

"This is weird," Lucy said.

But she got up on one knee in the chair and lifted her chin toward the mic.

"Just start talking?"

"That's it."

She hunted back through her brain. "Okay—there's five kinds of hunter cats in New Mexico. You and I actually have four of one of the kinds—the domestic kitties. That's why there aren't more quail around. They're efficient."

She heard Dad chuckle.

"Most of us can deal with those felines—that's the big word for cat," she went on. "Except when they don't find the litter box or they won't let you sleep in. And you usually won't see like a lynx, or a cougar, or a jaguar, which are the other kinds of wild cats in New Mexico. Not unless you go way up in the mountains."

"Which you won't be doing, by the way, so don't you and J.J. get any ideas."

"Da-ad!"

"Sorry. Go on."

"You don't usually see bobcats either, but I totally did. And the sheriff even proved it by the piece of fur it left behind. I guess that's dumb to put in my report."

"People like personal anecdotes."

Lucy wasn't sure what that was. She just wished doing a report in class was this easy.

"What else you got?" Dad said. "What would you say if you were on the air?"

Lucy grinned and pointed her voice toward the microphone. In radio voice, she talked about all the things she'd read about during class. As she rattled off facts like how the tufts of hair made it easier for the bobcat to hear, she wondered if she sounded like her mom. She tried to think of a fact Mom would pick out.

"Female bobcats do not 'hang out' together," Lucy said, "In fact, they won't even wander into each other's ranges. But whether they're boys or girls, you have to be careful, like not to leave food out, and you should bring your small pets inside at night, which isn't easy if you have a cat like Artemis Hamm or Mudge." She glanced over her shoulder. "Is that a personal anecdote?"

"It is, and it's perfect."

"And I want to say one more thing."

"Go for it."

Lucy squared off in front of the microphone again. "A bobcat is just a big version of Artemis or Marmalade, so I don't think the one that's trying to find food in our neighborhood should be 'destroyed.'" She made quotation marks with her fingers the way Mora did. "I think the Wildlife Manager people should take her back up in the mountains where she belongs. Thank you."

She looked over her shoulder at Dad and saw him flip off a switch. She whirled her chair around.

"Were you recording that whole time?"

"Why not?" he said. "You were great. You can play this for your class tomorrow, and you're good to go."

"I made mistakes, though—"

"I can edit those out." Dad gave her the sunlight smile. "It would be nice if we could just do that in life, wouldn't it?"

"Do what?"

Dad swiveled around in his chair too, and his eyes hit just about right on Lucy's. "I'd love to be able to go back and erase my mistakes, wouldn't you?"

Lucy shrugged. "I guess so."

"Since we can't, though, we have to do our best not to make them in the first place."

"I try."

"I know you do." Dad felt on the top of the desk, found a bowl of wrapped butterscotch candies, and offered her one. Lucy was glad to pop it into her mouth, which was way dry after so much talking.

"The thing is," Dad said, his candy tucked into his cheek, "some mistakes we don't see coming because we change as we get older. That's why we have parents—well, *you* do. *A* parent."

Dad held out his hands and Lucy put hers in them. "I'm not out to keep you from doing the things you want to do."

Lucy chewed at her lip, and Dad waited. He'd said they could talk about anything. And he'd just helped her with the hardest thing ever. And he *was* Dad—

She pried her hands away and got up on her knee again. "I want to talk about ODP. You said you wanted me to have a childhood, and Dad, I think it *is* my childhood, which is practically over anyway and—"

"You heard me talking to Aunt Karen."

"I shouldn't have been listening, but, this is, like, huge for me. I'm great at soccer—that's not bragging—even Mr. Auggy says so. And nobody else on my team is serious and I need to get even better and I can't if I don't get more training."

"You're amazing at soccer, Luce, but I don't think that's the only thing that's involved here. I have to know all the facts before I let you do something like this."

"But if you know them all and they aren't bad, will you let me at least try out?"

Dad directed his eyes at her in that way that made her sure he could see. "I don't know, Lucy. You're just going to have to trust me on this."

"But, Dad—I want to do this so bad! I have to!"

He seemed to wait until her voice came down from the ceiling. "All right, here's the deal. I'll do my part. I'll get all the information, and we'll sit down and talk about it. Meanwhile, you do your part."

"I'll practice every minute I can, and I'll—"

Dad put up his hand. "No, your part is to be your Lucy-best. Period. We have a deal about J.J. We're going to work on your homework together more, like we did today. Those things are just as important as being picked for this program."

No. Nothing was as important as that.

But it didn't matter. She could do all that other stuff and still be the-best-the-best-the-best at soccer. She had to.

"Okay," Lucy said. "It's a deal."

She started as soon as they got home, flashing through the rest of her homework, shoving her clean laundry into drawers, and finally heading for the backyard to practice dribbling only with her left foot, and then only with her right, and then going back and forth. When she'd gone from one end of the yard to the other without losing the ball once, she stood at the top of the porch steps and accepted the admiring cheers of an imaginary crowd, eyes closed, arms up to embrace them.

All she heard was Mudge growling outside the gate. It swung open, and J.J. appeared. He stayed there, watching from under his shag of hair. He didn't have to flash his fingers to signal "MAJOR Problem."

Lucy flew to him.

"Something up?" she said.

"Toolshed," he said.

"Okay," Lucy said, and led the way back to the shed where Dad kept the gardening stuff.

She and J.J. closed the squeaky door and sat on their usual upside-down buckets. Lucy didn't ask any questions and let J.J. unhunch his shoulders before he "dished," as Veronica would have put it.

"They said I have to see my dad and that Weasel Lady next Saturday."

She nodded. She was becoming a big believer in how much better it felt to just get it out.

"I'm not gonna," he said.

"How are you going to get out of it?"

"You gotta help me."

He shook the shag of hair out of his eyes, and Lucy saw the pleading in them that didn't show up in his voice. He never let anybody see that. Except her.

"What do you want me to do?" she said.

"Let me hide in your room."

"My dad'll be home. You know he'll know, even if he can't see you."

"Not if I'm under the bed."

"You can't hide under the bed all day!"

"I'm *not* gonna see my dad."

He stood up so fast the bucket turned over. The way his arms flew out reminded her of Mr. Cluck himself, and Lucy's heart pattered in her ears. J.J. was darting his eyes all around as if he were snagged in a trap.

"I'm hidin' in here, then," he said. "But you can't tell anybody."

Lucy opened her mouth to say that of course she wouldn't. It was what she had promised a hundred times for J.J. But other words crowded in. *If you get into trouble with me because of J.J. again, I'm going to have to forbid you to see him.*

"What did Januarie say?" Lucy said.

J.J. scrunched his face up. "What?"

"Did she say your dad was different when she had to see him. You know, nicer?"

"He'll never be nice—not to me."

"But the Weasel Lady will be there—"

"Are you gonna help me or not?"

Lucy slowly shook her head. It was the hardest move her neck ever had to make.

"Why not?" J.J. sounded like he was spitting.

"I can't."

"What if you do? You'd just get grounded. You said you didn't care if you got grounded."

"It's not that."

Even in the half dark of the toolshed, she could see his blue eyes looking straight into her. Best friends knew when you weren't telling everything. And he was her best friend. Which was why she couldn't

92

tell him what Dad said, that she couldn't see him if he got her in trouble. One dad hurting him was one too many.

"Then what is it?" J.J. said.

Lucy cringed. His voice was all thick, like any minute he might cry. Lucy had never seen J.J. cry, and she wasn't sure she could stand it. She had to think of something.

And then she did.

"You know I want to try out for the Olympic Development Program," she said. "If I get in any trouble, my dad won't let me."

That was true. Lying for J.J. wouldn't be her Lucy-best.

But neither was the hurt that pinched J.J.'s face in. It was worse than tears.

"It's not like I care more about soccer than I do about you," Lucy said.

"Yeah, you do."

He kicked the overturned bucket, and Lucy clamped her hand over her mouth so she wouldn't scream. When he shoved open the door and let the light in, she saw his mouth tremble and shiver until he pulled it into a straight, hard line.

"Wait, J.J.," she said.

He did, and when she got to the doorway with him, she saw it wasn't because of her. Sheriff Navarra was standing at the bottom of the back porch steps, peering at them over the tops of his sunglasses. Next to him was Gabe.

Why didn't the whole toolshed sink into the ground and take her and J.J. with it?

Beside her, J.J. was so still Lucy was sure he'd stopped breathing. Lucy marched across the yard.

"I guess you want to see my dad," she said in a too-loud voice. "He's inside. I'll get him."

But Dad stepped out the back door and cut her off from her only means of escape, except to run off with J.J., who was already at the gate. From the way Gabe's face was all twisted up like it hurt not to laugh, she knew that would only make things worse—if that was even possible.

"The sheriff's here," she said to Dad.

And his evil son who was going to spread it all over school tomorrow that she and J.J. were together in the toolshed. Whatever it was the Navarras came for, she hoped they'd get it over with fast. She knew her sixteen freckles had disappeared into a sea of red-face.

"What's up, Sheriff?" Dad said.

The sheriff looked at Lucy. "Your bobcat's at it again."

Since when was it *her* bobcat?

"It got into Mr. Benitez's dumpster behind the grocery."

"I guess it's really into garbage," Lucy said. It was the Lucy-best she could do under the circumstances.

"It's into more than that. Took out some chickens down at Pasco's mother's place. Somebody else saw it prowling along the irrigation ditch like it was looking for food." He took off his sunglasses, still looking at Lucy. "I thought you were exaggerating, but we may have a serious situation here. I want you to keep this number right by the phone, and if you even think you see it around here again, you call." He fished in his shirt pocket and pulled out a small piece of paper. "This is Wildlife Management."

As Lucy took the paper from him, she heard a growl from the direction of the gate again. Even Gabe jumped. She decided not to tell him it was only Mudge.

"I aired one PSA when we first saw it," Dad said, "I'm doing another one tomorrow. We're telling everybody to keep their small pets inside until this is taken care of."

Gabe jerked his head toward the gate, where Mudge was still grumbling on the other side. "Yeah, that cat'll have yours for lunch so fast."

"Thank you for that," Lucy said coldly.

"So, she's got the number, Ted," the sheriff said for what seemed like the eighteenth time.

"We'll put it on speed dial," Dad said.

Finally, Sheriff Navarra put his sunglasses back on and headed for the gate.

"You got that number, Luce?" Dad whispered, and with a grin went back in the house.

"How you doing, son?" Sheriff said to J.J. at the gate.

"So, Lucy Goosey."

Lucy dragged her gaze from a very uncomfortable J.J. to Gabe, who was still standing at the bottom of the steps with his arms folded so that his hands were in his armpits. Ickety-ick

"What?" she said.

"What were you and the J-man doing in the shed?"

"Planning how to take you out on the soccer field."

"Gabe. Let's go."

Gabe backed toward the gate. "I'm gonna leave you alone with your boyfriend, Lucy Goosey."

But J.J. wasn't alone. When Gabe and his father finally went out through the gate, Mr. Auggy stepped in. She'd forgotten he'd be over for their usual Sunday night supper. One look at J.J., though, and they had their heads bent together—Mr. Auggy talking in that low, kind murmur he seemed to save for J.J.

Lucy shoved the paper into her pocket and found her soccer ball and kicked it all the way to the back of the yard. It bounced against the bobcat tree and rolled off as if it were trying to get away from her. She couldn't blame it. Right now, she didn't know how to be with herself either.

"You don't have to kill it, Captain. The thing's already dead."

Lucy looked back at Mr. Auggy as she started down the yard. He stood next to J.J. with his hands parked lazily in his pockets. His small smile was very small. J.J. wouldn't even look at her.

"I hope you aren't that hard on the macaroni and cheese," Mr. Auggy said.

Lucy picked up the ball and shrugged. Mr. Auggy nodded at it, and Lucy tossed it to him. He held it in front of him with both hands. "A soccer ball takes a beating in the name of good sport," he said. "I hate to see it take one because somebody's having a rough time." He looked at her over the top of it and then at J.J. "Anything you need to talk about, Captain?"

She almost blurted out everything, told him that J.J. wanted to hide, and that she couldn't help him, and that somebody had to, and that she wanted ODP but she didn't want it more than she loved J.J., only other people thought she loved him like a boyfriend and she didn't want a boyfriend—she didn't even want a bra—

And then suddenly she was crying. Lucy Rooney never cried either. Yet there she was, sitting on the steps with tears pouring down her face and little squeaks coming out like the quails who cried for no reason at all.

The back door gave its small groan, and Dad was with them. He squatted and felt for Lucy's shoulder.

"What's going on, champ?" he said.

Lucy couldn't answer him. She looked up at J.J. and hoped with her streaming eyes that he would give her a signal that said, "We're okay."

But he clamped his mouth shut, and Lucy knew he wasn't going to say or sign a word, or listen to one either. Not even from her.

When the gate closed behind him, everyone was quiet. Even Mudge. Because something was very different now.

8

"Where did you get that, Januarie?" Dusty said Monday when they were getting ready to leave Lucy's for afterschool soccer practice.

Lucy stopped throwing her leg over her bike to see what she was talking about. Januarie was poking her thumbs clumsily at what appeared to be a video game.

"Mora gave me it," she said.

Lucy and Dusty exchanged looks.

"She did! Ask her!"

Lucy would have, except that Mora was several steps ahead of them on the sidewalk, jabbering into J.J.'s ear. He was riding his bike, and Mora was tripping along beside him, mouth going. Lucy's teeth tightened. He wouldn't even look at her all day, much less listen to her. He hadn't even told her that her CD presentation on bobcats was the best project in the whole class, like everybody else did. But now he was letting Mora talk his earlobe off, and he didn't even like her.

Lucy got on her bike and pedaled up to them. Maybe if she told him she didn't have to spend all her time getting ready for the ODP try-outs—maybe if she said they could lie around out on the desert like he wanted to, giving the cloud shapes hilarious names the way they always did when the weather got warm like this in the spring. Or ride their bikes in and out among the teddy bear cholla, laughing like the coyotes. Maybe if she told him that, he wouldn't be mad. He'd listen to her.

"Don't run over me," Mora said when Lucy joined them.

Lucy swung to the other side of J.J. and rolled her eyes at him. He didn't look at her.

"We were having a private conversation," Mora said. She put her hand on J.J.'s handlebar so he had to slow down. "Do you mind, Lucy?" she said.

Lucy did. But J.J. took that opportunity to shoot away from both of them. Mora planted her hands on her slim little hips.

"You know, if you don't want to go out with J.J., you could at least let me have a chance to."

"Whatever," Lucy said. She jammed her feet on her pedals and left Mora in the dust. It was time for her to do her Lucy-best at the only thing she seemed to be able to do right.

As soon as everybody arrived, Lucy had her team doing stretches while they chanted out their cheer: "The Dreams don't die!" And when Mr. Auggy blew the whistle, she was ready. Maybe if Mr. Auggy saw that they could score a whole lot more goals if he let her attack, he wouldn't hold her back at midfield.

It looked like things were finally going her way. Gabe had a good shot at a goal, but for once, Oscar was paying attention and dove on top of the ball. Although he hollered that he'd swallowed his tooth-pick, he was pretty pleased.

"Guess what—you're not supposed to have stuff in your mouth," Carla Rosa told him.

"Get ready for the goal kick," Lucy told her team.

Veronica and Gabe didn't back up very far. Carla Rosa was making the kick since she was practicing defense and Mr. Auggy was covering her goal for her.

She seemed to be in slow motion as she placed the ball precisely in the corner of the box and set herself up to kick it out to the side, just the way Mr. Auggy had taught them.

"Take your time," Gabe said, his voice all drippy with sarcasm.

"Guess what—I am."

Carla Rosa brought her leg up to kick, but she hit the ball on its top and it skipped lazily, right at Veronica.

"Get it in!" Lucy called to her.

Veronica looked at the ball as if it were a stranger who'd just rolled onto the field. And then she sprang to life, planted her foot, and made a perfect hockey stick with her other leg. But the ball didn't go over the goal line. It went to Gabe, who had J.J. all over him.

"To you, Gabe!" Veronica cried, *after* the ball was on its way to him.

There wasn't a chance he could capture it, much less make the goal. J.J. had it and was dribbling toward Emanuel before Gabe seemed to know it was coming. He grabbed at J.J.'s sleeve, and Mr. Auggy blew his whistle.

"Watch it, Gabe," he said.

But Lucy's eyes were on Veronica. "You totally could have scored a goal!"

"Nuh-uh." Veronica did her I'm-trying-to-impress-Gabe giggle. "I'm too spastic."

"No, you are not." Lucy sighed in exasperation. "You could be so good at this if you would just try."

"Let's take a water break," Mr. Auggy said. "You ready for us, Miss Januarie?"

He had to ask twice, because Januarie was engrossed in a video game with Mora.

"What is that thing anyway?" Gabe grabbed it from Mora, who squealed and reached for it while Januarie pummeled Gabe's back with her fists.

"Grow up," Lucy muttered.

"Looks like they're just having a little fun to me, Captain." Mr. Auggy handed her a bottle of water. "No reason we can't have a good time, right?"

"Right." Lucy drained the bottle and wished break could be over so they could get back on the field. Because at least maybe Mr. Auggy was seeing that *she* should be trying to make goals—not Veronica, whose only goal was Gabe. Ickety-ick.

But there weren't anymore chances to score. The wind picked up, and every time anyone made a long pass, the ball was blown off as it floated through the air. Lucy could see nobody's kick was strong enough to keep it on course.

"In weather like this, you really want to play along the floor," Mr. Auggy said.

"Guess what—it's not a floor," Carla Rosa said. "It's the ground."

"We call it a floor in soccer, Miss Carla." Mr. Auggy looked a little weary. "What do you say we knock off for today? It's getting too windy for us to have much fun."

"This is perfect," Veronica said to Lucy and Dusty. "I just got a movie this weekend. You guys wanna come over my house and watch it?"

Lucy dug her watch out of her sweatshirt pocket. It was only 3:45.

"We have time to practice on our own," she said. "We could do turn drills—we don't even need the ball for that, and I have cones at my house so—"

She stopped, because Veronica was drawing a heart in the dirt with her toe, and Dusty was looking from one of them to the other. Only Carla Rosa was nodding, bouncing the sequins on her hat.

"I'm tired of soccer for today," Veronica said. "I really want to just kick back."

"That's okay," Lucy said. "Me and Dusty can just—"

"You know what?" Dusty toed an arrow through Veronica's heart. "I don't think I want to do any more drills either. No offense." She looked up, eyes pleading. "You're not mad, are you, Bolillo?"

Mad, no. Disappointed, maybe. Surprised? Hello! What happened to Lucy and Dusty being the serious soccer players, even though Veronica wasn't?

"We're gonna go ahead and go," Veronica said. "Okay?"

Lucy shrugged and said, "Sure." Dusty hugged her, but it was hard for Lucy to hug back.

"Guess what?" Carla Rosa said when they'd gone off to get their backpacks.

"What?" Lucy said. If you didn't answer Carla Rosa, she'd just keep saying "Guess what?" for days.

"You can't stay here by yourself."

"I know." Lucy tried not to sound prickly.

"We could go to your house, though."

Lucy looked at her quickly. "We?"

"I'll practice drills with you."

"You?"

"Guess what? I like soccer. Even if I stink at it. You could teach me."

Carla Rosa was actually the last person on the team Lucy wanted to practice with, but since everybody else, including Januarie and Dusty—and J.J.—was taking off like they'd just been let out of school early, she was Lucy's only choice. It was that or kick the ball against her back fence, and Mr. Auggy had already said that wasn't okay. Yikes. What *was* okay anymore?

So Lucy and Carla Rosa rode their bikes back to the Rooney's house, and Lucy set up cones in the backyard like two goals so they could try to score on each other. When Lucy was making all the points, she decided to get rid of the ball and just practice turns.

"We're gonna start from this tree and have a race," Lucy said.

"To where?"

"You get to decide, only don't tell me. When you get there, just turn around and run back to the tree."

Carla wrinkled her nose. Lucy had never noticed before that it was kind of a cute nose. "Guess what?" she said. "I'll win."

"Right—unless I can turn around fast enough when you do."

"Oh." Carla Rosa didn't seem to get that, but she carefully planted one leg ahead of her and said, "On your mark, get set, go," and took off—actually much faster than Lucy had ever seen her run. Lucy went after her and caught up, but she couldn't get ahead because she didn't know when Carla Rosa was going to turn. The little redhead got almost to the porch before she changed directions and with a shrick headed in the other direction. Lucy laughed too, although she wasn't sure why. It just felt good to run, that was all.

"Now it's my turn," Lucy said when they got back to the bobcat tree.

But Carla Rosa was looking up at it, fingers tracing the claw marks. "Is it in there?" she said.

"What?"

"That top cat."

Lucy smothered a giggle. "You mean bobcat?"

"Yeah."

"No, it's not in there. It only climbs down it—and not every night."

Carla Rosa gave a little shiver. "You and J.J. are so brave."

"Not really," Lucy said. Hearing "you and J.J." made her droop. "Okay, you ready? Remember, I might not run as far as you did."

"Ready," Carla said, and she set her face as if *she* were trying out for the Olympics. It nearly made Lucy want to cry again.

But instead, they ran and turned and laughed until the shadows of the Mexican elder and the bobcat tree made it hard to see, and Lucy said maybe they should knock off for the day.

"You did pretty good, though, Carla Rosa," she said.

"Guess what? I still stink."

"Not that bad, though."

Carla Rosa grinned as if Lucy had told her she was superior. Then she pointed toward the back gate. J.J. was just slipping in, his skinny body almost disappearing as he turned sideways.

"Hey, J.J.!" Lucy cried. "Come see what Carla Rosa can do now!"

She knew she was speaking in exclamation points, but she couldn't help it. She was missing him so much.

J.J. barely looked her way. "Can't. Gotta get Januarie."

"I'll get her!" Lucy said, and bounded across the yard. Artemis Hamm streaked right across her path, and Lucy groped the air to get her balance. She fell headlong into J.J., just as the back door opened and Januarie appeared.

"I'm tellin'," she said.

"Tellin' what, moron?" J.J. said.

"I'm tellin' Mora that you two are messing around."

"You're not going to tell her that," Lucy said, "because it's not true."

But Mora was already in the doorway, eyes narrowed at Lucy.

J.J. brushed off his jeans and headed for the gate. "You gotta come home, Januarie," he said over his shoulder.

"I'll walk you." Mora was halfway down the steps before Inez showed up behind her and said, "Mora. Stay."

Mora let out a loud "Uh!" and flounced up the steps.

"Guess what?" Carla Rosa said. "She's mad."

"Good," Lucy said under her breath. At least now she wasn't the only one.

When she turned back to the gate to call to J.J., he was already gone.

Lucy didn't feel much like talking at supper, until Dad told her his news.

"I ran your PSA this morning."

"You put me on the radio?"

"I told you that you were great, and you were. A lot of people agree with you about not destroying the bobcat. I got calls through the whole show." Dad chuckled. "Somebody saw it walking on a power line at dawn — doing a tightrope act."

"Can they do that?"

"Evidently this one is very talented. She's a piece of work."

"You think she's a girl too?"

Dad paused in the wiping up of mole sauce from his plate with his tortilla. "I absolutely do. No boy would be that subtle."

"What does that mean?" Lucy said.

"Well, how do boys fight?"

Lucy rolled her eyes. "They punch each other and knock each other down on the ground and roll around."

"And then it's done, right?"

She considered that. "Yeah, then it's like they're best friends or something."

"And how do girls fight?" Dad's face was twinkling.

"They don't hit each other — usually. They mostly talk about each other behind their backs and call each other names and stuff." Lucy rolled her eyes again. "And it goes on for, like, ever. Once you fight with another girl, you can hardly ever be friends."

Dad laughed, a sound that was like sand pouring into a bucket. "I guess that's why girl bobcats don't cross each other's territory. Could get ugly."

"Yeah," Lucy said. "It could."

She was even more convinced of that the next day after school when she and Mora sat at the kitchen table for Bible study with Inez. Mora turned sideways in her chair, so that half her back was to Lucy, and she got her own bowl of salsa for dipping chips instead of sharing Lucy's. Lucy could just imagine her, with tufts of hair on the tops of her ears, doing a tightrope walk on a power line at dawn.

"You remember Senor Jacob and his two *esposas*?" Inez said.

"Leah and Rachel," Lucy said.

"Show-off," Mora muttered.

"Today we go to Genesis, the chapter twenty-nine, the verse thirty-one." Inez thumbed the onion-skin-thin pages of her Bible. "Poor Senora Leah. She knows Senor Jacob does not love her. His heart, it belongs to Senora Rachel. You can feel the pain, no?"

To Lucy's surprise, Mora said, "Yes," without the usual smart aleck edge in her voice.

"The Bible says El Senor sees the pain in Senora Leah."

Sometimes Inez used "El Senor" for the Lord. It made Lucy imagine God with a thin black moustache like Reverend Servidio. In her mind, God looked more like — well, a Spirit she couldn't quite see, like the sunlight in Dad's smile. It was just there. It didn't need a face.

"So El Senor, he blesses Leah with babies. One boy, and then another, and then another, until she has four."

"That's a blessing?" Lucy said.

"The boys, they have more value than the girls then."

Though Lucy said, "Nuh-uh!" Mora looked like she might actually agree with Inez. She was further gone into boy-craziness than Lucy had suspected.

"Senora Leah, she thinks Senor Jacob will love her more because she gives him sons."

"It's not like she could have helped it if she'd had girls." Mora looked at Lucy for the first time that day. "You do know where babies come from and all that, don't you?"

Lucy's face burned. "Yes. I'm not an idiot."

"Well, I just thought since you don't have a mother—"

"Neither do you!"

"I do too—"

"She's not here!"

"She's coming back for me—"

"Enough!"

Lucy looked, startled, at Inez. She never raised her voice, but she had just sliced through the air hard enough to send Mora back to her seat. Lucy too was halfway across the table. She sank into the chair and mumbled, "Sorry."

Inez waited for a minute before she folded her fingers like a stack of small sausages on her open Bible. "You see how the two Senoras will fight—just this way."

"Why?" Lucy said, only because she wanted the dangerous flash to go out of Inez's eyes.

"The Lord does not give babies to Senora Rachel. That means great shame for her." Inez shook her head. "It is first time Senora Leah has something her sister cannot have. Senora Rachel is now *celoso*."

"That means jealous," Mora said.

"I get that," Lucy said.

"Now she knows the pain of Senora Leah all those many years—to feel not so good enough."

Lucy found herself nodding.

"So—Senora Rachel send her maid, Senorita Bilhah, to Senor Jacob to have babies for her."

"No, she did not!" Mora cried.

Lucy frowned. "That doesn't make any sense. If Bilhah, or whatever her name is, had the kids, they would be hers."

"No. They belong to Senora Rachel. Two boys."

"That's not fair!"

Lucy looked at Mora, who had said the same words, right along with her. Mora sucked her lips in.

"Then Senora Rachel, she says——" Inez ran her finger down the page, lips moving. "She says, 'I have had a great struggle with my sister, and I have won.'"

"Won what?" Lucy said.

"Jacob, silly." Mora put her chin in her hands. "So, go ahead, Abuela."

"Senora Leah, she cannot let her sister win. She sends her maid, Senorita Zilpah, to Jacob——"

"And *she* had kids too?" Mora rolled her eyes. "These girls were serious."

"I bet the babies were boys, huh?" Lucy said.

Inez nodded. "And Senora Leah, she has two more sons—and a daughter."

Lucy sighed. "Finally."

"So——" Mora spread her fingers out like fans. "The count is Leah nine. Rachel two."

"It's like it was a contest with kids!" Lucy said. This was unbelievable.

"At last——" Inez went back to the page. "God remembers Rachel, and she has a son, her own. 'God has taken away my disgrace,' she said."

"I hope she was finally satisfied," Lucy said.

"No, no, no. Senora Rachel, she names her son Senor Joseph, and then she says, 'May the Lord add to me another son.'"

Some people just never had enough—they always wanted more. Lucy sneaked a glance at Mora, who was nodding as if it all made sense to her.

Maybe the story wasn't so unbelievable after all.

That night when Lucy went to the Book of Lists, which was right where she'd left it, on top of the Easter dress, there was only one list to be made to God.

How I'm Like Rachel

～ I don't have a mom. I don't think Rachel had one either, or she never would have let her husband trick her own kid out of her guy. I don't get the whole boyfriend thing, but even I can see how totally WRONG that was.

- I like to do stuff boys mostly do. Rachel tended sheep, and I play soccer. I wonder if she really wanted to get engaged when she was only twelve years old. I wonder if she and Jacob were just best friends. Like me and J.J. — used to be. And it was just other people who thought they were boyfriend and girlfriend.

- I'm mad at Mora the way Rachel was mad at Leah. I don't like that Mora is all trying to be friends with J.J. and he won't say hi to me or signal me. And I can't do anything unless I help him get away Saturday, and I can't.

Lucy blinked at the page. She wasn't talking about Rachel anymore. She tried again.

- I bet Rachel was WAY mad when Leah got to have Jacob when he didn't even want her — and then Leah got all the babies, even though I don't see what the big deal is about having babies. Ick — I don't even want to wear a bra. I wonder if they had bras back then.

- It kind of seems like, sometimes, God, you like other people better than you like me. Like they're the ones who are superior. I bet Rachel felt that way too.

Lucy started to put her pen down, yet something else nagged at her. It was like she wasn't finished yet, but what else was there to write?

"I'm done with Senora Rachel," she said to Lolli, who appeared to be done as well, judging from the bored look on her round, black face. "Am I supposed to make a Leah List? I'm not like her—" She gnawed the pen. But Mora was another story.

How Mora's Like Leah

Could that be? Lucy chewed on the end of the pen some more until Artemis pounced from the windowsill and investigated.

"It isn't food, silly."

She put the pen to the paper.

- ∿ Mora doesn't have a mom either, really. It's like her mother doesn't exist.
- ∿ Mora wants J.J., and he doesn't even like her, does he? That's kind of like Leah and Jacob.
- ∿ Mora's doing all this stuff to get J.J. to like her. I bet she's even using Januarie. That's not that hard to do. Leah used what's-her-nose — Zipper or something. I wonder why they didn't have names like us.
- ∿ Mora's mad at me because she thinks J.J. likes me as a girlfriend. Only he doesn't. I don't even think he likes me as a friend anymore.

Lucy looked up at the first list and felt funny in her stomach. The lists were a lot alike. Weird, she thought as she closed the book and gathered up Artemis. Because she and Mora were so not alike.

At all.

9

Every day that week was like vaccination day to Lucy. She woke up afraid of being stung, and all her fears came true.

J.J. didn't come to the back gate to go to school together in the morning or to ride with her to after-school soccer practice. He never did bunny ears or devil horns from his bedroom window or just showed up at the back door for a before-bed talk. In fact, he didn't even look at her in class or at lunch or on the soccer field. She didn't understand why Gabe and Oscar and Emanuel and Veronica—why anybody thought they were even friends anymore.

That hurt way more than the teasing ever had. It hurt more than Mora snapping at her all the time and Januarie acting like Lucy smelled bad. It even hurt more than Mr. Auggy not letting her score goals, keeping her at midfield to direct everybody else to score them. It was as bad as being so upset with him that she didn't even want to tell him about ODP anymore. It was worse than Dad not saying anything about it at all, as if he'd forgotten about her dream.

That was probably why that Thursday she felt as if an entire porcupine had emptied its quills into her. She was beyond prickly, and she wasn't sure why she even went to lunch. She sure didn't feel like eating.

The second she sat down at the table with the team, Gabe said. "Hey, Lucy Goosey. Don't you want to sit next to your boyfriend?"

"Guess what? She told you he's not her boyfriend." Carla Rosa shook her sequins. "Like a hundred times."

"She's a liar," Oscar said.

"Shut up, Oscar," Dusty said.

Half the table buzzed.

Gabe laughed like he'd just taken a whiff out of a helium balloon. "She says he's not her boyfriend, but I seen 'em comin' out of her old man's toolshed together."

Veronica shrieked, "Go, Lucy!"

"That's not true, is it?" Dusty said.

"You know something?" Lucy shoved her lunch bag across the table and stood up. "My *father* sees better than you people do. I'm gonna say it one more time: *I don't like J.J.!*"

She swept the table with her eyes, one person at a time. She stopped when she got to J.J.—her best friend, who looked like someone had just slapped him across the face. Someone named Lucy Rooney.

"That's kind of mean, Lucy," Veronica said.

"I didn't mean I don't like him—"

But there was no use. J.J.'s jaw clamped down, and Lucy knew he wasn't going to listen. Not even to her. He got up from the table, slam-dunked his lunch bag into the trash can, and shoved past three people to get out of the cafeteria.

"Do you see what you did?" Lucy said to everyone.

"I didn't do nothin'," Oscar said.

"You should go talk to him, Lucy," Dusty said.

"You don't get it—I can't!" Lucy backed up and knocked the chair over behind her. A hush fell over the cafeteria, and she could feel all eyes drifting in her direction.

"Guess what?" Carla Rosa pointed. "Here comes Mrs. Nunez."

Lucy didn't need the principal and her kindergarten voice right now. She needed to explain to J.J., and that wasn't going to happen. And once again, she felt the tears coming on.

Soccer drills at recess didn't go well, and neither did their after-school practice. J.J. was an icicle. Dusty didn't smooth things over when somebody made a mistake, and both she and Veronica smiled all sympathetic at J.J. every time he looked their way. Dusty didn't call her Bolillo one time. At least Gabe and Oscar and Emanuel stopped teasing Lucy. Now they just stared at her like she had grown an extra head.

Even Mr. Auggy seemed different to Lucy. She would have bet her soccer ball that Januarie had told him the whole story, although Lucy would never get that out of her because Januarie was acting like Lucy had become invisible. Mr. Auggy didn't call any fouls on anybody and made them play without keeping score. That was fine. Nobody was making any goals anyway.

By the time she got home, Lucy couldn't stand it anymore. She had to talk to J.J., and the only way to do that was through Januarie. The kid couldn't have changed that much in just a week. Surely Lucy could still make her feel important, the way she used to. Although, she couldn't give her expensive toys like Mora did. She could only imagine what Januarie had told *her* by now.

How did things ever get so complicated? Just a week ago, all she'd thought about was trying out for the ODP. Now even that didn't seem as important as making things right with J.J.

So just as Januarie was leaving Lucy's house by the back steps, after whispering in the living room with Mora while Inez was calling her to go, Lucy grabbed her by the sleeve of her sweater and tucked a chocolate rose from Claudia's into her hand.

"Yum!" Januarie said, and then her round face flattened. "What do you want?"

"What makes you think I want something?"

"Because you never give me candy unless you want something. When you just want to give me food, it's like a carrot or an apple or some other nasty thing."

Januarie was getting smarter. That must be because she was nearly nine.

"Okay," Lucy said. "I need you to give J.J. a message from me."

Januarie stuck the whole rose in her mouth before she said, cheeks bulging, "He doesn't want to talk to you."

"How do you know?"

"I just know."

She avoided Lucy's eyes as she chewed. Lucy took her face in both of her hands so she had to look at her. Goo escaped from the crinkles in her knot of a mouth.

"Did he say he didn't want to talk to me?"

Januarie tried to pull away. Lucy didn't let go.

"He didn't say it—but I know. I'm his sister."

"Januarie—"

"Okay—Mora said he didn't. She said he *probably* didn't after what you said at lunch."

"Which you told her." Lucy folded her arms. "You know I didn't mean I don't like J.J. at all. You know I meant I don't like him as a boyfriend, which I've been saying all along—" She could feel tears coming again. She blinked them away. "Why am I telling you this? I can't trust you anyway."

"You're crying."

"I am not."

"I never saw you cry before."

"And you're not seeing it now either." Lucy smacked at her own eyes and pointed down the steps. "Forget I even asked you. Just go home."

Januarie's voice went up into a Chihuahua whine Lucy hadn't heard since Mr. Cluck had been gone. "It scares me when you're sad." She swallowed the glob of chocolate. "Maybe I could tell J.J. something. Mora wouldn't care, I guess."

Lucy covered her mouth with her hand and waited until the tears went away. "Just tell him to come here, to the backyard, after supper. Tell him to wait till it's dark and to go to the shed. Just tell him that."

Januarie's own eyes were brimming.

"You know what?" Lucy said. "You shouldn't do everything Mora tells you to."

"I don't!"

"Good. Just, good."

Januarie looked as if she'd just been hit in the face with a soccer ball. Then she turned and waddled to the gate.

Lucy stayed on the back porch until Dad called her in. She missed the little pest. She missed J.J. She missed everything that used to be.

She did feel guilty that she was going to sneak out into the backyard and meet J.J.—just in case Januarie did tell him and he did come. But with the bobcat still on the loose, Dad would never let her. And she

112

couldn't talk to J.J. with Dad around. If he heard that J.J. planned to hide out on Saturday, he would have to tell on him. If she could just make J.J. understand, she could talk him out of it. She knew she could.

When they'd finished the dishes, Dad went into the living room to listen to NPR.

"Join me?" he said. "There's popcorn in it for you."

Lucy swallowed as if she had a mouthful already. This was hard. She was never going to disobey him again after this.

"I'm gonna go—sit around," she said.

"O-kay." Dad looked as if he was going to ask a question, and Lucy held her breath. But he just said, "Love you, champ," and went into the living room with Marmalade meowing at his heels for him to sit down and make a lap.

Lucy waited until he turned on the radio before she grabbed her coat and slipped out the back door. She shivered even in her ratty jean-jacket as she sank to the top step. The day's warm air had chilled, but she knew it was guilt that made her cold inside.

It wasn't all the way dark yet. She could still see the clouds scudding across the sky, and over the mountains, the sunset was like a ladle full of gold, ready to be poured away. It was so pretty, she wanted to cry again. What was up with that? And what if J.J. was so mad at her he would never watch clouds or anything with her ever again?

And then she heard the noise, back by the shed. She skipped two steps getting to the ground and was halfway there before her feet even touched.

"J.J.?" she said in a loud whisper.

He didn't answer. She squinted into the shadows as she moved, and at first, she was sure she saw the toolshed door open. But she laughed, nervously. It was just Artemis, slunk down low, going after some un-suspecting lizard or something.

"How did you get out?" Lucy said.

She got a growl for an answer. Only it wasn't Artemis Hamm's kitty-cat snarl. This was deep and rich, as if it came from something bigger.

Because it did.

Lucy scooped Artemis up and stuffed her under the jacket so she couldn't claw her way free. Beyond that, she couldn't move. She could only listen, and look for movement.

And there it was. Slinking down the tree just six feet away. Long tufts of hair at the tips of its ears. The tufts twitched, and a spotted head moved down the trunk of the dead tree. The big cat sniffed, and her lips pulled away from long points. Canine teeth. Powerful jaws. Lucy could see it on the page: *Bobcats can often kill their prey in one powerful bite.*

She squeezed Artemis, who growled in the confines of the jacket. They ate rabbits, rats, foxes . . . and house cats.

A bobcat can lift ten times its weight when it has a notion to, Lucy had read. She swallowed hard. She didn't even have to do the math to figure out she needed to get out of there.

She took a step backward. The bobcat's head swiveled, and yellow-green eyes stared at her. Unafraid.

Never breaking her gaze, the bobcat dropped almost soundlessly to the ground and crouched, just the way Artemis did when she stalked. Only this was no kitty Lucy could gather in her arms and scold. And she herself was not a mouse who could scamper away.

The bobcat padded silently forward, teeth bared, until she was only three feet from her. Lucy could hear her breathing. She could hear her own heart pounding. And when a whimper escaped from Lucy's lips, it sounded like it came from some other terrified person.

Run! her mind screamed at her.

But another voice whispered, "Don't move."

Again she whimpered, because the bobcat crawled toward her, eyes still focused on Lucy's face. She was so close Lucy could see her pinpoint pupils, see her nostrils flaring with Lucy's scent.

"Don't move," someone whispered again.

If the bobcat heard, she paid no attention. Her head and shoulders went low. Lucy knew that position — she was gathering her energy to pounce like all cats did. She sprang at Lucy, claws extended — and then with a yowl she dropped. Something — someone — grabbed Lucy from behind and pulled her backward into darkness. The toolshed door slammed shut, and Lucy tumbled to the plank floor, on top of a wiry, lanky body that was breathing even harder than she was.

"J.J.?" she whispered.

"Shhh."

Lucy listened. There was a scratching sound, and then a thud on the other side of the fence. And then a deep growl from inside Lucy's jacket.

Lucy ripped open the snaps just as Artemis Hamm dug her first claw into Lucy's chest. Artemis leaped straight for the door, dragging her talons down it as she continued to snarl.

"Dream on," J.J. said.

Lucy giggled. And then she chortled. And then she held her sides as she laughed and laughed. Until she started to cry.

"Aw, Luce, don't do that," J.J. said. "Don't cry."

But Lucy couldn't help it. She hugged her knees into her chest and sobbed as she shook. Artemis kept clawing at the door, and J.J. groped around in the dark. Something thumped, and Lucy felt him drop beside her.

"What was that?" she said.

"Something fell on my head. Ow—"

"Lucy!"

"Dad?" Lucy crawled for the door. "We're in here!"

She could hear his footsteps and his cane—and she froze.

"Dad—the bobcat might still be out there! J.J.—"

J.J. finally got to the door and pushed it open. Artemis sprang out as if she were going to take the bobcat down with her own paws, and Lucy followed, still crying and shaking. She plowed into Dad, who put his arms around her and held on until she thought her ribs would crack.

"It's gone," J.J. said, voice zipping up in the air.

"Then it *was* the bobcat." Dad pressed his face into Lucy's hair. "I heard it."

"She was ready to jump on me," Lucy said. "And then J.J.—" She pulled away from Dad. "J.J., how did you get her to—"

The words froze on her lips. J.J. drew his hand back from his head. It was dripping red.

"You're bleeding!" Lucy said.

"Who's bleeding?" Dad said.

J.J. stared at his palm. "Something fell on me in the shed."

"Lucy—how bad is it?"

The ground seemed to roll under Lucy's feet as she stood on tiptoes to look at the top of J.J.'s head. Blood drenched his hair as it spurted from a gash as long as her pinky finger.

"It's bad," Lucy said. She was sure she was going to be sick, but she swallowed hard and pushed J.J. to the ground by the shoulders.

"Make him sit," Dad said.

"Did that."

"Go get his mom."

"No," J.J. said. His voice was like a thread. "Mr. Auggy."

"Call him, Lucy. And the sheriff. And get me some towels."

Lucy felt like a robot as she did everything he said. And that was a good thing. At least robots didn't cry.

The tears didn't well up in her again until after Mr. Auggy had arrived and taken J.J. to the emergency room in Alamogordo so his mom could stay home with Januarie—and called to say J.J. had ten stitches and looked like a tough guy now that he'd survived a battle with a pick. Lucy held the tears back until after the sheriff had questioned her and determined that the bobcat was definitely still on the prowl and was more dangerous than he'd thought. He also told Dad he ought to keep his kid inside after dark. If he could.

Only after all of that, when Lucy was wrapped in a blanket next to Dad on the Sitting Couch with a cup of milk-and-sugar tea, did she cry again. But that didn't stop Dad from using the pointed voice he hardly ever brought out unless she was in big trouble.

"I thought we had a deal about J.J.," he said.

"I'm sorry," Lucy said. "I needed to talk to him."

"You didn't think to ask me?"

Lucy couldn't answer.

"You're not taking care of what I love. Or of what you love. J.J. could have been mauled right along with you."

Lucy hugged the blanket tighter around herself. Didn't he know she'd thought of that a hundred times while he was plastering towels on J.J.'s head until they turned red? It was her fault. It was all her fault.

"I'm glad he was there to throw a hatchet at the bobcat. But you shouldn't have been out there in the first place." Dad shook his head. "Lucy, I don't like to give orders and make threats. I thought I didn't need to do that. But when I do, I have to follow through." He smeared his face with his hand. "I said if you got into any more trouble with J.J., you wouldn't be allowed to hang out with him. At all."

No. This couldn't be happening.

"No more J.J. for a while, until I feel like you and I are on the same page again. Obviously you're going to see him at school and soccer practice—I'm not saying you can't talk to him—but that's it. No hanging out together other than that." He seemed to look right at her. "Do you understand now what I was saying about this big Olympic program you want to get into? Things like this make me think you aren't ready, Luce. Now, are we clear about J.J.?"

All Lucy could do was shake her head and cry.

"I'll take that as a yes," Dad said.

For once, he didn't "see." He didn't see at all.

10

All the cats except Mudge joined Lucy on her bed the next morning. Dad was in the kitchen making his usual breakfast noise. The Book of Lists was next to her where she'd written in it last night, because it was the only place now where she could say whatever she wanted. At least God didn't tell her she was wrong about everything.

But she felt as alone as she probably would have if she'd been standing out in the middle of the desert with only the cactus to talk to. She didn't even look forward to going to Saturday morning practice. In fact, for the first time ever, she wished she didn't have to.

She put her hand to her forehead. Maybe she did feel sick. Too sick to put up with Dusty and Veronica ignoring her and Gabe and the other boys staring at her and Januarie blabbing to everyone that J.J. had busted his head open at her house while the two of them were in the shed in the dark. Too ill to practice without J.J. and think about him being with his dad and Weasel Lady—all because she, Lucy, couldn't help him—

Lucy whipped the covers over her head and burrowed down. That was it. She wasn't going.

"Luce?" It was Dad at the door. "We need to be ready when Mr. Auggy gets here."

We?

"He's picking us up at eight thirty."

"Why?" Lucy said from under the blankets.

"The town council's coming to the practice today. Everybody wants to see how the team's coming along."

Nuh-uh. Not today. Nuh-*uh*.

But there was obviously nothing she could do about it. Just like everything else. Mr. Auggy was there at 8:30, and Lucy had to climb into the backseat of his Jeep.

Mr. Auggy looked at her in the rearview mirror and said, "J.J.'s visiting his dad this morning."

"Too bad it had to be during practice," Dad said.

"Unfortunately, we can't argue with the court. Besides, he's in no shape to play yet anyway."

But he was in shape to have to face his mean father? Lucy just didn't get it. As she looked out the window, she wanted to cry again. Everything made her want to cry. The flowers blooming out of the tops of the short squatty cacti. The fruit trees all in puffy bloom — apple and quince and peach and cherry. The orchard of pistachios still waiting to bust into blossom. The prettiness had her blinking hard to keep the tears from falling.

"It's a beautiful spring," Mr. Auggy said.

Dad cocked his head toward Lucy. "Are the pistachios out yet?"

"No," she said in a small voice.

"They're always the last," Mr. Auggy said. "Must be that whole boy-girl thing."

Dad chuckled. "Did you know there were male and female pistachio trees, Luce?"

Lucy groaned inside. No wonder they didn't want to come out. The boy-girl thing just messed everything up.

It was hard to play that day without J.J. there and with everybody else acting all weird. They ran around the field like a bunch of cats that Lucy couldn't possibly herd.

But she had to. What if they looked like kindergartners out there and Mr. Benitez, who owned the grocery store, stopped buying their uniforms when the team started outgrowing them? And Gloria wouldn't keep them in balls and cleats and shin guards? And Dusty and Veronica's moms didn't think they were worth making banners for next time they had another team to play? What if the whole town decided they were a joke and sold the field, and all their dreams blew away like so much cottonwood fluff?

Lucy couldn't let that happen. They were the Dream. Her dream. Her only way to get to the Olympics.

A lump formed in her throat, and she swallowed it away. All right, no matter what, they were going to show the town today.

"Come on—both teams!" Lucy said to them as they took their positions on the field. "The Dreams don't die. Do your best!"

"Or you'll yell at us?" Veronica said.

"Just remember, Lucy Goosey," Gabe said. "Just 'cause you're mid-fielder doesn't mean you're the boss of us."

Lucy looked at Dusty, but she was adjusting her ponytail—which she never did once she was on the field. Lucy's heart began to sag.

But she caught it halfway down. Okay, then. If no one was going to listen, it was up to her.

Right away, from the kickoff, Lucy's team had control of the ball, because J.J. wasn't there to take it away. Neither Emanuel nor Dusty was as good as he was at defense, and Oscar, who was taking J.J.'s place while Mr. Auggy played goalie, was no help at all. Dusty did finally get the ball close to the goal, only because Veronica wasn't guarding her like she should have been. Lucy opened her mouth to call instructions to her, and then she clamped her mouth shut and went for it herself.

She surprised Dusty by running right at her. With one well-placed foot, Lucy had the ball. It was a long way back to the other goal, and Mr. Auggy was there defending it. Veronica stood on the other side of midfield at the left, dangling her long arms and her lower lip, and Gabe danced in front of Emanuel who was trying to attack along the right wing.

It was like looking at a diagram with little X's that Lucy could move wherever she wanted them. Nothing could have been clearer: she should get the ball to Veronica and call for Gabe to get ready for her to pass it to him—which, of course, she would. Then Gabe would score—or at least make a try against Mr. Auggy.

She drove hard, straight toward Veronica, dribbling without missing a beat. She could hear Dusty coming up behind her and Oscar shouting at Carla Rosa.

And then she didn't hear anything. She beat past Emanuel who loped along beside her, and she blew by Veronica, and she barely noticed Gabe as she shot the ball like a bullet, barely missing his knee. Mr. Auggy had to jump for it, going off of one leg. He tipped it off to the side of the goal, and both Dusty and Veronica scrambled for it. The only thing Lucy heard was the town council, shouting as if David Beckham were on the field—just the way Mom would have been shouting if she had been there.

Dusty had the ball now and was setting up to pass it to Emanuel. Lucy got to it before Veronica did and made another shot toward the goal. This time, Mr. Auggy had to dive to catch it. It skipped off the top of his spread-out hands and bounced into the corner of the box.

"Score!" Oscar yelled. "Score!"

Lucy turned to Dusty. "Go ahead and kick it in for your team," she said.

"Why don't you do it?" Gabe said. "You're doing everything else."

Mr. Auggy blew his whistle. "All right—" he said. "I think we're done for today."

Felix Pasco had sandwiches ready, and Mr. Benitez provided two drinks for each of them. Claudia handed out miniature chocolate soccer balls she'd had made up. Mayor Rosa, Carla Rosa's father, just shook all the team members' hands, although he shook Lucy's the longest, like a bicycle pump, and told her what a great player she was and how lucky she was to have this team. Lucy knew she should have been on top of the soccer world.

But she also knew from the way Mr. Auggy was not smiling at her, not even a little bit, that he didn't think she was so great right now. She wished she didn't have to ride back with him, especially when Dad said he was getting a ride from Gloria, who was going to give him a haircut before he went home.

She decided maybe she should go ahead and apologize before Mr. Auggy had a chance to start chewing on her. But he didn't go toward his Jeep. He nodded for her to sit on the bottom row of bleachers, and before she could get her mouth open, he said, "April twenty-second."

"Excuse me?" Lucy said.

"April Twenty-second. That's our next game, against a team that's just started up in Mescalero. Sheriff Navarra's cousin is their coach. He set it up for us, and the town's ready to work toward Game Day."

Lucy couldn't help the tingle that went up her arms. "That's good, isn't it?"

"It can be. We have the skills. We have the talent."

Lucy heard a silent "but."

"Do we have the spirit, though, Captain?" Mr. Auggy said.

Lucy swallowed so she wouldn't start crying again. This would not be the time.

"Is this because I scored the goal," she said, "instead of passing the ball like I was supposed to?"

"That's part of it."

"What else?"

"I think you need to tell me."

I don't know! she wanted to shout at him.

Mr. Auggy reached into the net bag and brought out a soccer ball. He put it into her hands.

"This'll make it easier to think," he said.

Lucy smoothed her hands over it and felt herself sink down into the seat. "Why can't everything else make as much sense as soccer?"

"Maybe it can if we look at it the right way. Why don't we take it out there on the field and kick it around a little, see what happens?"

Lucy blinked at him.

"Come on—Knockout. First one who misses is knocked out."

He jogged lightly toward the nearest goal area, and Lucy followed, dropping the ball and dribbling it with her insteps. Mr. Auggy let her shoot it in, and then snagged it on the rebound, kicking it back in. Lucy caught that rebound and one-touched it back into the goal.

They went back and forth until Lucy was laughing between huffs of breath. When Mr. Auggy kicked it in the next time, Lucy re-bounded the ball and kicked it down the field. She took off after it, with Mr. Auggy laughing and running behind her as she dribbled back around and brought the ball to him again.

"Most things are as simple as that, Captain," he said, chest rising and falling as he rocked the ball back and forth with his foot. "You see what you have to deal with, you figure out how, and then you try it. If it doesn't work, you try something else. Just like soccer."

Lucy wasn't sure what he was talking about, but she nodded anyway.

"But just like in soccer, it isn't just you and the ball, is it? You have all those other people getting in the way." He smiled. "Soccer would be great if you didn't have to work with other players."

"No it wouldn't! You wouldn't even have a game!" Lucy tried to pry the ball from under his foot, but he kept a firm hold with his.

"I know what you're gonna say." Lucy ducked her head. "You're talking about how I have to be part of the team and not always want to be the star."

"I didn't think I'd ever have to talk about that with you. Until just a few weeks ago, you were the best team player we had. I told you—that's why I made you captain."

Lucy stuck her hands in her pockets and wished she could climb in there with them. "Sorry," she said.

"No sorry. It isn't just you, but you're the one who has the most influence. I say we try to figure out what's going on, what's making you want to score all the points all of a sudden." Mr. Auggy picked up the ball and held it against his hip. "I don't think it has that much to do with soccer—but let's figure it out the same way. You have a goal, right?"

She pointed down the field, but Mr. Auggy shook his head. "No—a Lucy Goal. What do you want more than anything?"

She felt the lump in her throat again. "I want to be picked for the Olympic Development Program."

He looked as if she'd just said she wanted to learn algebra. "I didn't realize you even knew about that."

Lucy shrugged, and Mr. Auggy waited. Lucy wasn't sure what else she was supposed to say.

"That's—that's a great goal, Captain. And I can help you with that." He shook back his hair as if he were also trying to shake a lot of different thoughts into place. "That's something you and your dad and I should talk about. I'm surprised you haven't mentioned it to me before this."

There were so many reasons, Lucy couldn't even get one of them out. Mr. Auggy nodded.

"We both have a lot going on in our lives right now, don't we, Captain? You know what I do when I find myself running around in circles?"

"What?" Lucy said.

"I think about my life like it's a soccer game, and I look at the whole field. I say, 'What are the other players doing? How can I get them to work together?'" He shifted the ball to his other hip. "Everybody's not working together in your game, are they?"

"Hello—no!"

"You might have to show them how then. You're a captain, Lucy. People look to you to sort things out."

"Not anymore. They're all trying to sort *me* out."

"What about Carla Rosa?"

Lucy scrunched up her face.

"You didn't notice how much better she played today since you worked with her on your own?"

"How did you know I did that?"

He wiggled his eyebrows. "I have my sources."

Lucy shrugged. "No offense to Carla Rosa, Mr. Auggy, but she could learn from anybody, if you know what I mean."

"Nope, I don't." Mr. Auggy twirled the ball on his finger and then tossed it to her. "But you'll figure it out. Like I said, look at your whole field, not just yourself. Nobody goes it alone." He backed toward the bleachers. "I better get you home. Oh, one more thing. Who teaches you how to look at your field and decide where the ball should go?"

"You do," Lucy said.

"Right. I'm your coach. Who's your all-the-time coach, you know, for your life?"

"My dad?"

"I don't know. Is he with you all the time?"

"Nobody's with me *all* the time."

"Oh," Mr. Auggy said. "I thought that's why you guys went to church. Huh."

It wasn't hard to figure out that he was talking about God. Du-uh. But all the way home, and in the backyard practicing her dribbling and in her room avoiding Dad, what Lucy couldn't figure out was how she was supposed to hear God coaching her from the sidelines. She wasn't like that girl Rachel. *She* knew what God was saying, even when she didn't like it.

"But *I* don't get it," she said to Lolli and Artemis. "I write all these lists to God—it's like I'm talking to him all the time. But he doesn't talk to *me*." She wriggled on the bed. "Mr. Auggy says it's like soccer—I still don't totally understand."

But it wasn't like she had a whole lot of other choices. Dusty said that when she was mad at one parent, she just talked to the other one. Maybe God wasn't the coach. Maybe he was the other parent she didn't have.

She sighed and opened her Book of Lists. What did Mr. Auggy say to do? Look at the "field" of people she had to "play" with?

People I'm Having Trouble Playing With
Big Note: This Is for You, God
∾ J.J.
∾ Dad
∾ Aunt Karen
∾ Mora
∾ Januarie
∾ Dusty
∾ Veronica
∾ Carla Rosa
∾ Gabe and Emanuel and Oscar, who are practically all one absurd little creep person.

Her hand hurt. And so did her heart. Because almost everybody she knew was on the list.

"God? Help, please," she whispered. And then for the first time in her whole life, she cried herself to sleep.

The eyes that looked back at her from the mirror the next morning were puffed up like Inez's sopapillas. Lucy was almost glad Dad couldn't see so he wouldn't ask questions. She was certain Dusty and Veronica wouldn't when she saw them at church. That made her want to cry again. She sure hoped God had been paying attention when she made that list.

"It's Palm Sunday," Dad said as they walked the short block to the church. "Look for Mr. Auggy. He said he might join us today."

She didn't have to look for long. Mr. Auggy was waiting on the steps, and Dusty and Veronica were with him. She hoped J.J. would be there too, but there was no sign of him.

They all had palms and were waving them in each other's faces and laughing. Lucy tried to just slide past, but Dusty caught her under the chin with her piece of palm and tickled her. Lucy closed her eyes so she wouldn't cry again.

"You know something, Lucy?" Dusty said.

Lucy didn't answer. She just stopped on the steps.

"You used to be way fun, and now—"

"You're like all serious all the time." Veronica planted herself in front of Lucy, waving her palm dangerously close to her own half-open mouth. "All you care about is soccer, and it's hurting our feelings."

"I do care about soccer," Lucy managed to say around the wad in her throat. "I thought you guys did too."

Veronica looked at Dusty, as if they'd agreed on an answer and it was Dusty's turn to say it. When she didn't, Veronica flicked the palm with her finger and said, "It's only a game, Lucy."

For the first time ever, Lucy thought that might be right.

11

The only thing that got Lucy through the rest of the day was the God list.

She went back to it again and again, trying to see how she could move the players around on the field. But no matter what Mr. Auggy said, it wasn't like soccer.

On Monday morning when Lucy crossed the street to the school, she saw Carla Rosa, sitting on the bike rack, fidgeting with her fingers.

"Guess what?" Lucy said to her. Carla just blinked at her. "You don't ride your bike to school."

"Guess what—I know. I was waiting for you."

"What's wrong?"

Carla Rosa fiddled with one of the sequins on her cap.

"What?" Lucy said.

"People are mad at you."

Lucy hiked her backpack up and started toward the support class portable building. "I know, Carla Rosa—you don't have to tell me."

"I know why."

"So do I."

"Nuh-uh."

Lucy stopped a few feet from the portable steps. "Yes, I do. It's because I'm trying to make the team better and everybody thinks I'm bossy and they think I was mean to J.J."

Carla Rosa was shaking her head. Lucy really wanted to snatch the cap off and ask her why she wore the thing when it wasn't winter anymore.

"I used to be mad at you all the time," Carla Rosa said, "but I'm not now."

"You're the only one."

"Guess what—that's right. And guess what else?"

Lucy just looked at her. She'd never noticed that, like her, Carla Rosa had freckles on her nose. She didn't count Carla's. She couldn't see her so well with the tears blurring her eyes.

"You're crying," Carla Rosa said.

"So sue me."

"I can't. I'm a kid."

Lucy laughed, right out her nose, and a bubble formed.

"Guess what—"

"I know!" Lucy wiped her nose on her sleeve.

"You wanna know why I used to be mad at you but now I'm not?"

"Sure," Lucy said.

" 'Cause you do everything better than me."

Most people do, Lucy thought. And then she was sorry. Because Carla Rosa was honest, and she noticed things nobody else did. And she was the only one talking to Lucy right now.

"No, I don't do everything better than you," Lucy said.

"Yes, you do, but then you showed me how to do it and now I'm not mad." Carla wrinkled her nose, folding the freckles. "But everybody else is."

"They're not mad because I do everything better than them!"

"My dad says that's why."

"Your dad? Like, your dad, the mayor?"

"He said it when we played Saturday. He said I oughta tell you. And guess what?"

Lucy followed Carla's pointing finger. Oscar and Emanuel were approaching, heads down, hands shoved into their pockets. Oscar, of course, had a toothpick in his mouth.

"They're mad," Carla Rosa said.

"Yeah, they are," Lucy said.

Carla shrugged. "Maybe you should teach them stuff and then they won't be."

"I don't think so," Lucy said.

But going into the classroom and sitting at the table with Carla Rosa felt a whole lot better than Lucy thought it would when she woke up that morning. Maybe she could cross Carla off the list. Could God actually be telling her something?

J.J. didn't come to school, probably because of his stitches. It was hard not having him there. Lucy wanted to ask him how it went with his dad on Saturday.

But it was also easier not having him there. At least she didn't have to watch him be his maddest at her yet.

She didn't try Carla's teaching suggestion at recess. Mr. Auggy was in charge, and she was okay with that. He gave her some small smiles and told her "good job" when she kept getting the ball to Carla Rosa in the passing drill. It wasn't the same as giggling with Dusty and hauling Veronica to her feet when she did a spastic fall and showing J.J. up in the shielding drill would have been. But it was something.

"Be ready for some intense practices after school between now and April twenty-second," Mr. Auggy told them when the bell rang. "What are we gonna do to the Mescalero Monkeys?"

"Are they really called the Monkeys?" Veronica said.

"Nah—I just wanted to make you guys smile." Mr. Auggy nudged Gabe with his shoulder. "Come on—if we're not having fun, what's the point?"

Everybody looked at Lucy.

"Right," Lucy said. "Let's have fun."

"Yeah," Gabe said. "Right."

As Lucy trailed home, alone, from school that afternoon, the only thing she looked forward to was seeing her list again. She had Carla Rosa on her team now, so maybe there was something else God had said that she'd missed.

The back gate flew open, and Mora burst out with her eyes shining. She didn't even seem to notice Mudge growling from behind the century plant. She just looked around as if she were expecting something. Her face folded just over her nose.

"Where is everybody?" she said.

"Not here," Lucy said.

"What about J.J.?"

"It's not my day to watch him."

Mora brought out her always-in-motion finger and stabbed it toward Lucy. "Did you guys have a fight?"

Lucy didn't answer.

"Is he coming over?"

"No. He can't."

Mora flipped her ponytail. "Why not?"

"Because my dad won't let him." Not that it mattered anyway now. J.J. wasn't even letting himself come over.

"Oh." Mora folded her arms neatly across the berry-colored top that tied in a bow in the back. "Well, then."

"If you want to talk to him, he's right there." Lucy pointed to the lanky figure on the rusty bicycle. He didn't have the bandage anymore, but Lucy was surprised he was allowed to ride his bike so soon. Dad would still have her on the couch if she had stitches.

He was just about to pass them, until Mora stepped right out into Second Street and put her hands on J.J.'s handlebars. Lucy stared as Mora got on her tiptoes and smiled like a toothpaste commercial into his face.

"Hi!" she said.

"Hi," J.J. said back. His voice shot up.

Lucy couldn't listen. She scooped up Mudge and slipped into the backyard, closing the gate behind her.

There was a silence so long Lucy was sure J.J. had ridden off across the desert. She couldn't help peering through the slats in the gate. Mudge looked with her. J.J. was still there, face red, teeth clamped down, hands opening and closing on the bicycle grips.

"She needs to leave him alone," Lucy whispered to Mudge, who purred in agreement. "She's not gonna get anything out of him."

But he did say, "Like what?"

Mora got on her tiptoes and cupped her hands around J.J.'s ear and whispered into it. Lucy watched as he grew very still. He didn't pedal his bike off like a mad dog. He just listened. To Mora.

"Maybe," he said. And then he looked back at the gate.

Lucy shrunk down, even though she knew he couldn't see her.

Mora looked too. "She's not the one," she said.

Lucy couldn't move. Not even to let Mudge go when Mora opened the gate and the cat struggled to be let down. Mora took the backyard in three leaps, and Mudge hurled himself onto the table and then hid underneath.

Mora was about to dance through the back door when Lucy finally found her voice.

"What was that about?" she said.

"That was about none of your business." Mora's nostrils flared so wide Lucy could have inserted a soccer ball in one of them. "You can't have it all your way, Lucy."

"What are you talking about?"

The fingers came out to talk. "You don't want him for your boyfriend, but you don't want me to have him either. But it's too late. J.J. needs me now."

"Needs you for what?"

"For what you wouldn't do because you're too selfish."

"Mora."

Lucy wasn't sure when the inside door had opened or how long Inez had been standing there. She was just glad she was there now. Lucy slipped past her and escaped to her room and closed the door so she wouldn't hear what they said to each other.

She dove for the bed and hugged her Book of Lists to her chest. She wasn't sure God had shown up for that scene, but Inez had. Maybe that was how God answered a prayer.

Lucy watched Lolli pop her head out of the toy chest and look around suspiciously. *Or Inez could believe whatever Mora was telling her right now. She was her granddaughter after all.*

Lucy sighed. Inez was just about the only person who wasn't on the list. She would love to talk to her. It had been so long. But who could she trust, and with what? She was feeing less superior by the second.

Maybe she could get past both of them and get to soccer practice and—and what?

What, God?

At least when Lucy passed through the kitchen, Mora had her head buried in her homework. Inez, however, seemed to see Lucy through the back of her head. She turned and tucked a tamale into Lucy's hand.

"Girls," she said. "Always there is tragedy."

That made Lucy a little less afraid the next afternoon, after another day of J.J.'s silence, to sit down at the table for Bible study. In fact, she was kind of anxious to find out if Leah and Rachel ever got things worked out. She definitely needed more information.

"Tricking Senor Jacob to marry Senorita Leah is not the last nasty thing Senor Laban does," Inez said as she opened her Bible.

Lucy nodded and nibbled the corner of a quesadilla. Mora dug right in.

"He also tries to cheat Senor Jacob out of the sheeps that belong to him. But El Senor, he will not allow that."

"I don't get that," Lucy said. "Did God just show up back then and tell people what to do?"

"It is the same now as then. El Senor is here."

"Right here, like in the room?"

"*Si*. Yes. Everywhere."

"Could we just get on with the story?" Mora said. She glanced at her pink watch like she had someplace to go.

"When El Senor is kind to Senor Jacob," Inez went on, "this makes Senor Laban very angry. And his hijos."

"Sons," Lucy said, before Mora could.

"Senor Jacob, he has it up to here with them—" Inez leveled her hand at her forehead. "So El Senor helps him make a plan."

"How?" Lucy said. "Did he send it in the mail or what? That's what I don't get."

Inez tapped her temple. "Senor Jacob, he pays attention to the things El Senor places before him. Example—he hears the brothers talking the trash about him, making the evil schemes."

"Uh-huh."

"And he takes that to El Senor when he prays. He asks for help. And he gets help, like we do when we pray and watch."

"So what happens?"

"If you'd be quiet for seven seconds, she'd tell us." Mora pounded her own forehead with the heel of her hand. "G-yah."

"Mora! *Basta!* These are good questions from Lucy. This is how we learn."

Mora flopped her head down on her arms, crossed on the table. Inez gave her a long look before she went back to her Bible.

"The problem with this plan is—Senor Jacob must take his esposas—"

"Rachel and Leah—"

"—and *los ninos*, the children, away from Senor Laban's country, back to where Senor Jacob come from. He is worry that his wives will not want to leave their father and everything they know."

"Okay," Lucy said, "so which one of them wanted to go, and which one wanted to stay? I know they had a fight about it."

The lines at the corners of Inez's eyes broke into rays like a sun in a little kid's picture. That wasn't something you saw often.

"They do not fight over this," she said. "At last, at last, they agree. They love Senor Jacob, and they will go with him. They choose him over their father."

"He was a jerk anyway," Lucy said.

"Ah, *si*. But he is still their father."

That tugged at Lucy, but she bobbed her head for Inez to go on.

"Now, because Senor Laban is the jerk, Senor Jacob must take his family away in the night. He does not tell Senor Laban he will go. Senora Rachel and Senora Leah, they help to get away. When they work together, they are—hmmm—"

Inez's forehead wrinkled like a stack of cinnamon sticks.

"Like a team?" Lucy said.

"Ah—*si!*"

"Seriously. They did?"

"*Si.* They take all their belongings. And Senora Rachel, she also takes the small statues that belongs to Senor Laban. They are his gods."

"His gods? I don't get it."

Mora groaned into her arms.

"Sit up, Mora," Inez said.

She was using the slice-the-air voice. Mora's head came up, and for a second, she actually looked afraid.

"Listen," Inez said. "And learn, like Lucy."

Lucy cringed. That wasn't going to go over well.

"She takes the gods that Senor Laban thinks are real, like good luck," Inez said. "We don't know why she takes them. Maybe she does not want her father to worship them anymore because she knows the real El Senor. Maybe she is only angry with her father. We don't know."

"I'm glad she ripped him off," Mora said. "He deserved it."

Lucy made a note to self: watch your stuff around Mora right now.

"When Senor Laban finds out his family is gone, he goes after them. He demands to know why Senor Jacob does this horrible thing to him."

"What?" Lucy said. "He was the one who was horrible!"

"We each see things through our own eyes."

"Well, du-uh." Mora put up her hand. "Sorry."

"But Senor Jacob, he tells the truth, everything he hear the brothers say, everything Senor Laban try to do to cheat him." Inez nodded wisely. "The truth is best. Senor Laban cannot argue. He tells Senor Jacob to take his family and go. But—" She smiled down at the page. "He is still angry about his gods. Where are they, he wants to know."

"I hope Rachel kept them." Mora sounded like she would spit if Rachel didn't.

"If Senor Laban can find them among the belongings, he can accuse Senor Jacob of stealing. Then all is lost, you see?"

"So—" Lucy made a rolling motion with her hand.

"Senora Rachel sits on the small statues when her father is searching. She is clever, yes? Senor Laban leaves, and he never knows Senora Rachel stole his gods." Inez smiled as if she'd been there herself. "Senora Rachel is at last thinking of somebody besides Senora Rachel. She is a different person now than before."

"It's like she grew up," Lucy said.

"And now you're going to tell us we have to grow up and stop fighting and work together, blah, blah, blah." Mora slanted down in the chair, arms folded. "Sorry, Abuela, but it ain't gonna happen. Not with me and Lucy. I can't wait for Mom to get here and take me away. One week, and then I won't have to—"

Inez slapped her hand on the table. Mora crammed her lips together. Lucy excused herself.

She got as far as the doorway to the hall before Inez said, "There is one more thing, Senorita Lucy."

Lucy turned. Mora had her head back down on her arms. "This happens to Rachel and Leah because El Senor, he is there with them, and they watch for what he places before them. He is here too." She tapped the corner of her eye, and she smiled.

Lucy smiled back. It was her first real smile in a long time.

In her room, she looked once more at her God list. She wasn't sure how she was supposed to ask God for all the stuff that needed to change. But it seemed like from the way Inez told it you just talked to God like you did everybody else. That was good, because she didn't know how else to say it except in lists. It was worth a try.

"If you can work things out between Leah and Rachel," she whispered, "then I know you can help me work it out with all my players. Even the ones that aren't in soccer. So please make me pay attention to what you want me to do. Amen."

She opened her eyes and half-expected to see some sign or at least hear a voice. There was only Artemis demanding to be let outside. She was sure God wasn't going to speak through a kitty. She would probably have to wait until tomorrow for instructions.

It was so windy the next day the team didn't have soccer practice at recess because the ball would have been swept away like the dust. Lucy was afraid Mr. Auggy would cancel the after school practice too. He said he would call Lucy's house to let her know.

"You all seem to gather there anyway," he said.

Everybody suddenly looked like they were examining the half moons on their fingernails, except Oscar, who just gnawed on his toothpick, and Carla Rosa, who said, "Guess what?"

"No time for guessing today, Carla Rosa," Mr. Auggy said. Lucy figured he really didn't want to know. No room for drama in soccer, he'd said.

The wind died down that afternoon, and everybody did gather at Lucy's, outside her gate. The boys punched each other a lot, and Veronica and Dusty sat against the fence and braided each other's hair. Lucy felt miserable. Mudge was beside himself, growling so loudly Lucy thought the bobcat was back.

He was especially testy when Mora and Januarie came out of the house and joined the group, although Lucy was pretty sure Mudge didn't see what she saw: that the two of them looked like they'd been planning some kind of takeover. Januarie's round, brown face was all chilly bumpy, like chicken skin, and she wouldn't look anybody in the eye. Mora clutched at her pink bag and giggled too loud and made even Gabe look as if he'd just sucked on a pickle.

"Why does she have to come?" Carla Rosa whispered to Lucy.

"That's what I'd like to know," Lucy whispered back.

Carla opened her mouth as if she were actually going to ask, but Mr. Auggy's red Jeep rounded the corner and they all rushed the curb.

Lucy was almost there when she felt a tug on her sweatshirt. She turned to see J.J. standing behind her, staring at the sidewalk. She could barely hear his voice when he spoke.

"I can't do it again."

"Do what?" she said. She could barely hear hers either.

"See my dad. He hates me."

"He said that?"

"I saw it."

Lucy knew exactly what he meant. She hadn't see Mr. Cluck in weeks, but she could still remember the way his eyes glittered when he yelled at J.J., right here on this very spot outside her fence. She shivered now. She could clearly imagine how J.J. must feel.

"Help me," he said.

"Yo — Captain," Mr. Auggy called from the car window. "Can you get your team there in ten? I think we can get a good forty-five minutes in."

"Yes!" Mora said.

As everyone else hopped onto their bikes or took off on foot, Lucy turned to J.J. "We'll talk," she said. "But we have to do it at practice. During the water break."

She couldn't see his eyes beneath his hair, but his shoulders weren't so far up to his ears as he got on his bike and followed the team. He twisted his head back toward her, and she hurried to get her bike.

Even as she did, Mora gave Januarie a small shove in J.J.'s direction. Januarie chewed at her lip and did an I-don't-want-to dance. Either that, or she had to go to the bathroom. But Lucy knew Januarie. Mora was using her for something, and Januarie, for once, didn't seem to care how important it was going to make her in Mora's eyes.

Lucy let herself down from her bike and walked it to catch up to her, but Januarie broke into a chubby, plodding run and grabbed the back of J.J.'s bike seat before he could take off.

Lucy got back on hers and sped around them. She'd talk to J.J. at practice. Dad said she could do that. And she would convince him that he shouldn't try to hide, that there were other ways. And he would listen to her.

She was suddenly lighter. J.J. was talking to her again. She would do her Lucy-best with J.J. *and* with soccer. Her whole life-field was going to be okay, just like Mr. Auggy said.

Her bike had wings as she crossed the highway.

12

While J.J. and Januarie and Mora sat on the bench, Mr. Auggy gathered them all on the field after their stretches, ball on his hip, small smile on his face. It looked to Lucy like he had to work to get it there.

"This is April fifth," he said. "How far away does that make April twenty-second?"

Before Lucy could calculate, Gabe said, "Seventeen days."

Show-off.

But Lucy stopped herself. Was that the way everybody else felt about her when she had the right answer all the time about soccer?

"Pretty smart, Gabe," Lucy said.

"I know," Gabe said.

Okay, so he was still an absurd little creep. But Veronica's eyes widened at Lucy before she went back to pulling up her yellow-striped socks with the butterflies on them. Only Veronica would wear butterflies for soccer.

"Cute socks," Lucy whispered.

"A little over two weeks," Mr. Auggy was saying. "In that time, we're going to concentrate on our teamwork. So—new rule." Mr. Auggy's smile turned into a line, like one in the dirt you didn't dare cross. "If anybody brings their personal crisis out onto the field and it interferes with the game, that player is going to have to sit out until I decide that person is ready to play with the team again."

"What's a personal crisis?" Carla Rosa said.

Everybody looked at the ground, except Gabe, who curled his lip at Lucy in an absurd-little-creep smile.

"Who can give Carla Rosa an example?" Mr. Auggy said.

Lips zipped as if an Artic wind had blown through. Gabe was still smirking at Lucy. She took a deep breath.

"Like me being all grouchy because people were saying J.J. and I were boyfriend and girlfriend. I took it out on everybody at practice."

Carla Rosa nodded the sequins. "And made us all mad at you."

"That was brave, Miss Lucy," Mr. Auggy said.

"Thanks," Lucy said.

"All right—are we clear on that?"

Heads nodded. No eyes met Lucy's, except Carla Rosa's. There was almost something wise in them.

"Can we just play now?" Gabe said.

Mr. Auggy grinned. "Absolutely."

"Women," Lucy heard Gabe say to him as the team got into their positions.

"I told you, don't try to understand them. Just enjoy them."

"No way!"

For once, Lucy had to agree with him.

It was still different without J.J., but Mr. Auggy said he needed to sit out until the stitches were removed and the doc said it was okay for him to play again. Lucy tried to praise everybody for every little good thing they did. She tried to stay at midfield. She even tried to get the ball to Veronica and coach her toward the goal. That didn't exactly work when Veronica kicked it too high and got Dusty right in the chin. She went down like a sack of stones.

Lucy was the first one to get to her. "You need a hand?" she said.

Dusty studied Lucy's outstretched fingers as if they might have lice. Finally, she nodded and reached her hand up. Lucy snatched hers away and clapped—and hoped Dusty would get it. *Please, let her think it's funny.*

"Very cute," Dusty said. She started to push herself up, and Lucy put her hand down. Dusty smacked at it, but Lucy thought she saw a tiny twitch at the corner of her mouth.

Lucy felt lighter again as she jogged back to center midfield. She might be able to cross Dusty off the list. Emanuel and Oscar were already acting like nothing ever happened. Maybe it was easier being a boy, especially those two, since they never seemed to know exactly what was going on anyway. Maybe she could cross them off too.

"To you, Lucy Goosey!" Gabe shouted.

Lucy grinned and went for the ball that was coming at her. Even as it sped her way, she stretched her neck to check out where it needed to go next. That's when she saw them: J.J. and Mora on the bench.

The ball smacked Lucy in the shin, but she let it roll away.

"Hey!" Gabe shouted.

She didn't answer. She just ran, past him, past Emanuel, past the sideline to get to where Mora was reading to J.J. out of a book. Her book.

Her Book of Lists.

"What are you doing with that?" Lucy screamed.

She grabbed the book and pulled so hard she yanked Mora forward with it. The long fingers didn't let go, and Lucy and Mora rocked back and forth. When Lucy heard paper rip, she screamed again, and this time, Mora turned it loose and scrambled off the bench.

Lucy didn't go after her. She turned the book around and stared down at it, her skin turning white under her thumbnails as she clutched it. There was a bite-size tear from the top corner of the right-hand page, but Lucy's eyes were glued to the writing. It wasn't hers. Someone else had scrawled a list on the paper—

Why I HAte J.J.

1. BeCAuse he is BetteR thAn me At soCKeR, AnD I CAn't stAnD AnyBoDy to Be BetteR thAn me At soCKeR.

2. BeCAuse he is pARt ApAChy AnD pARt wite AnD I'm ALL wite. AnD I think wite peOpLe ARe BetteR thAn AnyBuDDy eLse.

3. BeCAuse he mADe me feeL LiKe A LozeR BeCAuse he woh't Be my BoyFRienD.

4. BeCAuse he Lives in A ugLy house.

5. AnD thAt's why I woh't heLp him when he neeDs me.

The last line was hard to read, because Lucy's hands were shaking and the book wouldn't be still. Lucy couldn't be still either. She turned it toward Mora, who was now standing behind J.J., like he was her shield. His eyes were watery, and his jaw was clenched harder than Lucy had ever seen it.

"You ruined my book!" Lucy's heart pounded in her throat, and she had to scream to get around it. "You stole it, and you wrote stuff in it that isn't even true!"

Mora folded her arms and wobbled her head. "I found it. That stuff was already in it." She actually smiled. "You wrote everything in there, Lucy. You know you did."

Lucy shoved the open book in Mora's face. "This isn't my writing. I would never say this stuff. I know how to spell soccer!"

"Whoa, whoa—hold on." Mr. Auggy slipped his hand between the book and Mora's nose. "Back off, Miss Lucy."

"No! I won't! This is my private, personal, special—" But Lucy couldn't talk anymore. And she couldn't cry in front of her whole soccer team. She couldn't do anything.

"Miss Mora," Mr. Auggy said. "I would rather you didn't come to soccer practice anymore. Why don't you head on back to Lucy's?"

"No problem." Mora swished her ponytail as she turned to Januarie. "You come with me."

"Miss Lucy."

Lucy turned miserably to Mr. Auggy. The rest of the team was watching him, eyes waiting. Out of the corner of her eye, she saw J.J. take off on his bike. Just like that mad dog.

"I'm going to have you sit out the rest of the practice," the coach said. "Then we'll talk."

"But guess what? It wasn't Lucy's fault."

Surprised heads turned to Carla Rosa.

"I'll sort that out later," Mr. Auggy said. "Right now, I'm getting the crisis off the field so we can continue to play soccer. Understood?"

His voice was like some stern stranger's. He nodded Lucy toward the empty bench and then herded the team back to the field.

Understood? No, she didn't understand. And she couldn't sit there and watch her team, her dream, go on playing without her.

Lucy ripped off her cleats and her shin guards without even sitting down and shoved them into her backpack with her Book of Lists. She barely had her feet in her tennis shoes before she was on her bike, heading for home.

Except she couldn't go home. Mora was there, giving Inez some knotted-up version of what happened. Lucy never wanted to see Mora again. Or Januarie. Because it occurred to her as she rode and rode and rode, up and down every street in Los Suenos, that Januarie had found her Book of Lists and had given it to Mora. She thought of the day the book had ended up in her pillowcase. And the day she'd caught Januarie in her room, supposedly looking for candy. Hadn't Lucy and Dusty and Veronica all been impressed because Januarie scampered off when Mora said, "Don't you have something to do?"

"She had something to do, all right," Lucy shouted into the wind. It swallowed up her words, but she kept calling them out. "Mora made her steal my book. She gave Januarie video games so she would take my book and give it to Mora so she could ruin it. Mora messed it all up—and it was my mother's! My MOM!"

Lucy's front wheel wobbled, and she couldn't get it straight. She wasn't sure what took her off the road, but when she landed in the ditch, all she could see was dust whirling above her. When had it gotten this windy again? It was blowing so hard, Lucy struggled to get her breath as she tried to haul her bike up the slope. A gust plastered it against her, and Lucy fell backward with the bicycle on top of her. Her backpack cushioned her, and she kicked at her bike, hard, but it was as if some big hand were pressing it down. Lucy managed to get to her belly and slither out from under it—into another gust that filled her eyes with stinging grit.

With her head down and her eyes burning, Lucy crawled straight down the dry ditch until she felt a shelter above her. Must be a bridge—maybe the one they crossed to get to the soccer field. The fact that she didn't know for sure was the scariest thing of all. She pulled her knees into her chest and buried her face against her thighs. It couldn't blow forever. It couldn't sweep her away. Could it?

God, don't let it, please.

Lucy squeezed her shins in tighter and let the same words rise over and over into the whistling and the whining and the yowling. She felt something skitter across her backpack—maybe a hunk of sagebrush running from the wind. *God, don't let me get blown away, okay? I can't do anything. Please help me.*

She wasn't sure how long she stayed in her ball, praying into her own knees, before she heard the car. She still couldn't see, but she tried to claw her way up the side of the ditch, and she yelled even though her shouts were blown back at her.

"Don't let it go by, God! Please—help!"

The car stopped. The door opened. Lucy didn't know whether she was moving up or down but she kept on, until the wind carried her name to her.

"Lucy?"

"I'm here!"

Strong hands wrapped around her wrists, stronger than Mr. Auggy's muscles had ever looked to her. As he pulled her up as if she were a bag of feathers, Lucy knew she'd think of him as Superman from now on.

"Are you hurt?" he shouted into her face.

"No!"

"All right—stay low!" He planted his arms around her and pulled her to her feet and bent her at the waist the way he was. Together they battled the wind to the car, and Lucy hung onto him as he struggled to get the door open. She felt herself being pushed in the way she shoved her own stuff into her cubby. When the door closed behind her, she stayed curled on the seat until Mr. Auggy got himself in on the other side.

"You sure you're all right?" he said.

"Yes," Lucy said. "I'm sorry—"

"No, Captain. I'm the one who's sorry. I'll come back for your bike. Let's get you home first."

That wasn't so easy. The wind rocked the Jeep and blasted the windshield with sand. Lucy hoped Mr. Auggy could see better than she could, because it seemed as if they were driving through a sand dune.

"I bet you have a bushel of dirt in your eyes," Mr. Auggy said. "Hang in there. We'll get them washed out when we get to your house. If your father lets me in the house—"

Lucy didn't ask why Dad wouldn't. Mr. Auggy just sounded like everything was his fault. There was a lot of that going on.

They finally made it to Lucy's, and Mr. Auggy insisted on carrying her in over his shoulder, like a fireman rescuing somebody from a burning building. The first thing Lucy heard clearly when the wind was finally shut out was Dad saying, "Sam? Did you find her?"

"He found me," Lucy said. "You can put me down now, Mr. Auggy."

She barely had her feet on the kitchen floor before Dad was fumbling for her and found her and held on until she could hardly breathe.

"Smart girl, our Miss Lucy," Mr. Auggy said. "She knew to get under the bridge."

"Lucy—why did you run off in a sandstorm?"

"Ted—please." Mr. Auggy's voice sounded smaller than his smile ever was. "It's my fault. I should have handled things better."

As Lucy remembered what "things," her heart dove straight down. A few minutes ago, all that mattered was not being blown all the way to Alamogordo. But it was all back, all the things that didn't get swept away.

"You need to wash those eyes out," Mr. Auggy said.

"Yes." Dad's face drew lines down itself. "We can't mess around with eyes."

Mr. Auggy offered to help, but Lucy said no and escaped to the bathroom. After five minutes of digging into her eye sockets with a washcloth, she gave up and got into the shower. Between the tears and the water, she came out red-eyed, but she could see herself in the mirror. Her sixteen freckles and her wet bangs hanging in her face and her hazel-like-Mom's eyes. She looked sad. And a lot older than she had just yesterday.

Lucy could hear Dad and Mr. Auggy talking in murmurs in the kitchen, the kind that would stop if she came in and shift to too loud talk about what they should have on their pizza. She tied Dad's bathrobe on and padded to her room and pulled the Book of Lists out of her backpack.

Maybe she should give it a shower too. It had Mora on it. She'd touched it, and nobody was supposed to even know about it except Dad and Inez. Lucy used the corner of Dad's bathrobe to scrub at it. But then she sagged back against the soccer pillow.

She couldn't fix the inside. The page would always be torn, and Lucy had been more careful with it than she had ever been with anything in her life. The stuff Mora had scribbled in it would always be messy and misspelled. It would always be lies.

Feeling like she might just throw up, Lucy opened the book to Mora's list.

"Socker." "Apachy." "Wite." Lucy had always thought Mora was smarter than she was. Maybe she'd written it that way because she thought Lucy couldn't spell.

And maybe she'd said Lucy thought "wite" people were better than "everybuddy" else because Mora really thought Lucy felt that way.

But she couldn't possibly think Lucy felt like a "lozer" because J.J. wouldn't be her boyfriend.

Lucy studied the scribbly handwriting, and the words spelled like they sounded. Maybe Mora wrote all that because that was how *she* felt. Like a loser. Like white people were better than her Hispanic self. Like if she wasn't better than everybody else, she wasn't anybody at all.

Kind of like what Carla Rosa said.

Superior. Rachel over Leah. Leah over Rachel.

Lucy pulled at the page until it came loose at the bottom, and she tugged carefully at it until it was away from her book. She crumpled it up and tossed it toward the trash can, and Artemis Hamm pounced after it like a mini-bobcat. There. It was gone, out of her book.

But Mora probably wasn't going anywhere, not unless Inez quit. She had to work with the players who were on her field.

Lucy turned back to her last list — People I'm Having Trouble Playing With — and tried not to think about Mora reading it. If Mr. Auggy was right, it might actually be like soccer.

She turned the book sideways. What she was thinking of wasn't a list. But it seemed like something her mom would say was okay.

With careful strokes, Lucy drew a soccer field.

Each person on the list got an X and a place to be.

Carla Rosa was behind her, defending her. J.J. was still on the sideline — hurt.

She swallowed hard and kept drawing.

Dad was up in the bleachers. Maybe cheering her on, but knowing almost nothing about the game she was in. She didn't even invite Aunt Karen into the drawing. But Inez was on the bottom row of the bleachers, watching both sides. And Mora?

Lucy made her the goalie for the other team, because every time Lucy tried to score somehow, Mora kicked it back at her. Januarie's X went behind the goal area, ready to do whatever Mora told her to, even if it meant cheating.

Lucy chewed on the end of her pencil. What was she supposed to do with them? God didn't plunk an answer into her brain, so Lucy placed her Dusty and Veronica X's as forwards. Maybe they really did want to play with her, even if the three of them didn't always get it right. She hoped she could get Dusty to call her Bolillo again, even if the girl never scored a goal in her life.

She put Gabe way up front, where he always had to be whether Lucy wanted him to be or not. He was never going to listen to her, and maybe it didn't matter. She put Emanuel out in midfield where he could quietly do his thing. And, as for Oscar — she laid his X down at the other goal and tried to figure out how to draw a toothpick on it.

Lucy blew on the page so the ink wouldn't smear and studied it. It actually made sense, the way the whole field did when she was out there in the center, seeing where the players were and where the ball was and where it all needed to move.

She wasn't sure what to do with this field yet, but that's when you needed a coach. She said a prayer. And then she went for her clothes so she could talk to the other coach right now.

But Lucy stopped with one leg in her jeans. Mr. Auggy's voice was suddenly louder.

"He was gone when I finished practice," he said. She'd never heard his voice sound like that before, like he was scared. "His bike was gone, and I had to go look for Lucy."

Lucy let go of her jeans. Were they talking about J.J.?

"When was the last time you seen him?" said another voice. Sheriff Navarra's voice.

"The kids were having a little argument—"

"What kids?"

Lucy grabbed the robe again and tied it on as she tore for the kitchen.

"Luce?" Dad said.

"What's wrong? Did something happen to J.J.?"

Dad held out his arm, and she ran to it.

"Nobody's seen J.J. since soccer practice," the sheriff said. "Did you?"

Lucy tried to erase the last time she saw J.J. and shook her head. "We had a fight—Mora and I—and Mr. Auggy told me to sit out, and I got on my bike and left."

The sheriff shook his head. "I'm glad I have sons. All right, listen to me." His black eyes were serious. "Gabe says you two are tight, so if anybody knows anything about where he might have gone, it would be you." He put his hands on his hips. "You can't be protecting him—"

"I'm not! Honest, I'm not! He's not even talking to me right now."

Except that he'd been about to—until Mora ruined it.

The sheriff grunted, but Dad held up a hand. "That's true. Lucy's not allowed to spend time with J.J. And if she knew anything, she'd say so."

Mr. Auggy went for the door.

"Where you going?" Sheriff Navarra said.

"I'm going to go look for him."

"I have some more questions for you."

"Save them," Mr. Auggy said, and he was gone.

The sheriff turned on Lucy again. "Where do you *think* he would have gone?"

Lucy's mind was spinning so hard it hurt. J.J. had done it. He'd gone into hiding just like he said he would. And it was her fault. And Mora's.

"Lucy," Dad said. "This isn't to get J.J. in trouble. It's to help him. We're in the middle of a storm, Luce, and J.J. could be out in it."

"He might be in our toolshed," Lucy said.

"Gabe told me that. We looked there already. Where else?"

Under her bed. Out on the desert with the cholla cactus. Up in his room behind a sheet with a flashlight. Those were the places. Their places.

The sheriff scribbled things on a notepad as she talked, and then he looked at her again. His eyes were softer now. "Has he said anything to you about running away?"

Lucy shrank into Dad's bathrobe, but the sheriff just waited. What was the point? The answer was probably all over her face anyway.

"He said he wanted to hide so he wouldn't have to see his dad," she said. "And he wanted me to help him, but I wouldn't. That's why I don't know where he is."

She felt Dad's arm around her. It stayed there until the sheriff left.

"I'm proud of you, Lucy," Dad said.

"I'm not proud of me," Lucy said. And for what seemed like the hundredth time, she cried.

13

Lucy woke up so many times that night to look over at J.J.'s window that she could hardly drag herself out of bed the next morning. Dad told her she didn't have to go to school, but she couldn't stay home either. J.J. might just walk into the classroom like he always did. She had to be there.

She rushed out without getting her jacket, so she had to huddle inside her sweatshirt in the early morning chill. The sky was friendly—all horizontal stripes of white-foam clouds and gray mist and blueness like J.J.'s eyes. But Lucy had never felt so alone.

As she sat on the metal steps to the portable, she watched the watercolor stripes melt into the blue, but J.J. didn't show. Neither did Mr. Auggy. Only Carla Rosa greeted her halfway across the schoolyard, white sequins dancing in the sun. Lucy didn't even have to hear her to know she was saying, "Guess what?"

"J.J.'s missing," she said as she plopped down beside Lucy.

"I know."

"My dad told me. Guess what—my dad's the mayor."

"I *know*." Lucy held her head to keep it from exploding.

"The sheriff came to our house."

"What about the sheriff?" Oscar was suddenly there, hands in the air. "I didn't do nothin'."

"Shut up," Emanuel said to him. "Here."

He stuck a toothpick in Oscar's mouth and looked at Lucy. Oscar looked at Lucy, and so did Carla Rosa. The only one not there to wait for her to tell them what to do was J.J.

"I think J.J.'s hiding somewhere," Lucy said. "And if anybody knows anything, they have to tell."

"I don't know nothin'," Oscar said.

For once, Lucy wished he did.

Mr. Auggy didn't come to school, and Mrs. Nunez was their sub. Oscar usually messed with substitutes until they were ready to turn the portable over, but no one was in the mood, not even him. They just pretended to do the assignment and sighed and jerked their heads toward the door every time the wind rattled it. No J.J. No Mr. Auggy.

At recess, the team didn't get any farther than the cubbies in the sixth-grade hall. Dusty and Veronica each had Gabe by an arm as they dragged him to Lucy.

"He won't tell us," Dusty said, "but he'll tell you."

Lucy hugged her soccer ball, afraid to hear. "Tell me what?"

"Go ahead, Gabe." Veronica plucked at his jacket sleeve.

Gabe scowled until he looked more like the sheriff than Lucy was comfortable with. She was waiting for his beefy hands to go to his hips, when he said, "I'm just supposed to tell you, since you're the captain, that Mr. Auggy went out looking for J.J., even though my dad told him not to. My dad says you oughta keep the team going while he's gone. He says you're bossy enough."

Lucy sagged against the cubbies so she wouldn't go all the way to the floor in a puddle of disappointment.

"Just so you know," Gabe said, "I'm not taking orders from you."

"Shut up, Gabe," Dusty said.

"Guess what?" Carla Rosa shook the sequins. "If Mr. Auggy was here, he would buzz you for that."

"No, he wouldn't," Dusty said. "Gabe's being a moron."

"It's okay," Lucy said. "I don't even care about soccer right now. I just care about J.J.—and not like you all think. He's my best friend and he's missing and it's my fault."

"Aw, man, don't cry," Gabe said. He looked at Oscar. "Why do girls always have to cry?"

"Because we actually have feelings," Veronica said—through her own tears.

"J.J.'s coming back, dude," Oscar said. He poked Emanuel. "Ain't he?"

Emanuel just looked miserable. Everybody looked miserable.

"You really don't know where J.J. is?" Dusty said to Lucy.

She shook her head.

"Then what are we supposed to do?" Veronica was crying harder than Lucy and was wringing her hands like they were one of Inez's dishrags.

"Lucy'll find out, 'cause guess what?" Carla Rosa bobbed the sequins. "She's our captain."

They were all looking at Lucy with too-big eyes. Hopeful eyes. And she couldn't think of anything to say. She knew about things like sliders and shielding. She didn't know about things like this. But there they were waiting for her to make it better.

"Here's what we do," she said. "We stay together as a team, like the sheriff said, and we keep working on our skills so we're ready when Mr. Auggy and J.J. come back."

"What good is that gonna do?" Veronica said.

"Keep us from standing around crying," Dusty said.

Lucy nodded. "We have a game in sixteen days. We should practice."

Lights went on in Dusty's eyes. Veronica didn't look so much like she was going to burst into tears again. Carla Rosa was already happily bobbing her sequins.

"Okay, so, is it a deal?" Lucy said. "We practice after school?"

"We can't meet at the big field without an adult," Gabe said.

"Then we'll practice here, tomorrow, at the usual time."

"Guess what, tomorrow's a holiday," Carla Rosa said. "Good Something."

"Good Friday," Veronica said. "Sunday's Easter."

"Okay, so, Monday," Lucy said. "And anybody who wants to come to my yard any day this weekend, I'll do drills with you."

The boys all looked at each other like she'd suggested they wear bras, but the girls were shiny-faced and nodding.

"And J.J.'s gonna be back before any of this happens anyway, right?" Dusty said.

"Right."

Lucy was glad Mrs. Nunez came along and shooed them off to lunch. She didn't want Dusty to see the not-so-sure look on her face.

Dusty and Veronica went home with Lucy that afternoon to practice drills. Lucy liked that for several reasons, one of which was that she wouldn't have to deal with Mora alone. She wasn't sure she could even look at her without wanting to smack her. This was partly her fault too.

But Mora wasn't there when Inez brought out orange juice and cookies for them to eat at the patio table.

"This will not make it all right," she said, nodding at the food, "but it is easier to bear with something good." She shook her head. "I am sorry about your friend."

"I bet Mora's too chicken to show her face," Veronica said when Inez was back in the house.

Dusty passed the cookie plate to Lucy. "She's not a good friend to you. But we are."

Veronica raised her glass and nudged Dusty to do the same. "To Lucy!" she said.

"Why?" Lucy said. Her face was getting hot.

"Because." Dusty smiled at her. "You're our favorite bolillo."

Lucy took a good long drink of her orange juice so they wouldn't see her almost cry.

They dribbled up and down the yard that afternoon until they were worn out. But when Dusty and Veronica were gone, the fear pressed down on Lucy again like a big bad hand. It was getting dark, and J.J. was still out there somewhere. Maybe with the bobcats. Or in a ditch like she was. Somewhere thinking his best friend hated him.

She couldn't go there. She couldn't. She hurried into the kitchen with the dishes and found Inez scrubbing the tea kettle like she had to get it under control or it was going to turn around and bite her. Lucy looked around in surprise.

"Um, where's Mora?"

Inez made a low growling sound that reminded Lucy of Mudge.

Uh-oh. She wasn't speaking to Lucy either. Maybe a grandmother sided with her granddaughter no matter what hideous thing she did—unless, of course, she didn't know. Lucy put the dishes on the counter and started to back away.

"You make the lists when you talk to God, Senorita Lucy. I clean the pots."

"Oh," Lucy said. "Are you mad at God?"

Inez shook her head and kept scrubbing. "I am mad at one of his children. *My* child."

"You're mad at Mora too?"

"Mora's mother. My hija." She growled again. "I am not happy to say so. You want the tea?"

"Sure," Lucy said. "If you think the kettle's clean enough."

Inez looked up and gave her a surprising smile. "You always tell the truth. So I will tell the truth to you. Sit."

Lucy settled at the table with Marmalade on her lap and watched Inez make tea with movements as precise and fluid as a dance. Lucy knew she wouldn't say what she had to say until the cups were in front of them. Inez only did one thing at a time.

"Mora is with her mama today," she said finally. "She arrived from California yesterday."

Lucy stuck her spoon into her cup and stirred a little too hard. "Mora must be, like, hysterical."

"Oh, yes. Mora thinks her mama is queen."

"But you don't?"

"She is not a mama for Mora. Gone many months. Promises she does not keep. Many disappointments."

Lucy studied the way the milk swirled in her tea before she said, "I guess her important job keeps her pretty busy."

"No job is more important than being mama—or papa. Senor Ted, he has the important job, but he is a very good father to you." Inez lifted an eyebrow. "Even when you do not think so."

"How come Mora doesn't live with her father then?" Lucy said.

"Father left when Mora was only baby. He is—" Inez puffed out her hands. "Nowhere."

"So Mora doesn't really have a mom or a dad. I mean, she has you, and that's probably better than most moms and dads—"

"There is nothing better than mother and father who love you. I do my best for Mora, but I cannot be her mama." Inez ran her thumb back and forth across her lower lip. "Mora is *muy dificil*."

"Difficult?"

"Very difficult. Always she is looking for attention. Dancing on the stage. Having things other girls want." She cocked her head at Lucy. "What else, do you know?"

Lucy didn't even have to think about it. "Chasing boys."

"It is not good, but it is why. I think perhaps to understand Mora, it helps you."

They sipped their tea in silence while Lucy tried to move Mora's X. It wouldn't budge. Now she knew why Mora behaved like a spoiled brat, but it didn't make Lucy like it any better.

"I tell you this about Mora because I trust you," Inez said.

Lucy looked up from her cup. "I hope you don't trust Mora, because she lies."

She bit her lip, but it was too late. She'd already let it out.

Inez looked long and hard into her tea cup before she said, "Mora will sometimes lie to be big and important as she wants to be. This is why you are angry with her."

Lucy squirmed. "It's one of the reasons."

"But not the only. She has done something else very bad to you, no?"

There was no point in denying it. Inez seemed to be able to read Lucy's thoughts like they were printed on her forehead.

"She put lies in my Book of Lists," Lucy said without looking at her. "She wrote them like I had written them, and then she read it out loud to J.J. Now he thinks I hate him, and I think that's partly why he ran away."

Inez grew very still. "I am sorry for this pain for you."

Lucy felt those annoying tears starting up again. "I get why she does that stuff now, like you said. But I don't think I can ever forgive her. "

Inez got even stiller. Lucy felt her neck get prickly.

"You're gonna say I have to forgive her, aren't you? No offense, Inez, but I can't."

"I understand this." Inez poured more tea into her cup. The sound was loud in the suddenly airless kitchen Lucy wanted to run from.

"You know why I teach the Bible stories to you and to Mora?" Inez said.

Lucy wanted to say, "Don't change the subject!" but she shrugged. "Because my dad told you to?"

The eyebrow lifted again. "Because from them you learn how to be the young woman—like Senora Ruth and Senora Rachel and Leah."

"Yeah, I know."

"First thing you learned, from Senora Ruth—what must a girl do to become woman?"

"You have to love whoever comes to you from the heart of God, more than you love yourself, even." Lucy looked quickly at Inez. "You aren't saying I have to love Mora that way."

"You cannot now, no. But you can do the next thing, what we learn from Senora Rachel and Senora Leah."

"What? You have to share your husband?"

Inez's lips twitched. "No, thank El Senor. They fight and fight and fight and then—what?"

"They started working together." This was definitely going nowhere.

"But only after they can forgive the past. All the bad things."

"Their dad tricking them and Jacob not loving Leah and Rachel not having babies."

"Could you forgive that, Senorita Lucy?"

"I don't know," Lucy said slowly.

"But you must. To become woman, you must forgive what cannot be forgiven."

Lucy shoved her chair back. "I knew it. I knew you were going to try to make me be friends with Mora again. How am I supposed to do that when she tells me lies and steals my stuff and messes up my whole life?"

She stopped, because Inez was shaking her head.

"You do not understand—"

"I do, and it doesn't make any difference. Can I go to my room until my dad gets home?"

Inez stood up too, and stacked the tea cups. "Senor Ted will be home late."

"He didn't tell me."

"He is out with Senor Coach—looking for the *muchacho*."

The fear-hand pushed on Lucy again.

"They think he's not coming back, don't they?" Lucy shoved past the chair to the sink and made Inez meet her eyes. "They think they have to go get him because he's never coming back on his own—that's right, isn't it?"

Inez didn't answer. She just put her arms around Lucy and crushed her into her chest that smelled like tea and chiles and cinnamon. She held her there while Lucy cried.

14

Lucy fell asleep before Dad came home. She wasn't used to crying so much, and it wrung her out like Veronica's hands. Her eyes didn't open the next morning until Lolli skidded across her face on the way from the windowsill to the toy chest and Lucy's bedroom door flew open.

"Rise and shine, girl," Aunt Karen said as she breezed across the room. "We have eggs to dye, hair to curl."

"Why?"

"Sunday is Easter." Aunt Karen shoved Lucy's curtains open. "And you are not going to church looking like—"

She sat on the edge of Lucy's bed and took Lucy's not-even-awake-yet face in her hands. "Looking like you have carry-on luggage under your eyes. Lucy Rooney, have you been crying?"

"Yes." Lucy pulled away. "You would cry too if your best friend ran away."

Actually, maybe Aunt Karen wouldn't. It was hard to tell sometimes whether she really had any feelings at all.

"I bet you were crying even before J.J. went missing," Aunt Karen said. "And most of the time you didn't even know why."

Lucy stared.

Aunt Karen folded her arms. "Let me guess. You cry for no apparent reason and at the worst possible times. One minute you're so mad you want to rip people's lips off—"

"Nose hairs," Lucy admitted.

"And the next minute you want to hug them. Am I right?"

Lucy was still staring. "How did you know?"

"Hello! I was eleven once. And you think you're bad? You should have seen your mother."

Lucy sat up. "My mom did this?"

"Are you kidding? We'd be sitting at the dinner table, gigging hysterically about something, and our dad—your grandfather—would say, 'She'll be crying in a minute.' And sure enough, seconds later she'd burst into tears and go running to her room."

"She did, really?"

"And Daddy would say to Mom, 'What just happened?' and Mom would say, 'Hormones, Frank.'" Aunt Karen pulled her hand through her hair like she was raking it. "You know about hormones, right?"

Lucy's face went hot. "They're why you want me to wear a bra."

"It's also why you don't understand yourself right now. You definitely take after your mother." Aunt Karen tossed the newly raked hair. "I didn't dissolve into tears half as much as she did when it was my turn four years later. She'd cry over the cat getting her paw caught in the door. When her team lost their first game, she sobbed like it was the end of the world."

Lucy nodded. "I get that."

Aunt Karen gave the hair another rake. "No one's told you this part of the whole girl thing?"

"No."

"There's so much I could teach you if—"

Before Lucy could even start to groan inside, Aunt Karen licked her lips.

"Okay, well, we don't have time to cry now. We have things to do."

"What things?"

"Get dressed. We're going to Alamogordo to get egg dye, Easter grass—" She was still ticking things off on her fingers as she headed for the door. "And if I don't get to Starbucks, I may go into withdrawal."

"I can't go."

Aunt Karen stopped in the doorway, and Lucy steeled herself for a fight.

But when her aunt turned around, her face was almost soft. "I know you want to stay here until they know something about J.J., but, Lucy, that's only going to make the time drag. Let me help you through this. I'm not the enemy, you know."

She left the room, and Lucy climbed to the windowsill. J.J.'s window was still and empty … as empty and alone as Lucy's insides.

She climbed out of bed.

So this was Starbucks. Lucy took a look around as she slurped the whipped cream from the top of her hot chocolate. It smelled good, like cinnamon and morning, and people were calling out stuff in what must have been a foreign language. What on earth was a "low-fat, sugar-free, decaf vanilla latte?" Mora would know.

And then, suddenly, there was Mora herself, perched like a skinny bird on a stool at a tall table. She had a mug practically big enough to swim in before her, but she wasn't drinking out of it. Her enormous eyes were trained on the woman she was with.

"Isn't that Mora?" Aunt Karen said.

Lucy nodded and prayed her hardest that Aunt Karen wouldn't invite her over.

"Who's that woman?"

She had to be Mora's mother. She was almost as thin as Mora, and she wrapped her legs around the stool the same way. The dead giveaway was the hands, punctuating the air while she talked on her cell phone.

And talked. And talked. Lucy couldn't imagine having that much to say to one person in a single conversation. Meanwhile, Mora watched her almost without blinking.

Aunt Karen leaned across the table toward Lucy. "Now that is just rude."

"What?" Lucy smeared her napkin over her mouth. "Do I have stuff on my face?"

"No—the way that woman is totally ignoring her. If I were Mora, I'd snatch that phone right out of her hand."

"Um, I think that's her mom," Lucy said.

Aunt Karen gave them a look so long Lucy almost suggested she take a picture instead.

"There's only one thing to do," Aunt Karen said finally. She stood up, latte in hand. "We're going to introduce ourselves."

Lucy would rather have dumped her hot chocolate on her own head, but she followed her aunt to the tall table and tried to make herself invisible behind a display of Easter mugs.

"Hey, girlfriend!" Aunt Karen sang out as she wrapped one arm around Mora's neck and motioned toward the woman with her coffee cup. "Is this your mom?"

Mora gave the first real smile Lucy had ever seen on her face. Lucy could tell that it got there all by itself, without Mora telling it what to look like.

Aunt Karen set her coffee on the table and stuck her hand out to Mora's mother. "Karen Crosslin," she said, as if the lady weren't still carrying on a conversation on her cell phone.

The woman glared like Aunt Karen was the one being rude, muttered something into her phone, and flipped it closed with her chin.

"Gina Garcia," she said. Her voice sounded like an annoying boy playing with a Styrofoam cup. She looked at Mora from under eyelids heavy with something brown. "You know these people?"

"Mora and I are old girlfriends," Aunt Karen said. "And she and my niece—"

Mora looked around and seemed to shrink into her North Face jacket when she saw Lucy.

Ms. Garcia said, "Nice to meet you," as if it wasn't at all.

"Did you show your mom the dress I bought you?" Aunt Karen said.

"I haven't had a chance."

"Right. I'm sure you two have been talking nonstop ever since your mom got into town."

Mora nodded, but Lucy was pretty sure her mom hadn't gotten off her cell phone long enough to hear anything Mora had to say. Even now, she was reading the screen and punching in things with her thumbs.

"You'll see her in it Sunday," Aunt Karen said right into the woman's face.

"Not unless she gets up at five o'clock in the morning. I have an early flight out of El Paso. I have to get back to California."

"Mora's not going with you?"

"No." Ms. Garcia looked at Mora as if she'd just appeared on the stool. "Why would she?"

Lucy looked at Mora too, in time to see her stare into her cup like she wished she could dive into it. Lucy couldn't say she blamed her.

The cell phone rang, and Mora's mother flipped it open and turned her head. Aunt Karen put her hand under Mora's chin.

Lucy had never been more eager to get out of a place. But even after she and Aunt Karen were in the Toyota, headed for Wal-Mart, Lucy couldn't shake the sadness she'd caught from Mora like a bad cold.

"That woman doesn't deserve Mora," Aunt Karen said to the windshield. "I'd take that child in a minute. I could give the two of you so much—"

Lucy was grateful that she licked her lips and changed the subject to how Lucy should wear her hair for the Easter service.

Lucy had to admit later that the day did go faster than it would have if she had sat in her room watching J.J.'s empty window. She and Aunt Karen dyed two dozen eggs and put them in bowls full of grass and set them around the house. Several went into a fat glass vase in the middle of the table, which Lucy thought was a little weird, but Aunt Karen seemed thrilled with it.

At least they weren't shopping, and when Aunt Karen discovered Gloria's Casa Bonita Salon was closed that day, she didn't insist on trimming Lucy's hair herself but settled for watching *Ella Enchanted* while she painted Lucy's toenails.

By the time all that was over, Lucy was tired—too tired to resist the scary thoughts of J.J. she'd been chasing off between the egg-dying and the grass-arranging and the nail-polishing. The thoughts smacked at her and pawed at her until she fell into a troubled sleep on the Napping Couch.

When she woke up, Dad was there with her feet in his lap. His face was long and gray in the almost-darkness.

"You didn't find him," she said.

"Not yet, champ. But the good news is, we know his dad didn't take him. He's still around."

It didn't look like good news in Dad's slumped-over shoulders. Lucy sat up and slung her arm around them.

"Is there bad news?" she said.

"They found his bike finally. It was in the front yard with all the rest of the junk—took them a while to locate it. I don't know if that's good news or bad."

Lucy couldn't help feeling it was bad. If J.J. had left on his own, he wouldn't have gone without his bike. And he never, ever left anything important in that front yard.

"You guys are gonna keep looking for him, right?" she said. "Tomorrow?"

"Of course they'll keep at it. But I'm going to the station in the morning to record my shows so I don't have to work Easter Sunday. Then I think you and I need to just hang together."

"Can both of us look?"

Dad ran his hand over her hair. "We'll see, Luce. We'll see. What do you say we pray together?"

He'd already left for the station when Lucy got up the next morning. She did a scan of the backyard through the window in the kitchen door in the fading hope that J.J. would be crawling out of the toolshed, as if Lucy had told him she'd keep him safe there.

Instead, Januarie's round face appeared in the window. It was the first time Lucy had seen her since J.J. disappeared, and her jaw tightened. This was *her* fault too.

"Well, for heaven's sake, Lucy, don't make her stand out there in the cold." Aunt Karen opened the door, and Januarie hurled herself straight at her, burying her face in Aunt Karen's vest. Dad always said Januarie thought Aunt Karen hung the moon—must be all that girly stuff.

"Where have you been?" Aunt Karen said when she was able to peel the kid off of her. "I've been here twenty-four hours, and this is the first you've come to see me."

Januarie glanced at Lucy and then away, but not before Lucy saw that she looked guiltier than Artemis when they caught her with feathers sticking out of her mouth.

Lucy couldn't hold back. "Do you know where J.J. went, Januarie?"

"Lucy Elizabeth!" Aunt Karen's eyes flashed at her before she turned Januarie to face the egg-filled centerpiece.

"See what we did?" she said. "You like?"

Januarie nodded. "I wish we had that at our house."

"What does your family do for Easter?" Aunt Karen said. "Baskets? New dress for church?"

It was Lucy's turn to flash her eyes. Was Aunt Karen new around here?

"We don't go to church. And we aren't gettin' any candy because my mom's crying because of, you know, J.J."

Januarie looked warily at Lucy and backed toward the door. Her eyes were all over the place.

"I think I have to go now," she said.

"What—no French toast?" Aunt Karen said.

Januarie shook her head—and Lucy *knew* there was something way wrong.

"Don't be mad at me Lucy," she said. And then she wrestled with the doorknob and somehow got herself out the back door.

"Now what was all that about?" Aunt Karen said. "I swear, these mothers. Mora's treats her like she's invisible. Januarie's won't even let her go to church." She shook out her hair with her hand and went back to the coffee pot. "I guess I'm just going to have to open a home for girls."

Lucy moved toward her room before Aunt Karen could suggest that she, Mora, *and* Januarie all move to El Paso with her. She had enough problems as it was.

"I'm going to go help Dad at the station," Lucy called over her shoulder.

"Not until you help me make some Easter for that poor child."

Lucy made a U-turn. "What are you talking about?"

"You'll see," Aunt Karen said.

They spent the rest of the morning finding the dress with the most ruffles in southern New Mexico, with matching shoes, tights, and hair bows. Lucy hadn't seen that much pink together in her whole life. When they got back home, Lucy went straight to her room. One more pink ruffle, and she was sure she'd throw up.

The only thing that kept her from it was Carla Rosa showing up to do soccer drills at lunchtime. But even teaching her how to vol-ley—all over again—didn't stop Lucy from running to the gate every time Mudge growled and dashing inside with each ring of the phone. After only a half hour, they decided that was enough for the day. Then Lucy just sat at the patio table and waited for Dad.

He came home with the two deep lines still dug into the skin above his nose. When she said, "Hi, Dad," he twitched as if he hadn't sensed her there.

"I didn't mean to scare you," Lucy said.

"I was just lost in thought, champ."

He tapped his cane to the patio table and found his way into a chair. Lucy took a deep breath.

"I have to tell you something hard, Luce," he said.

Lucy was already shaking her head. "It's not true, Dad. J.J.'s all right—I know he is."

"I was just going to tell you that we don't know anything more about him, good or bad." He tilted his head. "You thought I was going to say something really bad, didn't you?"

"Yeah."

"I hate this."

"Me too."

"You want to know what I hate the most?"

Lucy wasn't sure she did, but she nodded.

"I hate that you already know everything doesn't always turn out the way we want it to, even though we pray hard and we work hard and we try hard to be the best we can be."

She knew he was talking about Mom, who didn't come home either. Lucy pressed her hands so hard into the table she could feel the diamond pattern making itself in her palms.

"Champ?"

"I don't want to talk about this anymore, Dad," she said.

"I know. It's hard—too hard for a girl who's only eleven."

Dad put his hand, palm up on the table. Lucy dragged hers to it.

"Just because we don't always agree doesn't mean I don't understand. I do. This is the very reason why I want you to have a real childhood, without so much pressure and responsibility." Dad winced as if a pain had just passed through him. "You've already lost so much, and it's made you grow up too fast in some ways. I want the other ways to go slower. Do you get that?"

She did. But she couldn't say it. All she could do was cry.

"That's my girl," Dad said, sandwiching her hand between his. "Just let it out."

"I hate hormones," she said through the blubbering. "I never cried before I got hormones."

Dad shook his head and squeezed her hand harder. "Don't ever think hormones are the cause of all your emotions, Luce. That's a lie men sometimes tell women to get them out of their hair."

She stopped crying long enough to say, "Huh?"

"It's something I learned from your mother. You have a right to be angry, and a right to be sad, and a right to try things your own way." He brought her hand up to his lips and kissed it. "What do you say we get through this together, champ?"

Lucy only hesitated for a mini-second before she thought about her soccer field. Maybe it was time to move Dad's X from the top of the bleachers, down into the game she had to play.

So she said, "Deal," in a voice that didn't try to hold back the tears.

"Good," Dad said. "Now, tell me about the sunset."

Lucy curled her legs up under her and gazed at the watercolor sky and became Dad's eyes again.

15

"You are so out of here, cat!"

Those were the words Lucy woke up to on Easter morning. Lolli leaped for the toy chest, and Lucy made a jump for her bedroom door with sleep crust still in her eyes. She almost collided with Dad in the hall, just as the back door slammed.

"Sounds like Aunt Karen has some feline issues this morning," Dad said.

She just better not have touched a hair on a kitty head, Lucy thought as she skidded into the kitchen ahead of Dad, ready to toss Aunt Karen into the backyard.

But her aunt was standing at the table, fluffing up tissue paper that stuck out of a basket—and sniffling. If Lucy hadn't known better, she would have thought . . . no, Aunt Karen didn't cry.

"You all right, K?" Dad said from the doorway.

"You try to do something nice in this house, and some cat has to come along and mess it up. I was up half the night working on this." Aunt Karen gave the yellow tissue paper a final, exasperated fluff and turned to Lucy, eyes wet. "In case you're missing anything out of here, blame it on that monster with the bad dye job."

"Artemis?" Lucy said.

"The one that's been squalling to get out of here all weekend. I just tossed it out the back door."

"She's a 'her'—and she's not supposed to be out because of the—"

"Missing from what?" Dad said quickly.

Aunt Karen picked up the bunch of tissue-papered fluff from the table. "From Lucy's Easter basket. I caught that animal tearing into it."

Dad chuckled. "That's what you get for putting catnip in there."

"That's for me?" Lucy said.

Aunt Karen handed it to her. It was so big Lucy had to use both arms to hold it.

"I wanted to hide it," Aunt Karen said. "That's what our parents always did on Easter morning. I always found mine right away. Your mother had to have ten thousand clues—it was all about the game with her."

"There's no way you could have hidden this. Dad, it's huge!"

"That's Aunt Karen. Go big or stay home."

"Exactly," Aunt Karen said. "So, don't you want to see what's in it?"

Suddenly, Lucy wasn't sure. It definitely smelled like chocolate, but if a bra was tucked into the Easter grass, she wasn't sure she could fake delight.

But what she discovered, once she pulled out an entire package of yellow tissue paper, she never would have guessed. She described each item to Dad as she found it.

Little net bags full of miniature chocolate soccer balls.

Juice boxes just the right size for her backpack.

A stuffed bunny in a soccer uniform identical to the ones the Los Suenos Dreams wore, complete with cleats, shin guards, and a ball.

Three pairs of soccer socks with no flowers, butterflies, or lady-bugs on them.

Easter grass loaded with jelly beans.

"Your mom always had jelly beans in her basket," Aunt Karen said. "I don't know if you even like them—"

"I love them," Lucy said, though she wasn't sure she'd ever had any before.

"I couldn't believe the selection that florist had," Aunt Karen said. "Who'd have thought you could find gourmet jelly beans in this town?"

"I'll take a purple one if you have any," Dad said.

"Who said I was sharing?" Lucy said, and then retrieved two purples and deposited them into Dad's mouth. He chewed happily.

"You're not done." Aunt Karen pointed to the basket. "Down in the bottom."

Lucy dug under the grass and pulled out a folded piece of paper.

"Read it," Aunt Karen said. "Out loud so your dad can hear."

Again, Lucy wasn't so sure she wanted to. What if it was Aunt Karen's plan for taking her and Mora and Januarie to El Paso to live with her? She unfolded the paper so slowly Aunt Karen said, "You're killing me, Lucy! Hurry up."

Lucy started to read. "'Subj: Re: Your niece. Date:—'"

"You don't have to read all that. Haven't you ever seen a printout of an email before?"

"No," Lucy said.

"One more thing I have to teach you."

"Who's it from?" Dad said.

"Read, Lucy. Where it says FROM."

"Nathan Quinn, Olympic Development Program."

Dad stopped chewing.

"He's the regional director," Aunt Karen said. "Read it, Lucy."

Lucy blinked at the page, where the letters refused to hold still. "'Dear Ms. Crosslin,'" she managed to get out. "'Thank you for the information you sent me about your niece. I don't usually review videos, but your email, phone call, and follow-up letter were all so compelling I made an exception, and I'm glad I did.'" Lucy squinted. "What does compelling mean?"

"What video?" Dad said. His voice was going into no-nonsense mode.

"The one I took of Lucy playing in the game against El Paso." Aunt Karen licked her lips. "Keep reading. No, let me."

She took the paper out of Lucy's hands, which were beginning to shake.

"'I will have to watch her play in person, of course,'" Aunt Karen read, "'but judging from the film, your niece is the caliber athlete we're looking for. If what you tell me is true about her lack of professional coaching and almost no playing experience, she has an exceptional raw talent that must be developed.'"

"Is he talking about me?" Lucy said.

"You're the only niece I have. 'It so happens,'" she read, "'I'm free April twenty-second and would like to attend her game. Please email me with the particulars.' Can you stand it?"

"He's coming to see my game?"

"It's part of your audition for the Olympic Development Program. Happy Easter, Lucy. Your life may be about to change."

And then she looked at Dad, and so did Lucy. He was sitting back in his chair, hands folded. His face was a hard mask that made Lucy's heart plunge. The words he was sure to say next tangled in her head like Easter grass.

No, Lucy, you need your childhood.

No, Karen, you've gone behind my back.

No, both of you. I make these decisions.

But as Lucy waited, mouth no longer tasting like jelly beans at all, he said none of them.

"I know you said to wait, Ted," Aunt Karen said. "But I really didn't expect this to happen so fast."

"Yes, you did," Dad said. "That's between you and me though."

This was the part where they would shoo Lucy out of the kitchen and she'd have to press her ear against her door to try to hear the argument that Dad was going to win—

"What do you say we celebrate the day?" he said.

Lucy stared. "Does that mean—"

"It means I'm proud of you, champ." He tilted his head. "What else do you think it means?"

Lucy looked at Aunt Karen, who had her arms folded and was smiling as if she herself had just been accepted into the ODP. Aunt Karen, who did whatever she wanted.

Lucy turned to Dad. "I think it means you and I still have to decide together whether I'm ready."

"How much more proof do you need?" Aunt Karen waved the paper. "This is the regional director!"

"You heard the lady, Karen," Dad said. "Now, what do you say we have some Easter omelets and some jelly beans and put on our new clothes and get to church? This is Easter, and we have some praying to do."

It wasn't like any other Easter Lucy had ever had. There was the dress, of course, and even though it was wrinkled from being in the bottom of Lucy's underwear drawer, it did make her look grown-up when she surveyed herself in the mirror. It also made her uncomfortable. She'd been so distracted at the store, she hadn't realized you could see through it.

But Aunt Karen didn't comment on the need for a bra under it. She actually said Lucy looked fabulous.

She also said, "Oh, Ted, if you could only see your daughter. She looks like a young woman."

"I'm sure she does," Dad said.

But Lucy figured he knew Aunt Karen was still trying to prove something. It made her want to go back and change into her jeans.

On that Easter day though, she didn't feel like the Lucy she'd been a week before, on Palm Sunday.

Her heels clicked like Aunt Karen's did when she stepped out onto the sidewalk. She felt taller than she had the day before as Dad took hold of her arm. And when Januarie called to them from behind her fence, Lucy was sure she knew how a mom felt. She wanted to pull Januarie from the midst of the rusted parts-of-cars and old lawn mowers and tell her J.J. was going to be okay and take her to church. Even if she was a disloyal little urchin.

Januarie was dressed hair bow to shoelaces in pink ruffles, and she clutched a little pink basket that had obviously come from Aunt Karen too. Nobody else could use that much tissue paper.

"Look what was on my front porch this morning," Januarie absolutely chirped. "I don't know where it came from!"

"Must have been the Easter bunny," Aunt Karen said.

She was smiling half a smile as she adjusted her sunglasses. On this Easter day, Lucy figured out that maybe somebody you thought was all wrong maybe wasn't.

So many things were different—the way the little church's walls seemed to bulge because so many people had gathered to celebrate

Easter, the way Felix Pasco and Mr. Benitez smiled at each other when the collection plate was passed, even though Lucy was sure they were competing to see who could put more money in it, and the way Gabe was scrubbed and gelled and pressed into his slacks and shirt and necktie. Lucy wondered if wearing a tie was as uncomfortable for a boy like Gabe as putting on a bra was for a girl like her.

Usually the Easter sermon was about something happy—du-uh, Christ rising from the dead. But that Easter day, Reverend Servidio talked about J.J., and how they all needed to pray as they never had before. Things had looked impossible to the disciples, he said, but look what happened: Jesus had returned.

The men all shifted their shoulders and fiddled with their ties. Lucy saw most of the women wiping their eyes. It was getting harder to celebrate.

After the service, Dusty and Veronica and Carla Rosa—all in baby-doll dresses and leggings not so different from Lucy's own out-fit—and Gabe gathered with Lucy on the church steps. Nobody smiled or talked about Easter baskets, though Dusty did tell Lucy she looked adorable. Carla Rosa whispered that, guess what, she could see through Lucy's dress. Lucy folded her arms. She wished J.J. were there so they wouldn't even be having this conversation. She prayed that he'd stroll in all uncomfortable in a tie next to Mr. Auggy.

But Mr. Auggy came out of the church alone and blinked in the sunlight. He seemed much smaller than he had just a few days ago.

"He looks so sad," Dusty said.

Veronica's eyes filled up.

"Aw, come on, no cryin'," Gabe said.

"Guess what?" Carla Rosa whispered. "He's coming over here."

Everyone looked as if they were being approached by a stranger—until Mr. Auggy opened his arms and they fell over each other like puppies to get to him—even Gabe.

"Oh, team," Mr. Auggy said. "You're just what I needed." He held on for a minute before he pulled back to look down at them. "How's everybody doing? You're all hanging in there, aren't you?"

Heads bobbed. Tears flowed. Gabe got his hand up and high-fived

Mr. Auggy, even though it wasn't cool. Then nobody knew what to say. Once again, they looked at Lucy.

"We're crying a lot," Lucy said.

"I'm not," Gabe said. "I'm just mad 'cause my dad won't let me help look. Man, I could get on my ATV and find the J-man—" He snapped his fingers. "Just like that."

"Don't do it, Gabe," Mr. Auggy said. "One missing team member's enough. You hearing me?"

"Yeah, well, so what *do* we do?"

"Guess what?" Carla Rosa said. "Lucy said we should play soccer."

Mr. Auggy's eyes seemed to flood over Lucy. "And the captain is absolutely right."

"It was really my dad's idea," Gabe said.

"Shut up," Dusty said.

Mr. Auggy let out a buzz that ended in a small, sad smile. "That's just what you can do to help, and I'm serious about that. You stay together as a team, and you get ready for that game. And in the meantime, I'm going to do everything I can to make sure J.J. is right there playing with us on the twenty-second."

"If anybody can find him, it's you," Dusty said.

"Go Mr. Auggy!" Veronica said, and she went into one of her little dances.

Mr. Auggy hugged them all again. But even in the comfort of the puppy pile, Lucy could hear her dad's words: *I hate that you already know everything doesn't always turn out the way we want it to, even though we pray hard and we work hard and we try hard to be the best we can be.*

Mr. Auggy let go, and the rest of the team scattered to their families. Lucy stayed, staring down at her orange toenails. Lucy had told Aunt Karen she wouldn't wear pink polish. But really, she would wear pink everything if it would bring J.J. back.

"Captain?"

She looked up at her coach.

"It's harder for you not to give up than most," he said. "But if you do, everyone else will too. It's not time yet." He put his hand to his chest. "I feel that."

"Then you just want me to coach the team?" she said.

"You got it. And keep thinking about everything you know about J.J. and even about Januarie that might help us find him."

He blinked so hard Lucy knew Dad was right. It must be a good thing to cry, because Mr. Auggy was about to do it.

"I'll think, and I'll pray really hard," Lucy said.

She thought he said thank you before he got away fast down the steps. She wished he was just going off to play soccer. She wished that really would solve everything. He himself had said to look at the whole field of players.

Had she done that? She'd mostly been thinking about J.J. What had Mr. Auggy just said—about—

She looked up toward the church door. Dad was deep in conversation with the mayor, and Aunt Karen, to Lucy's surprise, was actually talking to Claudia from the House of Flowers. Lucy ran down to Dusty, who was hanging on her mom's arm.

"Dusty," Lucy whispered to her, "would you tell my dad I'll meet him at home? I have to do something."

"Anything," Dusty said, and she scampered up the steps as if she'd been ordered to by the president.

Lucy got to the sidewalk in two leaps and was at the gate at J.J.'s in three more. Just as she'd hoped, Januarie was still there, twirling among the old stoves and tires in her ruffles. She looked like a pink cherub who for a moment had forgotten she lived in a trash heap.

When Lucy rattled the gate, Januarie stopped in mid-twirl. The glow evaporated from her face, and she twisted to run toward the house.

"Wait!" Lucy said. "I just need to talk to you!"

Januarie backed up, though she only got as far as the half-of-a-motorcycle that blocked her way. "You're gonna yell at me."

"Why would I yell at you?"

She shrugged, bringing two rows of ruffles up to her ears.

"Because you gave my special book to Mora?" Lucy said.

"She said she was doing it to help J.J.!"

Lucy bit at her lip. She actually did want to yell at the child. But she was going to save the hollering until after she got everything out of her. Lucy felt for a pocket—maybe she had some candy. But baby-doll dresses didn't have pockets, and besides, Januarie had a whole basket full of it, thanks to Aunt Karen.

"Okay, look," Lucy said. "If I promise to let you play in the game on April twenty-second, will you tell me everything you know about where J.J. went?"

Januarie's bottom lip trembled as she knotted her chubby arms against her chest. "You're not really gonna do that."

"Yes I am, Januarie. I would do anything—anything to find J.J. Come on—wouldn't you—even though he's hateful to you some-times and says he's going to lock you in the garage?"

Januarie nodded, but her eyes were swimming in confusion. Okay, too much at the same time.

"You can play, I promise on all my kitties' lives," Lucy said. "Just tell me everything J.J. said to you before he left."

"He didn't say anything to me. He doesn't tell me anything. He's just mad all the time."

Lucy could believe that, and her heart sank.

She was about to turn away when Januarie said, "I have to talk to Mora. That's why I came to your house yesterday. I think she made me do something bad—"

"Forget about it!" Lucy said. "I forgive you for letting her make you turn J.J. against me. This is way bigger—"

Januarie whipped her head toward the house, and for the first time, Lucy realized Mr. Cluck was standing on the crooked front stoop. Tall and mean-looking, lean and dagger-eyed. Next to him was a woman in a gray suit that made her look important. She had a long pointy face.

Weasel Lady.

"Get in here, Januarie," Mr. Cluck said.

His voice was hard, just the way Lucy remembered it. Weasel Lady put her hand on his arm and said, "Januarie, would you join us inside, please?"

Mr. Cluck held the door open until Januarie disappeared into the house and Weasel Lady followed her in. Lucy couldn't move, even as J.J.'s father looked down at her, across his ugly piles of rusted trash, and stuck his finger toward her like a knife.

"You," he growled. "Get off my property, and stay away from my family. Do it!"

Lucy did move then, and she didn't stop until she was in her room, holding Lollipop and rocking back and forth.

"I *will* find J.J.," Lucy told her over and over. "I will."

No, it was like no other Easter Sunday that had ever been.

Lucy didn't even have to make a list to know all the reasons she had to talk to Januarie now. She prayed without writing that night, and the next morning she was at the door to the third-grade classroom long before the teacher was. But the final bell rang, and there was still no Januarie. And when she got to the portable, there was still no J.J.—and no Mr. Auggy either. It was still up to her.

At lunchtime, no one looked like they were ready to grab their cleats and head for the field. Not until Carla Rosa said, "Guess what? It's the principal."

Before Lucy could turn around, something dropped to the floor beside her.

"These were left for you," Mrs. Nunez said. "You're to return them to me at the end of practice."

As she walked away, Lucy realized she hadn't even used her kindergarten voice.

"So what are we sitting here for?" Gabe said.

He picked up the bag of soccer balls, slung it over his shoulder, and headed for the door.

"Please, God," Lucy whispered. "Let this help."

On the field, Dusty made everybody laugh, even Emanuel, and Mr. Auggy had always said it was okay to have a good time at practice. Lucy wished she'd listened to him back then. Veronica got Gabe back into it by acting like she couldn't even do a throw-in unless he showed her how. Ickety-ick. But at least he thought he was all that again, and Gabe played best when he thought he was all that.

Lucy told Emanuel to fire balls at Oscar so he could practice making saves.

Emanuel made Oscar spit out his toothpick first. That was huge. Carla Rosa remembered almost half of what Lucy had taught her on Friday, and Lucy told her she was awesome. She'd never noticed what a big smile Carla had. Now if only she wouldn't hug Lucy all the time.

When Lucy took the bag of soccer balls back to Mrs. Nunez, she didn't use her kindergarten voice when she said, "Mr. Auggy would be proud of you."

She didn't mention J.J. None of the grown-ups at school did, as if by not talking about him, the kids might forget to be sad. Not a chance.

Since they couldn't practice on their big field without a grown-up, Lucy went home that afternoon and stayed in her room and tried to think of a way to get to Januarie, who obviously knew more than she'd had a chance to say yesterday. Lucy just needed some time with her, without Weasel Lady—or her father.

Even with the lady from the court there, Mr. Cluck had acted like he was going to tear into Januarie like a bobcat. Lucy felt as if someone had kicked her in the stomach. Why hadn't she just helped J.J. in the first place? Even not seeing him was better than not knowing where he was and thinking he was nowhere.

Please, God.

16

Inez let Lucy have dinner in her room while Dad went to a Town Council meeting. Inez was staying with her, and the last time Lucy had seen her, she'd gone into the guest room and closed the door. That left only Mora to get around, and she hadn't even looked at Lucy when she passed through the kitchen. Maybe she wouldn't even notice if Lucy slipped out.

Lucy nestled the Book of Lists into the underwear drawer and tip-toed to the door, where she pressed her ear to the crack. She could still hear the drone of the TV Mora had been sitting in front of ever since Lucy had gotten home. Even her own grandmother couldn't seem to stand the black circle of silence Mora had formed around her. There was no other explanation for Inez letting her watch that much television.

Lolli rubbed against Lucy's leg and gave a pitiful meow.

"Aw, man, I forgot to feed you guys," Lucy said to her.

But what a perfect excuse to go into the kitchen.

She scooped up Lollipop's black chubbiness and padded in her socks down the hall. Marmalade was parked by the kitty bowls, swishing his tail, and Mudge yowled from outside the back door, while Artemis complained bitterly from inside.

"You guys are way too cranky," Lucy said as she set Lolli on the floor and pulled the cat food bag out of the pantry. "It's not like any of you couldn't stand to miss a meal."

Mudge let out a particularly indignant squall at that. He was, after all, their curmudgeon-crabby-old-man. Lucy dumped a handful of Meow Mix into each bowl and opened the back door. Artemis Hamm bowled Mudge over as she sprang out.

"Get back in here!" Lucy said.

She went out onto the porch, but Artemis had already disappeared beyond the Mexican elder. Could it really be this easy? She took a step forward.

"What are you doing?"

Apparently not. Lucy groaned inside and turned to Mora, who was darkening the doorway with her body and her black mood.

"I'm looking for Artemis," Lucy said. Why did Mora have to pick this moment to start talking to her again?

"You better get in here before Abuela catches you." Mora's enormous eyes nearly disappeared into slits. "She's beyond grouchy today."

Lucy couldn't help laughing out loud.

"What's so funny?" Mora said as Lucy gave up her chance for escape and moved past her into the kitchen.

"*She's* grouchy?" Lucy said. "You're not exactly Miss Sunshine yourself."

"And you're loving it, aren't you?"

"Huh?"

Mora flounced to the counter and hiked herself up onto it. "I bet you're just laughing your head off inside because my mom dumped me. Admit it. I made your life miserable over J.J., and now you're glad *I'm* miserable."

Lucy shook her head.

"Liar," Mora said, and then she held up her hand and shook it like it was a pom-pom. "Whatever—maybe that's just how I would feel."

"Well, I don't." Lucy felt a lump forming in the back of her throat. "I know what it's like not to have your mom, and it's gotta be worse knowing you *could* be with her, only—"

"Only she doesn't want me. Is that what you were going to say?"

Lucy had to swallow hard to get the lump down. "Maybe that's not it. Maybe she really is busy with her job—"

"Too busy for her own kid? I feel like about this big right now." Mora held her fingers so close together they almost touched.

"I'm sorry," Lucy said.

"Then you're a freak."

184

"Why?"

"Because you're sorry after all the stuff I've done to you."

Lucy dropped into a chair and watched Mudge devour the last of the cat food while Marmalade and Lolli looked on with envy. "You messed up my friendship with J.J., and I hate that, but I've got worse problems than that now."

"Like what?"

Lucy's head came up sharply. Mora had stopped swinging her legs. "What could be worse?" she said.

"You don't know?" Lucy said.

"Know what?"

"About J.J.? That he's missing?"

Mora came off the counter and got her face inches from Lucy's. "What do you mean missing?"

"Inez didn't tell you?"

"I wouldn't let her tell me anything. I'm not talking to her—what do you *mean* J.J.'s *missing?*"

Lucy pulled back from her, and something bitter came up into her mouth. "Wednesday, after you showed him my book and made him think I hated him, he ran away."

Mora's face began to look like chalk. "Like he said he would, like you wrote about."

"Yes! And I was going to help him not do it—that day—only you showed him what you wrote—"

"Oh my gosh. Oh my gosh, Lucy!"

Mora dropped her face into her hands, but Lucy flew at her and pried her fingers away. Still holding Mora's wrists, she got her face close to the huge, now-frightened eyes.

"What—Mora, you know something!"

"You're going to be so mad at me."

"I already am. Who cares. What about J.J.?"

Mora opened her mouth, but another voice filled the air: a howling, screeching voice of pain, coming from the backyard.

Lucy bolted for the back door. The sick feeling in her stomach told her what she was going to see before she turned on the porch light.

The bobcat stood in the middle of the yard, with Artemis Hamm between her jaws.

"Artie!" Lucy screamed. "Let go of Artie!"

"Oh my gosh!" Mora cried from over her shoulder.

"Where's my soccer ball?" Lucy said.

Mora snatched it, bag and all, from the hook. Lucy grabbed it and hurled it toward the bobcat's head, but it hit the Mexican elder and bounced off, not disturbing a whisker on the wild cat's nose.

"Drop her!" Lucy shouted, and bounded down the steps.

Mora cried, "Lucy, no!"

But Lucy tore across the yard, screaming and waving her arms. The bobcat stopped shaking Artemis and trained her eyes on Lucy. Time stood as still as Lucy's heart, which she knew had stopped beating completely.

"Drop her," Lucy said again, whispering this time. "Just drop her and go away."

The bobcat let out a low growl and crouched, eyes still boring into Lucy, teeth still sunk into Artemis Hamm, who was now limp as a rag. Lucy looked around wildly, but there wasn't a pick or a hatchet in sight. She could pick up a patio chair, but it was too far away, and she would have to turn her back on the big cat. She wasn't sure she could move anyway, not with a cold, white fear crawling up her spine and freezing her to the spot.

"Please let her go," she whimpered, "Please, God, make her let Artie go."

A screech curdled the air, and for an awful second, Lucy thought it was the bobcat, giving her final, killer cry. But the horrific sound came from the back porch, again, followed by a clang that went through Lucy's head like she'd been hit with a hammer.

Something flew past her ear and landed inches from the bobcat's paws. A frying pan. And then the tea kettle. And then the pot Inez cooked her chili in. All to the tune of Mora screaming, "Help! Help! Somebody help!"

The big cat startled back, and Artemis Hamm dropped from her mouth. Lucy would have lunged for her if a barrage of kitchen utensils weren't still being fired from the back porch. The small kitty lay motionless as the bobcat jockeyed between dodging flying pots and looking hungrily down at her fallen prey.

And then something flashed neatly through the air—something that made the wild cat scream and flee, just as the biggest knife in the Rooney's kitchen stabbed into the ground. Lucy turned to see Inez on the porch, standing behind Mora, with a second knife poised for flight. She dropped it and pushed past Mora, who still had one more saucepan under her arm.

By the time Inez got to Lucy, Artemis Hamm was in Lucy's arms.

"Is she dead?" Lucy said. "She can't be dead, Inez. She can't!"

Inez pressed her hand to Artie's neck and shook her head. "There is life," she said. "There is hope."

Things moved in a blur after that. Dad was called from the Town Council meeting. The sheriff drove them all to the vet in Mescalero, siren blaring and lights flashing and the radio sputtering that Felix Pasco had been spotted going down Granada Street carrying some kind of animal trap and Mr. Benitez was following with bait.

"They're supposed to call Wildlife Management," the sheriff said. He didn't ask Lucy why she hadn't used that number he'd given her, instead of tearing out into the yard to save her cat. She was glad. She might not have been able to be polite.

Inez murmured things in Spanish, which Lucy hoped were prayers that made more sense than hers. All she could say was, "Please, please, please."

The blur turned into a picture all too clear when the vet took one look at Artemis Hamm and said, "I'll do what I can, but I can't make any promises."

Mora, Inez, and Dad sat in a row on a green, fake-leather couch. Lucy paced in front of them. How could they be still when right now Artemis was clinging to her kitty-life?

"I wish cats really did have nine lives," she said as she passed the couch for the fourteenth time. "Except bobcats. I know I said don't destroy them, but right now I wish they didn't have *any* lives."

"Not time for wishing," Inez said. "Time for praying."

Mora, slumped against the cold metal arm of the couch, let out a whimper. It was only then that Lucy remembered. She stopped pacing and stood over her.

"It's time for talking too, Mora," she said. "What were you going to tell me about J.J.?"

Mora tried to look down at her lap, but Inez caught her by the chin and lifted her face.

"What is this?" she said.

Dad leaned in from the other end of the couch. "What's going on, Luce?"

"Before the bobcat came — she said she knows something about J.J. —"

Inez barked some words in Spanish that filled Mora's eyes with fear. "*Habla!*" Inez said.

Mora nearly swallowed her fingers trying to cover her mouth. "I told J.J. I would help him hide," she said through them. "Because Lucy wouldn't."

"Help him how?" Dad was straining his neck forward. Lucy herself wanted to shake Mora until it all dumped out.

"I told him, before that day with the book, that he could hide in the back of Abuela's truck and stay in her falling-down barn she doesn't ever go in and I would bring him food."

Inez spit out a whole string of Spanish that made Mora talk faster.

"But then it seemed like he was going back to you — and when you and I had that fight, he took off, and then when I got back to your house, Abuela said my mother was here, and after that I forgot." She shook out her hands like she was trying to get something off of them. "What if he's out in the barn starving to death? What if he waited for me and I never came?"

Her words went high and hysterical. Inez grabbed her by the shoulders and held onto her, almost as if she were afraid Mora would join her voice on the ceiling.

"Lucy," Dad said. "Is the sheriff still outside?"

Lucy ran to the window and nodded, even as she headed for the door.

"Inez, will you wait here with the girls?" Dad said.

"I have to come," Lucy said.

She was halfway out to the patrol car when Dad called to her, "So do I. A little help here?"

Lucy guided Dad into the patrol car, already spewing out Mora's story to the sheriff. Dad put his hand firmly on her arm.

"You better let me tell it this time," he said.

But Dad barely got two sentences out before the sheriff started up the engine. "I'll get the Alamogordo police on it. After I drop you two off, I'll head down there."

"We're going!" Lucy said.

The sheriff turned all the way around in the seat and drilled his eyes into her. "Look, I'm not your dad. I don't let you do anything you want to—"

"I think she can help," Dad said. "If J.J. is hiding out there someplace, she's about the only one who can talk him out."

"We can get him out," the sheriff responded.

"Until he runs again."

Dad's voice was as don't-mess-with-me as it ever was when he lectured Lucy.

The sheriff sighed like he had sandpaper in his throat and turned back to the steering wheel. "I'll think about it," he said.

All the way down Highway 54 toward Alamagordo, Sheriff Navarra was on the radio, snapping out Inez's address and checking over and over to make sure some other policemen were on their way there too.

Lucy couldn't keep quiet either.

"Do you think he'd really starve, Dad? What if he's not even there? He has to be there, doesn't he?"

She knew she was battering him with questions he couldn't answer, but asking them kept her from snatching the radio out of the sheriff's hand and screaming into it, "Find him! Just find him!"

When Sheriff Navarra swished the car off the highway and onto a narrow dirt road, he turned his head sideways, as if he had one eye on where he was going and one eye on Lucy and Dad.

"Ted, she's going to have to stay in the car until I say so. *I* say so."

"Absolutely." Dad pulled Lucy into him. "It's for your safety, Luce."

"Okay," Lucy said, and pasted her face to the side window. Moonlight bathed the side of the road, flowing with spring grass until they reached a low rock wall that stretched all the way to a short driveway. Was J.J. hiding behind the wall?

Or beyond that weathered fence, which itself hid beneath thick new piles of flowers with their blossoms shut in sleep?

She got up on one knee and searched the silhouettes of buildings as the sheriff brought the cruiser to a stop in front of a low house with rounded off corners. Behind it were all kinds of square shapes in the darkness, maybe a gardening shed, perhaps a chicken house. And far, far beyond them, the tall, teetering form of an old barn.

"Back there!" Lucy cried. "Mora said she told him to hide in the barn!"

"Stay," the sheriff said.

Dad took hold of Lucy's hand and kept it between his while Sheriff Navarra climbed out of the car as if he were moving in slow motion. Two other police cars pulled in, one of them with its lights flashing.

"Dad, they're going to scare him to death," Lucy said fiercely. "He's never going to come out."

"Just give it a minute," he said.

All of the policemen and the sheriff disappeared, though she could hear them calling out J.J.'s name in voices Lucy knew he'd never answer to. A minute grew into longer than she could sit there without begging Dad to let her get out.

"He's probably more scared of being out there all by himself than he is of these guys," Dad said. "If he's here, Luce, it's been five days. That's a long time to find out how bad things aren't."

Lucy tried to focus on that. Mora hadn't been here until last night. Inez never went out to that barn, Mora said. J.J. always had snacks in his backpack, but could that last for five breakfasts and lunches and suppers? And what about coyotes? What about bobcats?

She couldn't stand it another second. She grabbed for the handle, just as the sheriff pulled the door open.

"We can see him in the back of the barn," he said. "He's asleep under some blankets. You can come if you do exactly what I say."

"Luce," Dad said.

"I will," Lucy said.

Nothing felt real as she almost-ran beside the sheriff with him holding onto her sweatshirt sleeve. The chilly spring night air, the shadows of Inez's pistachio trees falling across her path, the slatted wood door hanging halfway off its rusted hinges—it had to be out of a story she and J.J. would have made up when they played on the desert.

But when the sheriff let her go into the barn alone, the sight of J.J. curled up in the corner on a pile of burlap sacks, covered with a ratty blanket, was more than real. His shag of hair fell over his eyes, just like always, and his shoulders were hunched up to his ears the way she'd seen them a hundred times when he wasn't sure but he didn't want anybody to know it. When she saw the stale-looking sopapillas and pieces of hardened tortillas piled on his backpack, she felt sick to her stomach. J.J. had been eating out of Inez's trash.

"J.J.?" she whispered.

He stirred a little and then snuggled back under the blanket like a very young boy. She wanted to sit with him until the sun came through the cracks and he woke up by himself and wouldn't be scared.

"Lucy?" the sheriff hissed from outside.

"Okay," Lucy whispered back.

J.J.'s eyes flew open and stared at her. She had only seen them look that frightened once—when he was staring at his father.

"It's just me," she said. "It's just Lucy."

J.J. bolted up, kicking the blankets away and whipping his head around.

"Don't run, J.J.," Lucy said as she got to her own feet.

He stood there, breathing hard, blinking, until he seemed to see her at last.

"You found me," he said. His voice was fuzzy, but it still went skyward at the end.

"Yeah," she said.

He cocked his head as if he were listening to something outside.

"I bet you're hungry," Lucy said. "Hello—rotten tortillas? Inez has better ones at my house."

J.J. wrapped his arms around himself. She could see him trying to keep his face from crumpling.

"I'm sorry I didn't help you before," Lucy said. "But I'm going to now, I promise. Let's just go home."

She could see his eyes behind the hair that had grown even shaggier. Tears shimmered through it.

"Okay," he said.

And then a beam of light drove across the barn and Sheriff Navarra said, "Everything okay, Lucy?"

The light hit J.J.'s face and bounced away. But it stayed long enough for Lucy to see the flash from behind the shag of hair. *You tricked me*, it said. And then J.J.'s jaw clamped down, and with his shoulders hunched, he walked slowly toward the sheriff.

There were so many cars in Inez's driveway when they got there Lucy wasn't sure which one they put her in until she and Dad were halfway home in Mr. Auggy's Jeep.

"Thank you, Lucy," Mr. Auggy kept saying. "Thank you, thank you."

Lucy was sure J.J. wasn't thinking the same thing in whatever car they'd stuck him in, wherever they were taking him. He would never talk to her again. They wouldn't grow up together in the desert and celebrate the springs.

But at least he was safe.

Inez was in the kitchen making tea when they got back to Lucy's house. Mora was wrapped in a blanket on a chair, her eyes almost swollen shut from crying. When Dad told them J.J. was okay, she bawled some more. Lucy herself was all cried out—even when Inez told them that the vet said Artemis had made it through the surgery. If she got through the night, she was likely to live out the rest of her eight lives. Even when the sheriff called and said J.J. was spending the night at the hospital but he was fine—and that Felix Pasco and Mr. Benitez had trapped the bobcat and were taking her up into the mountains tomorrow—none of that brought on any more tears from Lucy.

"Eat," Inez said, and set a bowl of soup in front of her.

Lucy couldn't even look at it.

"Eat," Dad said, "and talk."

"*Sí*," Inez said. She gave Mora a hard look.

"What you want to ask Mora, Senorita Lucy?" Inez said.

"Come on," Dad said, as if he heard Lucy shaking her head. "You know it helps to get it all out."

"Okay," Lucy said, before she could change her mind. "Why did you do it, Mora? I don't get it. Just—why?"

Mora looked at her grandmother, eyes begging. "Do I have to say it again?" she said. "I already told you—you tell her, Abuela."

Lucy nearly laughed. Like *that* was gonna happen.

"Okay!" Mora cried. "I did it because I hate soccer!"

Everyone in the kitchen said some form of "What?"

"We need a little more information, Mora," Dad said.

She spread out her dancing fingers. "Everybody's so into it—you are like way more serious about it than you ever were before. And Veronica and Dusty and that other girl you started hanging out with, the one with the weird hat—they're always with you doing soccer—and I just got left out all the time."

Lucy blinked. Who knew Mora even cared whether they liked her or not?

"And I thought me and you were getting to be, like, best friends, and then you had to like the same boy I did, and even after I told him I'd help him hide, he still went back to you, and I had to write all that stupid stuff in your book thing that wasn't true—and then you hated me and my mom didn't care about me—"

She flung her face into her arms on the table and sobbed, loud, until Inez had to take her into the bathroom.

Dad was shaking his head. "Who knew?" he said.

"All that time, Dad. He was out there by himself all that time, and we were all scared and she could have told us."

"I know." He was quiet for a minute. "Inez told me you and Mora worked together pretty well tonight, driving off that bobcat."

"Like Rachel and Leah," Lucy said, before she even knew she thought it.

"When you two were out there screaming and throwing things—which as I understand it was pretty effective—were you thinking about what Mora did to you and what you did to her?"

"No."

Inez slipped back in, and Lucy looked at her, because it seemed like it was time for her to say something, something she'd said before. What was it?

They'd been standing right here in this kitchen with the red-checked curtains and the tea kettle. Inez had been pouring the tea like she was doing this very minute, and saying—

"To become the woman, you must forgive what cannot be forgiven," Lucy said.

"Right," Dad said in a voice soft as a cloud.

Lucy stared into the soup, where alphabet letters swam in Inez's broth. X's. Mora's X was the goalie, always bouncing things back at her. But she wasn't in control of the game.

"It wasn't her fault J.J. ran away, huh?" Lucy said. "She just gave him a place to do it."

"That's right, champ. And you would have done the same thing a few weeks ago, before you started to grow up."

Lucy had to nod.

"Nobody knows yet why J.J. ran away," Dad said. "Not really. And it had to be something pretty serious for him to go that far away and never ask Inez to bring him back. He wanted to stay hidden."

Lucy sagged way into her chair. "He's sure never gonna tell me. He really hates me now."

"No, J.J. needs you."

"But I don't see how if he won't even listen to me."

Dad tapped his forehead. "I know you. You're so much like your mother. I was four years older than she was, and she still taught me how to be a grown-up." A sad smile crossed his face. "That was after I practically had to stand on my head to get her to notice me. She wasn't into boys either."

"Just like I thought," Lucy said.

"But that isn't where I'm trying to go with this." Dad's eyes went straight to Lucy. "Mr. Auggy is like a dad to J.J. now, but even he says J.J. doesn't trust anyone like he does you."

"But J.J. thinks I turned on him, me and Mora. He thinks we ganged up on him. Like I'm just like all the other girls now."

Dad smeared his hand over his mouth, as if he were hiding a smile, but Lucy saw it in the crinkles around his eyes.

"It isn't funny, Dad!"

"No, it isn't, but, Luce, boys are a lot less complicated than you think we are. When we get confused about something, we have two ways of dealing with it. We either punch somebody out and feel like we're in control again, which, of course, J.J. isn't going to do to you."

"He better not! He knows I could kick his tail."

"Precisely. But don't let your Aunt Karen hear you say that."

"What's the other way?"

"We act like it isn't happening until it goes away." Dad chuckled. "Or until some woman straightens it all out."

"You think that's what J.J.'s doing?"

"I can almost guarantee it."

Lucy ran her finger around the top of her glass. "What if he won't talk to me, Dad? Seriously."

Dad didn't hide his smile this time. "Since when did you and J.J. ever speak in complete sentences anyway? You say a word, he grunts, and somehow you both get it."

"Yeah, that's kinda how it used to work with us."

"I guarantee you, champ, J.J. wants things back the way they were as much as you do. But you're the more grown-up one in this pair. He can't do it without you."

"So—it really is like Jacob and Rachel."

"*Si*," Inez said from the doorway.

Mora trailed in behind her and stood in front of Lucy. When she spoke, her voice was tiny.

"If he talks to you again, Lucy," she said, "I will be the happiest person in the world—I swear. I mean, if you can be friends with me again—after what I did, then J.J. will be friends with you. Seriously."

No one said anything. No grown-ups poked Lucy and told her she had to forgive Mora. It just came up in her, and out of her, and onto the pretty girl who thought she had to trick people into being her friend.

"Yeah, we're friends," Lucy said. " 'Cause I sure don't want you for an enemy."

Mora flung out her arms, but Lucy ducked.

"Just 'cause we're friends doesn't mean I have to hug you, okay?"

"Okay—okay—hey!" Mora's eyes widened. "J.J.'s real name isn't Jacob, is it? That would be so freaky."

"No."

"Is it close? Jason? Jonathan?"

"Does anybody want to tell me what we're talking about?" Dad said.

"This is the girl thing, Senor Ted," Inez said. Her eyes were no longer flashing like knife blades at Mora.

She made up pallets on the floor in Lucy's room for them to sleep on, but Lucy was sure she wouldn't be able to close an eye until she saw J.J. again.

"I'm gonna pray all night," Lucy said to Dad when he came by to tuck them in.

Of course, she didn't. She was almost asleep before he even left. But she did say to Mora, "I wonder if it was this hard for Rachel and Leah being without a mom. They didn't even have an Inez."

"No," Mora mumbled, "and they didn't have a Lucy."

But they did have God. Lucy prayed until the dreams took over.

17

The next morning, Inez woke them up with the news that Artemis had made it through her surgery and the night.

"Senor Kitty Doctor, he said Senorita Artemis was 'in the shreds,'" Inez told them, using her fingers in Mora quotations marks, "but he sews the organs back together and gives her the blood transfusion. We will bring her home and be careful about the infection." She left the room muttering that she had to make some special soup for Senorita Artemis.

"We totally saved that cat's life," Mora said.

"Us and God," Lucy said. Because it seemed like more things were working that way.

But it only made her a little less sad about J.J. He was home, and he was safe. But he wasn't her best friend anymore. She'd told God that would be okay, but it sure didn't feel like it.

Inez took Mora home right after that. Lucy had barely finished her cereal when Dad came in the back door with a lady Lucy thought she'd never seen before, until she was actually sitting at the table.

Weasel Lady.

Although up close, she really didn't look like a pointy-nose animal at all. She reminded Lucy more of the grandmother in a family of plump elves, with a twinkle that lurked in her eyes as if it were waiting for just the right moment to come out.

"Luce," Dad said, "this is Winnie Warren. She's with Child Protective Services."

"You're J.J.'s court lady," Lucy said.

"I'm sure he has other names for me," Winnie said. The twinkle got closer.

"Do I have to tell you what they are?" Lucy said.

She laughed right out loud then. Lucy knew her mouth was dropping open the way Veronica's did.

"Your father tells me that you and Jedediah are very close," Winnie said.

"I call him J.J."

"Of course. He's never shown me his J.J. self. He seems to think I'm the enemy, and you can't let the enemy see your real self, right?"

"I guess so."

Dad found Lucy's hand on the tabletop. "We're not asking you to tell anything about J.J., Luce. I think you've already said everything you know. We just need you to listen."

Lucy nodded. "If it'll help J.J., okay."

Dad tilted his head toward Winnie, who zeroed in on Lucy.

"Even though J.J. is completely protected during his visits with his father, he seems absolutely terrified. He tries to hide it—I'm sure you can imagine that."

"Oh, totally," Lucy said. "Nobody ever knows J.J.'s scared."

"Except you."

"Well, and you, 'cause you just said it."

"I see it because I'm trained to. You see it because he trusts you."

"He used to. I hope he still does."

Dad squeezed Lucy's hand.

"I think there are some things about the way Mr. Cluck has treated J.J.—and not Januarie—that J.J. is afraid to tell us. I think he's frightened that it will come out when we're all together. Does that make sense to you?"

"I think so," Lucy said. "It's like if you knew how horrible his dad really was to him, something bad would happen." She squeezed in her shoulders. "He's pretty mean."

Winnie sighed. "If J.J. would just talk to me, I could reassure him that nothing is going to happen to *him*. It's his father who will be punished."

"And you want me to get him to talk to you," Lucy said.

"I would like that, yes, if you feel comfortable doing it."

"Huh," Lucy said. "I wouldn't be comfortable at all. But I'll do it."

Winnie gave her a long look, even as she said, "Mr. Rooney, you were right. You have a very mature daughter here."

"There's only one thing," Lucy said. "J.J.'s dad can't be there when he talks to you."

"Absolutely not."

"Then I can tell him that?"

"Please do. And remember, if he doesn't agree, it isn't your fault."

"When can I do it?" Lucy said. Her mouth was already going dry, and if she didn't do it soon, she'd get all tangled up in being afraid J.J. was going to tell her to go away and she'd just hide under the covers with Lollipop.

"How about right now?" Winnie stood up. "J.J.'s over at his house with another 'court lady,' and I don't think his calendar is full."

"I'll walk you over," Dad said.

But for a minute Lucy couldn't get up. How was she going to make J.J. understand? The way Winnie talked wasn't going to work. Lucy and J.J. didn't talk that way. They just talked about soccer and—

Soccer.

"Luce?" Dad was at the door with his cane. "You coming?"

"Will you tell him to meet me on the front porch?" Lucy said. "I have to get something from my room."

Lucy had waited so long to talk to her best friend and had missed him so much it ached inside her. But when she saw J.J. pick his way through the junk in his yard toward Dad, who was calling to him from the fence, Lucy wanted to slow time down some more.

Didn't she need another minute to be sure what she planned to say was the right thing? Or maybe an hour to go over the soccer field diagram five or six or a hundred more times? Or at least a week to be certain J.J. was going to understand about the X's?

But she didn't even have a second before J.J. was standing on the bottom step of the front porch, while she sat at the top, on the soccer drawing, jaw clamped down. *Please, God—help!* Why couldn't she be like Mora right now and just blurt it all out?

"Did you hear about Artemis?" she said, sounding not at all like Mora, she knew.

"Bobcat get her?"

"Yeah."

"She dead?"

"No way. She's too tough to die."

Lucy watched J.J. swallow like it hurt. She was afraid to even go after the lump in her own throat.

"Mora lied about me," she said around it.

"She's a freak."

"She can't help it."

Lucy stopped. What was she doing?

Whatever it was, she kept on. "You and me know what it's like to only have one parent."

J.J. grunted.

"She doesn't have any, really, so she lies."

J.J. folded down to the step like that hurt too, and sat stiff as a stick.

"You haven't told Weasel Lady why you're scared to see your dad, have you?" Lucy said.

"No."

"She doesn't know all the bad stuff he's done to you, does she?"

"No."

"Why were you scared to tell her?"

J.J. swallowed so hard Lucy could hear it. "If I told her everything, she'd put us in a foster home."

Lucy stared. "She'd even take you away from your mom?"

"My dad would find us. He said that the first time Weasel Lady made me see him." Another swallow. "He said he'd find me and do even worse stuff."

Lucy's insides were shaking. "He said that in front of Weasel Lady?"

"She went up to the counter to get our drinks. That's when he said it."

J.J.'s chest sagged like he was worn out from saying so much. Lucy scooted down to the step just above his, leaving the field drawing behind.

"I'm sorry I didn't help you," she said.

"I thought you'd fix it." J.J. shrugged. "You always do."

Lucy shook her head. "*You* have to fix it, J.J."

"How?"

"I don't know—"

Lucy watched J.J.'s jaw clamp down, and her heart started a dive she had to stop.

She grabbed the drawing of the soccer field from the top step and spread it out between them.

"What's this?" J.J. said.

"It's how I figure stuff out about life."

J.J. grunted, and his jaw muscles tightened so hard she could see them.

"Clam up again if you want," Lucy said, "but I'm gonna show you this anyway."

She pointed to an X she'd drawn near the goal. "That's you. You've got the ball, and you could shoot it right in. That's like getting everything back like it should be—that's the goal."

J.J. stabbed a finger at the goalie X. "Who's this?"

"Your dad."

J.J. turned his head, but Lucy stuck the drawing in his face.

"You have to get the ball in there, past him, or you're just always gonna be scared and running."

J.J. took the drawing and frowned at it. "I can't get past my dad," he said.

"Not on your own," Lucy said. "See, that's what I learned from Mr. Auggy and Inez and my dad. I'm the captain, but I can't do it all. Nobody can, and we're not supposed to. We gotta work together. See—" Lucy showed him an X positioned to shield J.J. "This is Weasel Lady."

"I hate her."

"She's on your side, moron! She's not gonna send you to foster care. It's your dad that's gonna get punished."

J.J. peered at her from under his shag of hair.

"And these X's are our whole team, and we're trying to keep it together because we want you back." She heard her voice shake. "If you don't do this, J.J., you'll just always keep running away and I won't ever see you again and I can't stand that. I can't!"

"That's what my father wants. He hates you and your dad and Mr. Auggy."

J.J.'s voice went high. His Adam's apple bobbed, and he looked twelve-year-old awkward. Yet he narrowed his icy-blue eyes like a grown-up.

"Where's your X?" he said.

"I'm at midfield. I've got your back."

"So—when I go talk to Weasel Lady, you're gonna go with me."

Lucy hugged the drawing against her chest and closed her eyes and made herself not cry. "Of course," she said. "You're my best friend."

18

Why I Know God Really Does Listen, Even though I Wasn't So Sure for a While

- Mr. Auggy is back. Now we have our team for real, and our class, and Dad and I have our Sunday night macaroni and cheese with him. He doesn't even seem like he's mad at Mora or Mr. Cluck or anybody. Talk about forgive the unforgivable. It's like he took Bible study from Inez too.

- Dad's letting me hang out with J.J. Aunt Karen doesn't like it, but what else is new?

- Artemis Hamm is home and getting better. I think it's because all the other cats — except Mudge, of course — keep licking her stitches. There haven't been any more bobcat sightings, but Dad has me check the backyard every night at dusk and every morning when I get up. Together we have amazing eyes and ears.

- We have a new routine after school. Inez and Mora meet us at the soccer field with the snacks so we don't waste any practice time. J.J. still won't even look at Mora, but Inez says he'll learn about forgiveness if he keeps watching me and Mora in action. Meanwhile, Mora's over J.J. She says Gabe is cute. Ickety-ick! I made her promise not to try to steal him from Veronica. I'm sick of girl-drama.

∽ Mora told me sports bras are way more comfortable than the kind Aunt Karen was trying to buy me. She said she'd give me one of hers, but I said no. Dad and I took the bus to Alamogordo, and we got me some at Wal-Mart. It wasn't even all that embarrassing. And Mora was right about it being comfortable. Who knew I'd ever be taking bra advice from her?

Lucy stopped and rubbed her hands together before she wrote down the best one of all, the one that convinced her God really was listening.

∽ J.J.'s dad pitched a fit when Weasel Lady told him he wasn't allowed to see J.J. and Januarie for a long time. It was such a big fit, they put him back in jail. God, I hope you're listening when I say I'd sure like to see a big ol' miracle happen and J.J.'s dad be a great dad like mine. Okay, so maybe even half as great. J.J. deserves it.

Lucy sank back into her pillows and studied her hand. It didn't even hurt like it used to when she put that much stuff on her list. Writing and praying were getting a lot easier.

"Hey, champ—you up?" Dad said outside her door. "It's Game Day."

Like she had to be reminded. It hadn't seemed like April twenty-second would ever come, and then Veronica and Dusty's moms' banners were going up and Gloria was putting all the girls' hair in French braids—because she said that would keep it in place for the game better than ponytails—and Felix Pasco was holding a night-before-the-game team supper at the café and Mr. Benitez was giving them each a new red warm-up jacket with Los Suenos Dreams on the front in blue and their names on the back in white. He didn't even put his grocery store logo on them. Mr. Auggy beamed over all of it, though he said they shouldn't eat the chocolate soccer balls Claudia gave them until after the game.

"Until after we beat them Monkeys, right, Mr. A.?" Oscar had said.

Lucy felt a flicker of fear now as she remembered the look on Mr. Auggy's face. Sure, he smiled and said, "You betcha." But Lucy caught the tightness of his already small smile. They'd missed a lot of practice time with him. Were they really ready to take on another team?

Lucy threw back the covers and reached for her soccer ball, which she'd tucked under the bed before she went to sleep.

"We have to be ready," she said to it. And not just because the whole town would be watching. And not just because they really had a chance to win this time.

That was a lot. But it wasn't everything.

She hugged the soccer ball tighter and remembered the night after she and J.J. talked to Winnie, the un-Weasel Lady. Lucy and Dad went to Pasco's to celebrate, and over grilled cheese sandwiches, Dad said, "I don't know about you, Luce, but I think you're ready."

"Ready for what?"

"Ready for what? Ready for the most important thing in the world that you want so bad."

Lucy set her half-eaten sandwich on the plate. "You mean the ODP?"

"I do, and the fact that you even had to ask convinces me even more that you're ready."

Lucy got up on one knee. "I don't get it."

"The people who love you had a lot of concerns about this. I thought it might cut short your childhood. Mr. Auggy thought it was too much Lucy-focus and not enough team-focus. Even J.J., I think, was afraid you'd get so wrapped up in it you'd forget about him. Maybe all your friends felt that way." He shook his head. "But I don't think any of us need to be concerned about those things. You put your dream aside while you were helping J.J.—and Mora—and Carla Rosa—"

"Dad?" Lucy said.

"What, champ?"

"I gotta know this: how come you're blind, but you see absolutely everything?"

"Because that's one way you're just like me," he said. "God made us just to know stuff. And I know we need to let this guy from the ODP come watch you play."

Lucy sat back in her chair and let the rest of the grilled cheese go cold. Could this really be happening? Could Dad really be letting her audition for her dream program?

She looked up at the picture of her team and the banner that hung above it. And then she looked at Dad's sunshine smile. And she knew what he meant. That he was looking at her whole field—and all the players were working together.

"You up for it?" Dad said.

"Are you gonna be there, like, cheering me on?" she said.

"All day long, champ," Dad said. "All day long."

Today was that day. Even before she was out of bed, Lucy heard the Toyota pull up, and she rode the rug down the hall to the bathroom. If Aunt Karen had that Nathan Quinn person with her, Lucy didn't want to be caught in her pajamas. She was nervous enough about making a good impression. But when she came out, scrubbed and dressed, only Aunt Karen was in the kitchen with Dad.

"Nate is down at Pasco's having breakfast," she said, "and if he survives that, he'll be at your game." Aunt Karen's eyes shone as she rubbed Lucy's arms. "Are you ready to knock his socks off?"

"I guess so."

"There is no guessing about it. You're going to be fabulous. How many goals do you think you'll score?"

"I don't—"

"Nate says he's seen some of his candidates make six or seven in one game." She laughed. "I don't know—is that a lot?"

"It's impossible!" Lucy said.

"It's okay, Luce," Dad said. "You just play your best—" He frowned at the tabletop. "The way Mr. Auggy has taught you to play."

Aunt Karen swatted her hand at the air. "Nate will be able to see around that, I'm sure. He's looking at your raw talent, and when you're chosen, *his* people will shape you."

Lucy was glad Mr. Auggy wasn't there in the kitchen.

"Enough with the pressure, Karen," Dad said. "This is Game Day. It's a celebration."

"Oh, it's going to be. From what I can gather, Nate watching Lucy is just a formality. She's practically in." She picked up her purse. "I'll see you at the field. Oh, and lunch is on me at the Tularosa. I already told Nate."

"Is she going out with that guy or something?" Lucy said when she was gone.

"Let's forget about Aunt Karen and concentrate on the game, huh?" Dad said.

There was nothing Lucy wanted to do more.

Mora's dance team was already cheering when Lucy and the Los Suenos Dreams arrived at the soccer field. Inez was behind the counter at the refreshment stand, helping Felix Pasco, and she stopped to smile a rare smile at Lucy. She put her hands together at her chest, and Lucy felt a flood of love. If Inez was praying, it was going to be all right.

The Mescalero team went out onto the field to warm up first, and the Dreams watched from behind the field building.

"They're only about as big as monkeys," Oscar said. "That's good, ain't it?"

"Guess what?" Carla Rosa said. "They aren't really called the Monkeys, are they?"

"They're the Mescalero Mountain," Mr. Auggy said, smiling his small smile at them for real. "And we're going to climb it, aren't we, team?"

They let out one big Los Suenos Dreams whoop as they ran out onto the field, amid the even louder whoops of their whole town. Lucy felt it all fill her chest. She was ready to play, and that was all that mattered.

She saw right away that the rest of her team was ready too.

From midfield, she yelled for the defenders to build a wall, and they blocked the Mountain's first attempt at a goal before it even got close to Oscar, even though he looked like he was going to move that Mountain if he had to.

From midfield, she cheered for Carla Rosa to keep dribbling until she could get the ball to Dusty. And she volleyed with Veronica to keep the other team from snagging the ball until they could get it to Gabe. And she yelled like a wild woman when Gabe slid the ball right past the goalie for their first score.

The first half was over before Lucy even felt tired. The score was two-nothing, Dreams, both goals driven in by Gabe.

"You are, like, amazing!" Veronica said to him when they were all gulping down water behind the refreshment building. "I love that. Go, Gabe!"

Gabe grinned like, well, like an actual monkey, Lucy couldn't help thinking.

But then he said, "Hey, Lucy Goosey. Thanks for getting the ball to me."

"I love that!" Veronica said. "Go, Lucy!"

"Go, everybody." Mr. Auggy put out his arms, and they all huddled around him. "You're playing like a team, and I'm so proud of you."

"Go, us!"

Dusty put her hand over Veronica's mouth.

"Keep doing what you're doing," Mr. Auggy said. "But just one thing. If there's an opportunity for Lucy to score, I want you to help her."

Gabe blinked. "You mean, like give her the ball? Why?"

"Because it's important for her today," Mr. Auggy said. "Okay?"

"I love that!" Veronica said, between Dusty's fingers.

But Lucy shook her head. "Only if it just works out that way, you guys. Let's don't mess up what we got going."

Mr. Auggy motioned toward the field, and with a second-half whoop, the team headed for it. Lucy took off after them, but Mr. Auggy said, "Hold on, Captain."

"Uh-oh," Lucy said. "Did I do something wrong?"

"No, I just—"

"You don't have to set it up for me to score. I'm not pouting about that anymore. I get it about being a team—"

"You women!" Mr. Auggy's small smile was big. "If I could just get you females to stop filling in the blanks!"

Lucy put her hand over her mouth and said, "Sorry," through her fingers. It must be from hanging out with Veronica and Dusty—and, of course, Mora.

"I met Coach Quinn, the guy from the ODP," Mr. Auggy said. "He's impressed so far, and he'd like to see you take a shot at the goal. No pressure to score—this is still about the team."

"Okay," Lucy said. Her blood was suddenly ice cold.

Mr. Auggy rubbed his hands together. "I'm proud of you, Captain. You've worked hard for your team, and for J.J. Now let's see if we can't do something for you."

A whistle blew—right through Lucy. This was it, everything she'd dreamed of.

And suddenly, she was terrified. Her legs were stiff, and her hands even stiffer as she joined her team on the field. Only her heart seemed to be moving—five times faster than usual.

"You okay, Lucy?" Dusty said when Lucy caught up to them.

Lucy couldn't exactly say that she was. Suddenly it wasn't just two kids' teams playing on a spring morning. It was as if she were out there alone, maybe even naked, and somebody important was watching only her.

The ball was in play, and a girl from the Mountain took charge of it. J.J. swam around her, making it almost impossible for her to move. When she tried to pass to a nearby player, it bounced too high and went straight for Carla Rosa's head.

"Head it, Carla!" Lucy cried. But as Carla's sequins froze, Lucy remembered that was one thing they hadn't worked on. No one else was around but another member of the Mescalero team, and the Dreams all seemed to be backing off.

"Take it, Lucy!" Dusty hollered.

Lucy was miles from the goal. Dusty was in a much better position. But Lucy charged for the ball—and straight into the Mountain girl.

A whistle screamed, and everyone turned to statues. Except the girl, who dropped on her backside and clutched her shin.

"Are you hurt?" Reverend Servidio, the referee, said as he reached a hand down.

"Hello! She kicked me!"

"Guess what? She didn't do it on purpose!" Carla Rosa nudged her head under Lucy's arm.

"That's a foul," the Reverend said. "Direct kick for the Mountain."

"Bad call!" Lucy heard Gabe yell.

"You want me to call a foul on you, son?" The Reverend stroked his thin mustache. "I have to be fair."

"It's all right," Mr. Auggy called from the sideline. "Focus, team." He pointed at Lucy.

She tugged at her braid and tried to think. "Okay, make a wall!" she shouted. "Oscar—you're open on that side—

But Mountain Girl didn't give them a chance to get shoulder to shoulder, or even for Oscar to get to the space on the far side of the goal. Her kick went straight in.

The Mountain did take time to cheer themselves. Feeling like she had a weight hanging around her neck, Lucy managed to tell J.J. to take the goal kick, which got past the still-celebrating Mescalero players. Dusty took it and dribbled like Mr. Auggy's mad dog until she was wide open. Her head came up toward Lucy.

"To you, Bolillo!" she said.

But Lucy froze. Dusty passed the ball cleanly toward her, and she couldn't move.

Not until a chorus of voices went up in words Lucy didn't understand until the ball was nearly at her feet. "The Dreams Don't Die! The Dreams Don't Die!"

It was as if someone else's legs ran through it, and someone else's foot directed the ball on first touch, and someone else's body took off away from the defenders who were suddenly scrambling for the ball.

Veronica was ahead of her.

"To you!" Lucy called.

Veronica didn't wait for the ball to come to her. She ran to it and passed it off to Gabe. He dribbled toward the goal, but the Mescalero defenders had pulled it together and were turning themselves inside out to get their feet on the ball. It was a mess—but Lucy saw a hole.

Veronica obviously didn't see it. She ran way out of position to get to the other side of Gabe.

Lucy ran into the hole and yelled, "Gabe—to me!"

Gabe looked like she'd just saved him from detention and passed the ball right through the opening. They were still far enough from the goal for Lucy to dribble forward until Gabe could get into position to shoot. All she had to do was send it between the two defenders, and he could run onto it.

"Through!" she called as she danced the ball away from an oncoming Mountain member and shot it to him.

Gabe was on it before the defenders seemed to know Lucy had passed it. But instead of going straight for the goal, he too called, "Through!"

Lucy ran. The ball was there to meet her, and there was nothing between her and the goal except the goalie himself. He was crouched like he'd been waiting for her all morning.

Lucy lofted the ball. It was almost over his head before he came up and smacked it with the heel of his hand. But Lucy followed her shot, charging into the goal. When the ball came back at her, she snapped it with her foot, and it went straight into the corner. Lucy slid and came down on her bottom.

A rush of voices came at her from the bleachers. And then a whistle blew.

"Who fouled?" Lucy said as Veronica stretched her hand down to help her up. "Did I do it again?"

Gabe's face came into view over Veronica's shoulder. "No, Lucy Goosey—the game's over. We won!"

Lucy was at the bottom of a pile of screaming teammates when Aunt Karen opened it and tugged Lucy's arm.

"You can do this later." Her eyes had news in them. "Come here."

She half-dragged Lucy away from the Dreams to a tall man who looked a little like a giraffe leaning against the refreshment building with his arms folded. When Lucy got closer, he stood up straight and stuck out a long arm and swallowed Lucy's hand with his. Lucy had to bend her head completely back to look up at him.

"I'm Coach Quinn, Olympic Development Program," he said. "Great game, Lucy."

Lucy knew there were athletic things she was supposed to say, but all she could think of was, "Thanks."

"You were fabulous," Aunt Karen said.

Coach Quinn seemed to ignore her as he kept his eyes pointed down at Lucy. "I understand you're interested in the ODP."

"I am."

"Good. Because we're definitely interested in you."

Lucy knew the smile that spread across her face went from earlobe to earlobe and would have met at the back of her head if it could have. It was happening. Her dream was coming true. She looked around for Dad. He had to hear this—

"So, what do we do next?" Aunt Karen said.

Coach Quinn still kept his gaze on Lucy. "Just as soon as you get settled down in El Paso, let me know, and I'll start the paperwork. This was your tryout—the rest is just—"

"El Paso?" Lucy felt her smile dissolve.

"You're moving to Texas, right?" For the first time, he looked at Aunt Karen. "That's what I understood you to say."

"Right—"

"Wait," Lucy said. "I don't get it."

Coach Quinn looked from one of them to the other. "I'm the ODP rep from Texas—I can only take Texas residents. I explained that to Karen."

Aunt Karen pressed a hand to her chest. "I totally understand that, and it isn't a problem."

"Yes, it is." Lucy's voice went up like J.J.'s and stayed there. "I live in New Mexico."

Coach Quinn lifted an eyebrow at Aunt Karen before he turned back to Lucy. "Huh. I thought this was all arranged."

"It will be," Aunt Karen said, shooting her eyes into Lucy.

Lucy's heart shot straight downward. She took a step back, straight into a familiar chest.

"Stay, Lucy," Dad said. He looked up, though not far enough, and put out his hand. "Ted Rooney, Lucy's father."

As Coach Quinn shook Dad's hand, he looked as if he had no idea such a person existed. Lucy was pretty sure he didn't.

"I think you and I should have met before this conversation got started," Dad said.

"I didn't realize — "

"I'm sure you didn't, and that's not your fault."

Aunt Karen made a face, and it was all Lucy could do not to wipe it off with her hand. She was sure Dad could feel the rolling of Aunt Karen's eyes.

"No worries, though," Dad said, "because the decision is really Lucy's. And she hasn't been given a chance to think about it because she didn't have all the information." He put his hand on her shoulder. "You take all the time you need."

Lucy's heart had already landed in the pit of her stomach, but she could see her soccer field floating in front of her, with all the X's in their places. Here. Right here.

"I live in New Mexico with my dad," she said, "and this is where my team is. I'm not moving to El Paso." She looked at Aunt Karen. "Ever."

"I'm sorry you wasted your time," Dad said.

Coach Quinn nodded down from his lofty height. "It's never a waste of time to see that kind of talent, both in a player and in her coach. It was a pleasure."

"We appreciate that," Dad said.

Lucy stole a glance at Aunt Karen. She didn't look like she appreciated anything about this.

"Don't be bummed, Lucy," Coach Quinn said. "Mr. Rooney, if Lucy wants to try out in New Mexico, I can give you the name of the person to call up in Albuquerque. I'll definitely recommend you to her." He put his hand out to shake Dad's hand, and when he didn't respond, Coach Quinn took hold of it and squeezed it. Lucy was liking him more by the minute.

Aunt Karen, on the other hand—

As soon as Coach Quinn was gone, Lucy turned on her heel to disappear too. But Aunt Karen got her by the sleeve and twisted her around.

"Have you lost your mind?"

"No," Lucy said. She yanked herself away.

Aunt Karen raked a hand through her hair and turned on Dad. "Ted, you are depriving her of the opportunity of a lifetime. Do you know how many strings I pulled, how much time I spent arranging this?"

"Under false pretenses," Dad said. He felt for Lucy's shoulder. "Go celebrate with your team, champ. I've got this handled."

Lucy believed that. And she couldn't get away from Aunt Karen fast enough. Tears blurred the ground she stared at as she ran—straight into Inez. It certainly was her day for plowing into people.

"Tears on this happy day, Senorita Lucy?" Inez said.

"She did it again!" Lucy said.

Inez didn't even ask who. She just nodded and smelled like funnel cakes and understood the babbling that was coming out of Lucy's mouth.

"She tried to trick me into moving to El Paso with her—again."

"Ah."

"She's worse than Laban. I feel like Rachel—no, Jacob—who do I feel like, Inez?"

"You feel like Senorita Lucy."

"She's never gonna stop, is she? She's never gonna stop trying to take my mom's place."

Lucy put her fist to her mouth, but the tears were already coming. Inez folded her arms around her.

"She will try. But she can never be, because your mama, she is always there."

"I wish she was *here*."

"She is still caring—like Senora Rachel." Inez put her hands on Lucy cheeks and looked into her face. "Long time after she has died, when Senora Rachel's great-great-many-great grandchildren are driven from their homes in much sadness—the Bible says they can hear Rachel, crying for her children."

"You mean, like, from heaven? They could actually hear her with their ears?"

"Perhaps with their hearts." Inez brushed a strand of hair out of Lucy's streaming eye. "You have learn about your heart—how to love, how to forgive."

"You're gonna say I have to forgive Aunt Karen."

"What do *you* say?"

"I have to forgive the unforgivable if I'm going to be a real woman."

"*Si.*"

Lucy looked back to the concession stand, where Aunt Karen stood with her arms folded against the words Dad was saying to her with his hands.

"What she did is pretty unforgivable," Lucy said. "But I think my Dad's doing it."

"Senor Ted, he is a Jacob."

Lucy sighed. "Then I guess I better be a Rachel." Her throat got thick again. "It's hard, Inez."

"*Si.* It is hard to be the woman. And it is joy."

Lucy was about to point out that she wasn't exactly feeling that at the moment, when warm, sweaty arms crept around her waist from behind.

"Lu-cee," Januarie said. "Come on—Mr. Auggy said we could eat our chocolate soccer balls now, and everybody's waiting for you."

"Why?" Lucy said as she twisted to look down at her. She was surprised she wasn't actually drooling.

"Because," Januarie said, "it's never as good without you."

She tugged Lucy's arm, and Lucy didn't really have much choice but to go with her. The team stood in an excited knot, bouncing and stuffing their faces with chocolate.

All except J.J., who stood a little apart, watching her. Lucy left Januarie and went straight to him.

"Did you make it?" he said.

"Yeah."

"But you're not goin'."

"Nope."

"How come?"

Lucy looked up at his shaggy hair, where blue eyes peeked through and understood everything.

"I have to stay here," she said.

J.J. nodded. And then he smiled. And then he nudged her until she nearly fell over.

And Lucy felt the joy of being an almost-woman.

1

Lucy wrote, "Reasons Why I Hate Aunt Karen," then she stopped and rolled the pen up and down between her palms. Dad always said "hate" wasn't a people-verb. It was a thing-verb. It was okay to hate jalapeno peppers in your scrambled eggs, which she did, and rock music that sounded like soda cans tumbling in a clothes dryer, which Dad did. It wasn't okay to hate human beings. Even Osama bin Laden. Or Aunt Karen.

Lucy drew a squiggly line through her words and wrote below them,

Reasons Why I Wish Aunt Karen Would Move to Australia:

Dad would say that was fine. Not that she was going to read it to him. Or anybody else. This was extreme-private stuff.

Lucy scowled at the page. The scribble messed it up, and she wanted to be so careful writing in this book. Anything to do with Aunt Karen made her mess up worse than usual. She would have to put that on the list of reasons. But she started with,

— Because Australia is as far away from me and Dad and Los Suenos, New Mexico, as she can get.

— Because she probably wishes our cats would move there.

The very round, coal-colored kitty on Lucy's pillow raised her head and oozed out a fat meow.

"Don't worry, Lollipop," Lucy said. "You're not going anywhere."

The cat gave Lucy a long, doubtful look before she winked her eyes shut, but she continued her nap with her head still up, as if she wanted to be ready to leap into the blue-and-yellow toy chest that Lucy kept propped open with a wooden spoon—for just such occasions—should the cat carrier, or Aunt Karen, appear.

Lucy leaned against her giant stuffed soccer ball, propped her feet on the blue-tile windowsill above Lollipop, and went back to the list of reasons.

— Because she wants me to learn to give myself a manicure.

She looked down at her gnawed-to-the-quick fingernails and snorted out loud.

— Because she says a ponytail isn't a real hairstyle.

Lucy flipped hers so it play-slapped at the sides of her face. She could see its blondeness out of the corners of her eyes. Yellow and thick and straight like her mom's had been. Not all weird and chopped-off and sticking out the way Aunt Karen's did. That was supposed to be a "style."

Lollipop's legs startled straight, and her claws sunk into Lucy's faded blue-and-yellow plaid pillowcase. She sprang to the window-sill—in the slow-motion way her chunky body insisted on—and pressed whisker-close to the glass. Lucy crawled to the headboard and leaned on it to peer out.

Granada Street was Saturday-afternoon-in-January quiet. Even J.J.'s house across the road looked as if it were trying to nap behind the stacks of firewood and tangle of rusted lawn mowers and pieces of cars piled around it. Dad asked Lucy just the other day if the Clucks still had everything but the kitchen sink in their yard. She reported that now there actually *was* a kitchen sink out there.

But there were no doors banging or Cluck family members yelling, which was what usually made Lollipop switch her tail like she was doing now. Unless the kitty saw something in the spider shadows of the cottonwood trees on the road, there was nothing going on out there.

At least it wasn't Aunt Karen already.

A Lucy Novel
Written by Nancy Rue

New from Faithgirlz! By bestselling author Nancy Rue.

Lucy Rooney is a feisty, precocious tomboy who questions everything—even God. It's not hard to see why: a horrible accident killed her mother and blinded her father, turning her life upside down. It will take a strong but gentle housekeeper—who insists on Bible study and homework when all Lucy wants to do is play soccer—to show Lucy that there are many ways to become the woman God intends her to be.

Book 1: Lucy Doesn't Wear Pink
ISBN 978-0-310-71450-7

Book 3: Lucy's Perfect Summer
ISBN 978-0-310-71452-1

Book 2: Lucy Out of Bounds
ISBN 978-0-310-71451-4

Book 4: Lucy Finds Her Way
ISBN 978-0-310-71453-8

Available now at your local bookstore!
Visit www.faithgirlz.com, it's the place for girls ages 9-12.

faiThGirLz!
the beauty of believing

Sophie Series
Written by Nancy Rue

Meet Sophie LaCroix, a creative soul who's destined to become a great film director someday. But many times, her overactive imagination gets her in trouble!

Book 1: Sophie's World
IBSN: 978-0-310-70756-1

Book 4: Sophie Steps Up
ISBN: 978-0-310-71841-3

Book 2: Sophie's Secret
ISBN: 978-0-310-70757-8

Book 5: Sophie's First Dance
ISBN: 978-0-310-70760-8

Book 3: Sophie Under Pressure
ISBN: 978-0-310-71840-6

Book 6: Sophie's Stormy Summer
ISBN: 978-0-310-70761-5

Sophie Series
Written by Nancy Rue

Book 7: Sophie's Friendship Fiasco
ISBN: 978-0-310-71842-0

Book 8: Sophie and the New Girl
ISBN: 978-0-310-71843-7

Book 9: Sophie Flakes Out
ISBN: 978-0-310-71024-0

Book 10: Sophie Loves Jimmy
ISBN: 978-0-310-71025-7

Book 11: Sophie's Drama
ISBN: 978-0-310-71844-4

Book 12: Sophie Gets Real
ISBN: 978-0-310-71845-1

Available now at your local bookstore!
Visit www.faithgirlz.com, it's the place for girls ages 9-12.

Introduce your mom to Nancy Rue!

Today's mom is raising her 8-to-12-year-old daughter in a society that compels her little girl to grow up too fast. *Moms' Ultimate Guide to the Tween Girl World* gives mothers practical advice and spiritual inspiration to guide their mini-women into adolescence as strong, confident, authentic, and God-centered young women; even in a morally challenged society and without losing their childhoods before they're ready.

Nancy Rue has written over 100 books for girls, is the editor of the Faithgirlz Bible, and is a popular speaker and radio guest with her expertise in tween and teen issues. She and husband Jim have raised a daughter of their own and now live in Tennessee.

Visit Nancy at NancyRue.com

Available wherever books are sold.